Best Wishes

James F. Lucas D.V.M.

BIRTH IN
CHICKEN HO

BIRTH IN A CHICKEN HOUSE

A Collection of Stories by James Lucas, DVM

STONE TABLETS PUBLISHING

BEDFORD, IOWA

References used in this book are from the following sources:
•The King James Version of the Bible (KJV)
•Shane, George. "Cities, Towns, Farms Reflect Bright Era in Taylor County" Picture, Supplement to Des Moines Register October 19, 1953
•Shane, George. "They Went Back to Their Old Home Town" Picture, Supplement to Des Moines Register September 27, 1964

Cover Design by Lynch Graphics & Design

Library of Congress Catalog Number: 99-62983
ISBN: 0-9671823-0-1

"This is the day which the Lord hath made; we will rejoice and be glad in it" (Psalms 118:24).

Dedicated
to my wife

Kay Lucas

for the many rungs of
the ladder we've climbed
together.

CONTENTS

PREFACE

Life is about living, loving and caring for others, the love of God, loving our parents, loving our children, and loving and caring for animals. Will Rogers once said, "I never met a man I did not like." I feel the same although there were some folks I liked better than others and, I never met Hitler. If I tried, I found things I liked in nearly everyone … if I really tried.

Life is short. We must enjoy every day that comes along. Will Rogers, whose own life was cut short in a plane wreck, also said, "If you live life, death is a joke as far as fear is concerned."

When you think you have life all figured out God has a way of balancing the pendulum of time. After you set your goals to reach the top rung of the ladder, you begin to climb and climb. Just as the last rung comes into view, it happens. You step and the rung cracks, breaking in half.

My wife, Kay, and I were first featured in Picture, a supplement to the Des Moines Sunday Register, during the last days of high school. The feature spotlighted our lofty goal of first leaving our hometown for college and then returning to spend our lives together in Bedford, Iowa.

We had reached the goal in 1964 and Picture wrote a follow-up article boasting the "Home Town Kids Made Good." We both had graduated from Iowa State University. I had my DVM degree and had apprenticed with Dr. Don Anderson. Kay had her Master of Science degree in Home Management. The feature told of our community accomplishments and showed how our daily routine followed close to the life goal we had earlier imagined.

The veterinary practice was going well and Kay was teaching Home Economics. We were building a new home and joy of all joys, Kay was pregnant with our first child.

The _Picture_ article was timed perfectly. Our first son, Daniel James, was born on Sunday, the day the supplement was published. I was weary, due to lack of sleep, and left the hospital when things had settled down. I returned to Bedford with a fistful of cigars and candy bars. My wife, newborn son, and I were the talk of the town.

Then a call came later the same day that Daniel was having trouble breathing. With the help of a friend, Boyd Novinger, we rushed Daniel to Omaha where a team of doctors could not correct a birth defect in Daniel's heart. Daniel passed away on the third day, suffering from a pulmonary stenosis. The world drifted away. The ladder had snapped. The pendulum swung the other way.

Over the period of time it took for Kay and I to regain our spent strength, the support of the community never faltered. With their nurturing, we stood the ladder up again and climbed.

As we continued to climb, another rung of the ladder began to weaken. In 1986 while testing cows for pregnancy my left arm began to shake with tremors. This was the first symptom of Parkinson's Disease that drastically changed my life. Even though I practiced another twelve years it forced me into early retirement, yet allowed me the opportunity to begin writing.

I dedicate this book to my wife, Kay. She is my lover, secretary, the mother of our four children, my cook, housekeeper, organizer and inspiration for all I do.

I give thanks to my parents, Max and Dorothy, who never had the opportunity to further their education. Yet, their foresight led my brother, Donovan, and I toward the degree of veterinary medicine.

I honor my blessed children, Jamie Kay, Matthew Leroy, Shelly Sue, and Joseph William. They willingly helped me in my veterinary practice with hard physical labor and office duties. They were good apprentices who used their experiences as a springboard for life.

"This is the day which the Lord hath made; we will rejoice and be glad in it" (Psalms 118:24). Being a veterinarian gave me the opportunity to live full days and rejoice in each and every one. These days have turned into an experience of a lifetime and a story to share.

1
MY VET
PRACTICE

After spending six years of my life dreaming and preparing for the glorious veterinary vocation, I spent many more additional days and nights wondering if I had made the right choice. In the field, I found I loved the occupation and the excitement of the call. There was seldom a dull moment and every day offered up variety. Yet, so many times I found myself in situations that were out of control. The glory was elusive.

I had the opportunity to make the acquaintance of many different characters. With that, I eventually learned how to maintain self control by using wit and psychology. I discovered then the glory came from the love of life, the love of people, the love of animals, and the love of being able to help those animals and their owners.

In the early years, I was not always in control. If a client and myself were both mad, there was never a winner. Eventually, I found if a person became upset and you did not, he didn't know what to do next. This would usually settle the situation down. Still, you could not let the client run over you.

On one call, I had a very difficult delivery from a cow that had been trying to calve for two days. I wallowed for two hours dismembering the rotten fetus and taking it out in pieces. After I cleaned up, the owner offered to pay. When I told him the fee, he made out the check, handed it to me and began to complain about how high he thought the bill was. I lost my cool. I threw the check at him, told him to stick it where the sun didn't shine, and drove off.

This proved to be a very good decision. He came to town, found me, and apologized. I did accept the check this time, and he respected me thereafter.

Practicing veterinary science in Southern Iowa offered much diversification. Farms could have swine, cattle, sheep, horses, chickens, goats, dogs and cats that needed treatment.

Many of the people I worked for were products of the 1930's Depression. Thereafter, they developed the life-style as if another depression was right around the corner. These people had also lived through the era of no electricity or running water. They had outdoor toilets, and central heat and air-conditioning were unheard of. Roads were surfaced with dirt and horses were the main source of power. Most of the county's population lived in the country and small farms quilted the landscape. There were country schools about every two miles. Many families had five or ten children and raised most of the food they ate. Modern technology eventually came along and these small farms were gradually pushed into the future.

It was glorious to take care of small farmers' animals because they typically had only a small number in their herd. They really appreciated your service and could ill afford to lose even one animal.

One time, a client brought in a sick hen for me to examine. I was in a bit of a hurry, and immediately performed the standard procedure for diagnosing chickens. I killed the bird.

While examining the carcass in the post mortem, I asked, "How many chickens do you have?"

The owner answered, "I did have three." I felt awful. I had just killed one-third of his flock.

When I was practicing with Doc Anderson, we had a client who had lived through the hard times. This person, while very honorable, was one of the tightest people I have ever met. Doc Anderson had vaccinated his calves for Blackleg and had charged him one quarter for each doctored animal.

Some time later, the farmer had a cow have a calf. When the calf needed vaccinating, the client asked Doc Anderson to stop by and he did. After the vaccination, Doc Anderson was handed one quarter for one calf and no mention was made of the cost of the trip. Doc Anderson and I thought it was quite humorous. Regardless the distance, one calf or many, the rate was the same in the eyes of that farmer.

2
IOWA STATE,
HERE I COME!

The fall of 1957, I was rumbling toward Iowa State College in Ames in my old 1949 black Chevy coupe. The interstate highway system was not yet constructed, but the road was paved. I drove as fast as I could, heading for my first semester of life away from home.

My mind drifted back to Main Street and Bedford, the brick pavement and small agricultural town I was leaving. I was playing pool in the old Pool Hall with my friends. My future father-in-law, H.K. Russell, a prominent farmer and Angus cattle producer, was there, chalking his cue. He ambled over to my table and asked, "Why don't you go to veterinary school and make something of yourself?" I laughed at the thought.

I later began to think about that bit of advice. I told myself I was good veterinary material. I was a farm boy and had experience raising farm animals. I loved animals and I liked people. I wanted eventually to be someone in the community. I very much wanted to be rich. I thought I was the perfect candidate.

That's what young people feel when they want to become a vet. *"I love animals."* It's too bad it's not that simple. Earning the degree is an academically difficult track.

I rolled the old Chevy on up the road. The land was now flat when compared to the rolling hills of Southern Iowa. I could see beautiful farmland for miles. "Iowa State, here I come! I'm going to be a vet!"

I'd left behind a town where everyone knew one another. Little did I know that college teachers were there to teach and had no personal interest in getting to know you. They didn't care if I came to class or how I scored on a test. I thought it odd you had to carry a good grade point average when no one seemed to take interest. Good grades were the number one vet school requirement. You could be the most willing prospect in the world but you might not make it if you drew a teacher who enjoyed flunking students. You could flunk Algebra, Chemistry, Physics, Courtship and Marriage or English, none with any apparent bearing on being a vet, and get kicked out. Some students had to attend an extra one or two years of expensive school because of one bad grade they'd received. I lived in fear of the next test I wasn't prepared for and the grade I'd score.

I'd always hope for a good grade. A high grade point average meant I could be admitted before other pre-vet students who ranked below me. It was a cutthroat system, but somehow we pre-vets got along and worked together.

During the second year, nearly all of the students in my class had sufficient grade points to make application to veterinary school. I beamed when I filled out the application. I had it all … farm boy, 4-H leader, FFA officer, honors recipient. Now all I had to do was pass the oral exam. My confidence level soared, the one thing I was good at was words.

My first interviewer was Dr. Jeremaier, a retired down-to-earth practicing veterinarian who was working his last years in Anatomy Lab. He was great. I was left at ease thinking I would have no problem passing the oral.

The black cloud came without advance warning from the other veterinary students. Dr. Borkman was the most hated professor in veterinary college. To put it bluntly, he was the south end of a horse standing north. I stood erect before him and was cunning for his part of the interview.

Dr. Borkman first asked me, "Why do you want to be a veterinarian?"

Easy question, I thought, and began reciting from my mental list. "Well, Dr. Borkman, I want to be a veterinarian because of my love for animals, my love of people, and I can be my own boss."

There was a long silence. A big wrinkle locked on his forehead. If eyes could kill, his pupils were weapons. "Listen, you stupid little son-of-a-bitch. Will you love animals when the bastards bite you, kick you and half kill you? Will you love people when they treat you like shit, expecting you to perform miracles? And, if you think you'll ever be your own boss, you're full of shit. I worked as a practitioner for six years. When clients call, you go all hours. I was in the armed service for four years. When they say shit, you say what color. Now, I work for Iowa State, and they also call the shots. How in the hell do you think you'll be your own boss?"

I shook with fear and was speechless. A cold sweat broke out under my arms. I started to make a feeble attempt at words when he said, "Screw it, bring me the next candidate."

I thought I was dead and was sure I had failed the oral but miracles never cease to happen, I made it after all.

3
CALF LOOSE AT THE VET CLINIC

For January, it was an unusually nice day in Bedford. This time of year, the mean temperature was 11 degrees above zero. Today it would warm up to 62 degrees.

Curt Randolph was a client of Dr. Jim Cummings, a fellow veterinarian and partner. Curt had scheduled cows for pregnancy testing and e-coli scours immunization. Dr. Cummings badly wanted to do a scheduled bull surgery and he shyly hinted that I could do the Curt work while he operated. Curt and I had a disagreement years ago, but I thought this might be the time of reconciliation so I offered to do the work.

Time can heal old wounds. I took the Randolph call and everything was beautiful between he and I. We were enjoying the warm day and working the cows.

While Curt and I worked on cows a pickup and trailer backed up to the outpatient large animal surgery unit at the clinic. Without looking twice, the pickup driver threw the trailer gate open and out ran three calves into the pens. It didn't take long before the calves noticed the wide open pen gates on the opposite end. Freedom! They kicked up their heels in excitement at their chance to explore the outside world and off they romped down the old brick streets of our quaint town.

Little did the calves know that they would soon be honored with a roundup. An entire army of townspeople was eager to test its rodeo skills.

Tom, the driver of the pickup, realized the calves were loose and yelled, "The calves are out of this damned place." Tom was panicked. He tried to blame someone, anyone, at our facility for his narrow-minded mistake. Dr. Jim and Dr. Greg both saw the calves run by and yelled, "Oh, shit!" An elderly lady saw the calves run by her window and called the sheriff's office.

The sheriff's dispatcher sent out a two-way radio message. It hit the scanner airwaves in a flash. Instantly, a mob of would-be cowboys arrived, eager to join in on the calamity.

The more vehicles and people the calves saw, the wilder they became. The sheriff's posse arrived, then the city police. They were followed by the volunteer fire department, county employees and state highway commission boys.

Dr. Greg was pleading for calm as the chase picked up steam. On the way to a call, the ambulance became sidetracked and its personnel joined the melee. One of the ambulance personnel became so interested in the chase that the ambulance left without her when they continued on their call.

The herd was now running through the grass courtyard that surrounded the stately Taylor County Courthouse building. Courthouse employees came pouring out of the building and stood on the steps for a while. Soon, they too couldn't resist and joined the force.

The herd moved west across the street and through the yard of the Public Library. Some folks bravely attempted to run in front of the calves, and nearly got run over.

Two cowboys, Joe Kellogg and Dean Rowe were perched on the back of a pickup truck. They were attempting to rope one calf but the calf was faster than their lariats. Another calf was becoming exhausted and it began to move slower and slower. It was beginning to look like it would be happier in the pasture than running the bricks.

Three men with ropes caught up to the run-down animal and pinned it against a building. They threw ropes again and again but could not lasso even the stilled calf. After a few minutes, the calf caught its breath, bolted and ran away from the flying ropes.

The press arrived to film and take still photos. The vet clinic was becoming famous by now.

Then, as if by miracle, the mass of cowboys, vehicles and calves turned and were headed southeast, straight for the sale barn. A gate was opened, the herd was driven in, and the chase was over.

Back at the clinic, my two partners looked a little frazzled and weary. I had to comment, "If it will make you feel any better, I had a beautiful morning."

Greg and Jim looked at each other with menace. The look was meant for me.

4

JUNE 12, 1993

OH, WHAT A DAY

How would I ever live through it? It was Saturday, the sale barn's weekly sale day. I was overwhelmed with work. My partner was down and out, recovering from carpal tunnel surgery. My only hope for the day was the absence of rain. This might keep farmers working in their fields and away from the noon sale barn event. On that faith alone, I scheduled myself for 7:30 a.m. to castrate 70 head of 70 to 170-pound boars owned by Randy Elliott.

I got up at 5:45 a.m. and skipped a homemade breakfast knowing my Saturday secretary, Donna Eischeid, would be bringing a homemade roll. The mental image of the sweet treat would sustain me until 8:30 a.m. when Donna was scheduled to open the clinic. Before I left home, I asked my son Joe if he wanted to get out of bed to join me. He rolled over.

I left the house alone to check if Donnie, my ever-steady helper, had awakened. Donnie was up and I instructed him to eat breakfast and head to the office. I drove on down to the clinic to get my grip ready. I had a few minutes to spare which I spent studying the new sales tax formula and its inherent problems which had been presented by the State of Iowa. The phone interrupted me. It was Randy, asking if I would bring along shots to treat his dog as well. I repacked my grip and when Donnie arrived, we headed out the door. The sun was just beginning to rise. The fresh morning air engulfed our senses as we drove to New Market, a small town 12 miles west of Bedford.

Elliott's hogs were more than a handful because of their weight.

Donnie was in a heightened working mood and he handily threw the hogs down for the castration. The process went quickly, Donnie was throwing about as fast as I could cut. We finished up with a few smaller hogs that were penned in a farrowing house. Donnie and I said our good-byes to Randy and left the farm. On down the road, I happened to glance in my rearview mirror and saw Randy chasing us on his four-wheeler. I pulled over and Randy said, "You forgot to treat the dog." We returned to New Market for the Chow-Chow's vaccination. Once more we exchanged farewells and my mouth watered for that homemade roll.

Donnie and I got back on the road. About halfway to the office, my mobile phone rang. It was Everette Lee who lived just north of New Market. Everette had a colt with colic that required immediate attention. I whirled the truck around in the road and my stomach hungrily rumbled. I wished he had called ten minutes sooner.

On the road, Donnie and I came upon Lloyd Shaw. He had four bulls loaded in a trailer, all set to go to the Saturday sale. I was supposed to semen test them at 9:00 a.m. but I had forgotten about the appointment. I speedily hurried on to New Market to doctor Everette's ailing colt. As I was driving back to the office, I quickly called my disabled partner to make sure I had correctly covered the medicinal scheme for the colt. I made a second call to Donna to have her contact Ray Mercer, my lay assistant, to take my testing equipment to the sale barn and set it up for the Shaw bulls.

Donnie and I arrived at the sale barn and were met at the door by Steve Basler. He had a heifer in the chute that needed every kind of treatment in the book, none of which I could do with the supplies I had in my grip. I radioed Donna to have her gather up the list of necessary materials and I sent Jesse Beemer, a 10 year-old sale barn urchin, across the street to pick them up. I unloaded what I needed for Steve's heifer and was then ready for the bulls.

The bulls were ton bulls and as such were harder to handle than the earlier boars. The sale barn was full of curious onlookers, including Frank Jones. Everyone pitched in with commentary and watchfulness as I alone slowly finished the semen testing. I was lucky the spectators stood far enough back so the huge bulls didn't inflict injury upon them.

By now, my clothes were a royal mess and I wanted to slip over to the office to change. I walked in to discover a beehive of customer activity. Some clients wanted medicine, some a dozen eggs from Donna who sold fresh-from-the-farm produce on Saturdays and some clients just wanted to talk. It was 10:30 a.m. when I grabbed one of Donna's tasty homemade rolls. I gulped it down much like a near-drowned man taking in air.

I felt an urge to take a break and decided I'd go home to clean up. Before I stepped out the clinic door, in walked Marlene Smith with her Yorkie. The dog needed shots and Marlene wanted to talk about the season's possibility of heartworms. I told Marlene treatment probably wasn't necessary but someone else had told her it was. I figured someone knew something I didn't. Between phone calls I treated the Yorkie for the summer.

Jim and Sharon Moler came in and asked how busy I was. I feared I couldn't answer in a civilized manner and didn't have time to anyway. The Moler's proceeded to tell me we would be working 25 calves after the sale. I reluctantly shook my head yes to the 25 calves but before I was done nodding, they said they would have an additional 21 head or so and could I work them in?

Jerry Murphy, my farm help, drove up. He told me my cows were out in the Rowe's hayfield, the bull was in with the Rowe cows and there was a sick calf. I looked downhearted at Jerry. He said he could get things taken care of without me.

Both hands on the clock were heading straight up. It was nearly high noon. I slipped out of the office and at home I changed my clothes in record time. I was back at the sale barn by 12. There I met Winston and Jennifer Jones who had a load of cows to preg-check and bleed before they could be sold. I was sure pleased about the advance warning they had given me. I gathered up my help. The first cow of the Jones' had shit a bucket full in the chute. The second cow down the ramp kicked the shit all over me. So much for the clean clothes I'd spent the morning planning for.

Louis Birkenholz had been lingering around my office all that morning. He wondered about working his cows and calves, whether he could do it or if he needed help. He decided he could do it himself and I was relieved. He asked me if his cows would need worming before the month was out. I wasn't sure and told him 'probably not' and I made a mental note to get back to Louis.

I finished testing the Jones' cows at 1:00 p.m., sale break time. I was walking the cow's papers to the auction box when Jerry Davis, the auctioneer yelled, "You're wanted at the chute, Doc!"

Paul Jones had two more cows and a bull to test that he wanted to include in the sale. I rounded up all the equipment and tested the three that Paul had just requested. I hurried back to the arena so I could watch the cows sell. I was representing the Jones' herd.

Jerry again caught my eye and yelled, "Someone is back at the chute with something more to look at."

I ran back and found Gary Harl with a horse that had a cut leg. I talked him into wrapping the leg instead of suturing it but I didn't have any wrapping materials with me. I ran to the office, grabbed supplies, and ran back to the chute where I doctored the horse.

At the auction block I relieved Mark Spire who I'd put in temporary charge of handling my paperwork. My mobile phone rang and I very reluctantly answered it. A young girl needed medicine for her dog that had been sick for three days. The girl informed me she could pick up the medicine at the clinic, but she couldn't pay until Friday. I didn't have time to argue and I agreed to her terms.

Someone then called me back to the chute. A calf owned by Bob Cornell had a navel infection. I doctored the calf and turned to head back to the auction when Bob asked, "If you have some time, Doc, I need some milk replacer and mineral. Is anyone in the office?"

I turned again. "No, no one is in the office, but I'll get it." I hurried away.

At 2:00 p.m. I crossed the street and arrived back at the sale barn. Louis Birkenholz was there, hanging out at the sale. Louis had, by then, reached the conclusion that after the sale, he needed my help to run his calves and worm them and pour his cows. I strong-armed Ray and told Louis that Ray would help him. I gave Ray a list of things they'd need and told him to go with Louis, I had some pigs to vaccinate. I convinced Mark to do the vaccinations for me as the cows were beginning to sell and I needed to supervise.

An hour later I imagined things had slowed down enough that I could sneak away to the Moler place and work their calves. I headed for my truck and there stood Louis and Ray. They hadn't even left yet. They needed help getting the shots organized. I assisted them and sent them on their way. I hunted down Donnie and we headed toward the office only to be cut off by a red Chevy pickup with a screeching and honking horn. Inside the truck were Glen Hall and Glen Nickols.

"What're you doing?" they asked.

Warily I said, "Oh, nothing." The Glens had bought 23 calves at the sale and they needed treating. I agreed to do the work.

James Murphy, another helper, came into the office and wanted his paycheck. I wrote it.

Back at the sale barn, I found Gary Bolinger and Lenny Long leaving. With a little persuasion, they agreed to help me doctor the 23 calves. With the extra sets of hands, the calves went through quickly. I told Lenny I was in a hurry and I would pay him on Monday. "Mom said to bring the pay home tonight," Lenny told me. I went back to the office and wrote him a check.

"Let's get out of here," I hurriedly said to Donnie as we got into the truck. Out of nowhere, Dan Cline was standing at my window. He wanted to pay his vet bill. I climbed out of my vehicle and opened the office back up, did the paperwork and jumped back in. I cranked the wheel and had pointed the truck south before Tim Davison flagged me down. "I need a bag of calf feed," he said. I told Tim where the office key was hidden and to just help himself.

The mobile phone rang. The Moler's were confirming that the calves were ready, all 46 of them, and they were waiting for me. I needed to hook onto a chute for the Moler job as I had left mine in the country. It seemed the chute's hitching pin was in a bind, so I stomped on it. No go. I tried to pull it out. No go. I said a few choice words, got a hammer and knocked the pin out. I searched to find a small bolt that would hold it.

At last! Donnie and I were on the road. It was a relief to get away from the hubbub of the sale and clinic. Everything went like clockwork at the Moler's, we set and reset the borrowed chute and it worked smoothly. Now, we could go check on Ray and Louis as promised. I drove across country to the old Whipp place. Ray had gone and Louis had three calves left to process. I dumbly asked, "Are the cows done yet?"

Louis replied, "Of course not." Louis needed to change pens to sort the cows and calves.

In the meantime, Gerald Garner called and he had a sick cow. Jerry Murphy called again and said our sick calf was about to die. I told Louis to get the cows sorted, I would make the two calls that had just come in, then Donnie and I would return to help. Back to the sale barn we went. There I examined and doctored Garner's cow and headed out to Murphy's. On the way, the mobile rang. It was Patty Paxson. Her butcher calf was bloated badly and it needed help. I promised I'd stop after I finished at Murphy's.

Jerry's kids, Joe and James Murphy bounded out to greet me. They both assisted me in doctoring the calf which was a great help. Donnie and I then headed to Paxson's. We were in time for the calf, let the bloat out, drenched the critter and headed back across the country to Louis'.

Louis called me on the mobile. He had gone back to town to check on my whereabouts. I told Louis I was headed his way and he should go back to the country. I arrived before Louis and discovered that some of his sorted cows had gotten out of the corral. When Louis eventually pulled up, he was packing a cheeseburger and malt for me. Was I ever glad to see him! The roll I'd eaten at 10:30 a.m. had digested long ago.

Eight of the cows were still penned so Donnie and I worked them while Louis took off on horseback to round up the rest. After one cow was through, the phone rang. It was John East who was doing chores for Don Hensel. Don had a ewe down and John didn't want to lose an animal on his watch. I told him not to worry. The ewe would die anyway, but be sure and call the next day if it were still alive.

When the cows were rounded up, they worked well. I had Donnie run the chute and administer the rumen injector with wormer and the pour-on. Donnie felt very important with all that responsibility and I was running the cows to him for a change. I threw a "Lucas fit" only once when some Brahma cows gave us some trouble. It was 9:30 p.m. when we had doctored the last cow, loaded up and got out of there. Louis was very appreciative. I had to admit that the job had gone well considering the amount of time Louis had spent pondering instead of planning.

On the way back to town, the mobile broke my silence. I surely picked up the receiver as a reflex. After the day I had there couldn't have been any thought process involved. It had been three weeks but the splint had come off Patty Paxson's dog's leg. I told her to take the splint completely off and hope for the best.

Donnie and I were unhooking the chute back at the office when the phone rang there. A woman with a sick dog was on the other end. I told her, "Give the dog 2cc of combiotic and call me Monday. I am very tired."

Damn, it had been a fun day. Sleep nearly found me before I drove the few blocks home. Once I got there, I didn't have to hide.

5
GREG'S FIRST EMBARRASSMENT

In the 1990's I had reached the magical age of 50. It was sort of like dropping off the stage after performing for nearly 30 years. I began to wonder if I had paid my dues to the veterinarian profession. I looked in the round glass and it told me I'd better be thinking about whether I wanted to continue with the pressures of veterinary practice while also dealing with the unknown of Parkinson's Disease.

Now, more than ever, I was enjoying the regular routine. That wasn't always so. During the time that my kids were growing up, I wanted to be at all of their events and functions. The vet practice interfered with my desire to be a good father. Being a good father interfered with my vet practice. My life partner, Kay, helped me juggle my responsibilities by playing multiple roles. She was wife, mother, veterinary secretary, taxi-driver and bloodhound. Kay could always find me to send me on my next call.

A young lad from a neighboring town was the grandson of a client of mine. As a junior in high school, this boy had set a goal of becoming a veterinarian. His name was Greg Young. I had my doubts about Greg and his occupational choice. He was a "city" boy and was very quiet. He had worked on the farm with his grandfather but it wasn't the same as growing up there. I thought Greg's chances were slim to none of his becoming a successful vet. But, I also believed everyone deserved a chance. As a teenager, Greg and I agreed that he could ride with me on some calls.

As the years passed, Greg and I became close friends. I had seen his potential and I was making every effort to groom him to be an assistant of mine in my practice. Greg had the willingness and desire to attack the sometimes dangerous, sometimes frustrating, work-all-hours profession. I advised him that in order to be successful he had to be tough, enduring, resilient and resourceful. He needed to be kind to animals, never fail to do what was right and control his temper. I taught him that a customer was the most valuable asset, was always right, and when they called, they needed quick response. There is no place for independence. A veterinarian's client should never be afraid to call. At any time, your worst client could become your best.

After school, Greg returned to Southern Iowa and worked for the Adams Veterinary Clinic. It was a great experience for him, but soon after, he joined our clinic. By then, Greg and I had developed different habits. Unlike me, Dr. Young liked for his small animal clients to make an appointment for a visit rather than just dropping by.

It was a beautiful day in our little county seat town. The sun was arching over the majestic courthouse steeple. From the tall courthouse perch, you could overlook the entire town. The 120-year-old paving brick, which formed the streets, reflected in the sun as the morning moisture slowly evaporated.

Dr. Young opened the clinic door and there stood Laura O'Dell. Laura was married to Bob who was an all-time favorite client of mine. I had worked for most of the O'Dell family members, including father Bill and grandpa Al. The O'Dell's were shirttail relatives of mine, from generations back, but Laura was a stranger to Dr. Young. He knew Bob and Bill but, new to the practice, had never had the pleasure of Laura's acquaintance.

Laura asked if Greg would attend to her dogs. Greg hesitated and said with a little air in his voice, "I suppose so. However, I like for small animal clients to make an appointment before they drop in. Now, let's look at your dogs."

All seemed to go well between Laura and Greg. On Laura's way out, Greg reminded her, "Call for an appointment in the future. Otherwise you might be in for a long wait."

I visited with Laura before she left and didn't detect that Laura was miffed. Thirty minutes later the phone rang. The caller asked for Dr. Young. It was Laura. "Dr. Young, I want you to know that I was extremely offended by your reprimanding me for bringing in my dogs. Furthermore, my family has been with your establishment for years and years and has paid you hundreds, even thousands, of dollars. I don't deserve that kind of treatment. Dr. Lucas would never think of such a thing."

Greg tried to interrupt the conversation by saying, "I'm really sorry ...."

"Being sorry may not be good enough. Good-bye!" Laura said as she disconnected.

The look in Greg's eyes was distant. He wasn't angry, just very sorry he'd forgotten what I had told him. The next day a letter appeared on my desk written by Greg. It was addressed to Laura. In the letter, Greg spent two pages attempting to explain his actions. The letter was full of excuses. Greg never mailed it.

I swelled with a feeling of accomplishment and triumph. Greg had learned a lesson and the O'Dell's remained friends and clients.

6
JIM CLINE

Back at the clinic, we odd-manned to see who had to go to Jim Cline's. I lost. Yet while driving to the 102 River Valley I wondered if my partners had tricked me. Nonetheless, I figured it was my turn to go, so I loaded up the chute and Donnie Blake, my trusty helper.

Jim Cline was a very amiable young farmer who worked full time as a draftsman. His farm layout made me think that a blind man must have been the designer. Junk and old machinery piled everywhere; you could or could not imagine. It was a big job with eight cows, one bull, six calves and four pigs needing vaccination.

I pulled into the wrong side of the barn because Cline wanted me at the opposite corner. That corner had collapsed and was low to the ground. The penned cows would not be able to escape if I worked them from there. The lane was narrow and surrounded by broken gates and junk. There was no room to drive the truck in forward and turn around.

Jim said, "You'll have to back in." This included about 50 yards of backing but by going slowly, I positioned the chute into place.

"Oh, Doc," Jim said, "could you move the truck over about a foot?"

"No problem," I replied. I drove forward a couple of yards and began to back up, veering to the right. I felt a bump and then heard a big pffftttttt. I had run over a piece of iron that was sticking up out of the ground and ruined a nearly new tire. I took a deep breath, looked up at the blue sky, and kept myself from throwing a

Lucas tantrum.

"We'll need that gate laying over there to plug the hole in the barn door," Jim said. The gate must have weighed a ton but we got it moved into place. We set up our equipment and he said again, "Oh, I have a cow and a bull in the big lot I couldn't get in." So we took some medicated pour-on and fooled the two animals and got them treated. Now we could proceed with the others.

Rain began to fall. Systematically, Jim would drive an animal out of the lot, into the barn, through a maze of broken gates, and into the chute. The wild critters went through in unbelievably good fashion. We had help from Red, Jim's Blue Healer dog. Red was a persistent barker and bit the cattle as they went through the maze. Because of all of its barking, the dog could not hear its owner's pleas to let off. As one big cow ran out of the chute, the dog jumped at her, bit her on the side, and sent her into the side of my new truck, caving in the door.

"Oh, my," Jim replied. "Red, you'd better be good, or else." Or else is right, I thought to myself as I backed off yet another tantrum.

It had reminded me of Doc Anderson, my first partner, who was working calves for a client whose dog constantly barked and caused much commotion. It didn't bother the owner. When they finished, the client asked Doc Anderson how much the fee was for the procedure. Doc Anderson replied, "I'll do it for free, if you'll let me kill your damned dog!"

We thought we were finished when Mr. Cline said, "Oh, yes, I about forgot the bull calf to work. He's down in the other shed."

"Do we need the chute?" I asked.

"Oh no, we can tail him in the corner of the shed," Cline replied. We gathered up all the equipment and walked 50 yards to a dumpy little building. Water runoff was flowing through it. Even with the irrigation, piles of smelly feces were everywhere.

"I forgot to tell you, the bull kicks," Jim warned.

Jim had barely spoken when the bull calf gave a sharp kick and caught me square on the shinbone. The bull made a rapid lurch, momentarily suspended himself in midair, and came down flat on his side. He was bellowing and kicking trying to right himself. The bull had landed in a waste pile and rank, rotten matter covered

Jim and myself.

"Now why did you do that, you little rascal?" Jim asked of the calf. I was thinking of a lot worse things to say but kept my cool. The calf got on his feet and we managed to corner him up and finish his vaccination.

We gathered up the equipment, headed back to the truck and loaded up the chute. Then I asked, "Where are the four pigs?"

"Over in the other lot," Jim said. "We'll have to walk around." So we gathered up the equipment and once again made it around the barn.

"Hog dust really makes me sick. Could you please run the pigs out of the hog house and we'll pen them outside?" Jim asked.

"OK," I said. Donnie, who had been scrounging around for buried treasures until now, followed me and went inside the dirty, filthy, low-ceilinged farrowing house. Dusty spider webs draped from the roof to the floor. The four pigs were not pigs at all but hogs (big pigs). The hogs were startled when they saw strangers enter their private domain. They barked loudly and acted as if they would attack. They were running wildly about the pigsty in and out of water troughs. Water and dirt spewed everywhere, except out of that hole. Through the mist and dirt I spotted a gate. I could use that gate to direct the pigs where we wanted them to go. Luckily, I also had Donnie along, my strong-armed help. With the aid of the gate, he manhandled the pigs so I could castrate them.

Making our way back to the truck through the junk and broken down gates my client replied, "Now that really went well, didn't it?"

I lied, "Yes, it really did." It had only taken us two hours to do this big job and meanwhile I had a ruined tire and a dented door. "Yes, it just went great!" I spoke in jest.

On our way back to the clinic I got on the two-way radio and sang, "Oh, Beautiful for Spacious Skies" to my partners. They were impressed. I must have been in a good mood because a grin came over my face and I thought, this could only happen to a veterinarian. How lucky could I be?

7
BIRTH IN A CHICKEN HOUSE

February nights in Iowa can be breathtaking. Temperatures around 0 degrees can fall to 50 degrees below zero with the wind chill before dawn breaks. It was a cold wintry night when the phone rang at 1:30 in the morning. A voice on the other end slowly asked, "Were you sleeping, Jim?"

I immediately recognized the voice of Jim Wells, a good samaritan bachelor. I wanted to answer with "Oh, hell no, Jim, I was up canning tomatoes," but I didn't. Remembering Jim as being a good caretaker of his livestock, I was my usual, easy, cool self, considering what time of day it was.

"I have a cow that has been calving since 6:00 p.m. She isn't gaining so I figured it's about time to check her out," Jim told me on the phone.

I thought to myself, that's nice to know. I could have done this in the early evening if the cow's been laboring since 6:00. But I told Jim, "Okay, I'll be right down."

"And," he said, "I tried the other vet in Parnell so as not to bother you, but he said he doesn't do night calls anymore. I thought maybe you would help my cow."

I was even happier knowing I was second choice, but at least Jim was honest with me. I ambled to my coveralls and boots and headed out—on my way to Missouri.

Jim and I met in the drive where he informed me the cow was penned in the old non-electrified chicken house. He hoped I had a flashlight. Jim remarked, "She was real tame when I drove her in, but now she is a little nervous."

"Oh boy," I said, "it sounds like fun."

I stuck my head in the door of the dingy, little chicken house. It was a 1900's version of the old fashioned laying house where hens laid their eggs. Rows of unused nests lined the wall. I looked around for a pole to tie a rope to but found none. I could see no avenue of escape either, except for a small feed room. For my own protection I always looked for an escape route in case all hell broke loose. The cow warily looked at me but did not offer to charge. I walked on in with the equipment. I had a flashlight, lariat rope, a bucket of warm water, an obstetrics bag that contained a chain and a snare, and the calf jack. The jack is a tool about 6 foot long which helps deliver hard-to-pull calves.

I proceeded to get a rope around the cow's head on the first throw. Amazingly, she did not react wildly. I then threaded the rope through a hole around a support of the shabby building. I was positive this would restrain her. We got her tied short so I could make my examination. The calf was a normal presentation but the cow's pelvis was extremely small. Under these conditions, I feared doing a caesarean and went ahead to attempt a "normal" delivery. I placed the OB chains on the calf's feet and pulled. Its head went back. I put a head snare on and again applied pressure. There didn't seem to be birthing room so I put the calf jack in place and attached it to the chain and snare. As I tightened the tension of the jack, the cow became hysterical and lunged and jumped. All of a sudden the restraint rope released and the cow was loose. My 6 foot jack was firmly in place, sticking from behind her like a club. I yelled to Jim to get to safety as the 1500-pound animal was bucking through the dark building. As the cow banged around, the calf jack sounded like a gun firing every time it hit the floor. The swinging jack could have easily killed one of us.

The more the jack banged the wilder the cow became. For safety, I dove into the dark feed room and shut the door. Jim had retreated outside. In time, the cow tired and began to settle down. Not venturing far from my safe hole, I carefully retrieved my rope. I looped her again and retied her to the support. She didn't offer resistance. The unborn calf was surprisingly still alive and with one more hard pull, the calf came through the narrow pelvis.

A miracle had happened again. A new, vibrant, live calf flopped back and forth. It was trying to get on its feet but kept falling back down on its side. We released the cow and her maternal instinct kicked in as she aggressively began licking the newborn. She paid absolutely no attention to Jim or I.

"Isn't that something," Jim said. "It was a little trouble, but it was worth it."

"Yes," I replied. "It's always so great to get a live calf."

We made our good-byes and I then realized I was wide awake. I took a deep breath of fresh, cold air and saw that the stars were bright. There was a big, beautiful, full moon watching over. There was no wind and I felt a bead of sweat trickle down my neck. As I drove down the old Missouri road I crossed a wooden bridge that had no rails. The frost on the roadside weeds flashed on and off like Christmas lights, reflected in my truck's headlights. What a beautiful sight! I thought how most people were sleeping in the warmth of their beds and didn't even know what they were missing. I love being a veterinarian I told myself.

8
PIERRE,
BAD DOG

During the years attending veterinary school I wanted to believe I had chosen a glorious career. At Iowa State, I trained to rescue injured animals, treat sick ones and carry on in a routine manner. There were no classes in People 101. There was nothing to prepare me for every call.

Jan Hanna called around 10:00 one evening to discuss a problem she was having with Pierre, her large male Poodle.

"In the beginning," she said, "Pierre would sneak up on us or our visiting friends. Then he would stick his nose into one of our crotches. One time he stuck his entire head under a lady friend's dress."

"Oh," I replied, "did this alarm her?"

"Oh yes, very much so," Jan went on. "She said his nose was very cold."

"However," she continued, "that's not the half of it. Today he mounted me and then he mounted my daughter."

Trying not to think the worst I said, "You mean he was humping your leg?"

"No!" she emphatically said, "I mean he mounted me from behind and did the same to my daughter. When I tried to separate Pierre from my child, he bit me."

I couldn't believe it! I suggested to Jan that if it were my dog I would not put up with him anymore. I asked, "Do you want him neutered or put to sleep? At the very least," I continued, "I would have his nails trimmed."

Jan giggled at my comment.

Jan's husband tried to catch Pierre to bring him to the surgery clinic and Pierre bit him. They asked me to come to their house to capture the criminal dog. I gave Pierre an injection of tranquilizer with my pole syringe. Then I muzzled Pierre and transported him to the clinic.

Jan and the city police held dog court for Pierre. He was (unofficially) charged with assault, resisting arrest, lascivious acts with a child and indecent exposure. Pierre was convicted and sentenced to death, by lethal injection.

9
MATT
THE MUDBALL

Rain had fallen off and on for three days. The streams were running full, backing up to flood low-lying areas. The sun was shining now, making it a beautiful day in Southern Iowa. It was June. The trees were in full bloom, the grass was strikingly green and there were no weeds to block nature's beauty.

My son Matt, now 5 years old, was riding with me on a call. Charles Coolidge raised dirt hogs and he was an expert. Charles had asked me to bring along my small son. Matt was just the right size to crawl in and under the narrow farrowing crates to retrieve baby pigs and hand them out to us. Matt was his own expert. He slithered under the low slung gates, and one by one, quickly grabbed the fast little piggies. When Matt handed them out, I treated them with iron by injection. Chuck bragged on my son and that inspired Matt to work even harder.

As we were working, my mind wandered back to veterinary school. Dr. B. W. (Bud) Kingrey, our instructor in infectious diseases, had taken us on a field trip to see a swine herd that was infected with TGE, a highly fatal, fast spreading virus. After the visit I was the first to be back in the transport vehicle but had neglected to wash my boots. Dr. Kingrey instructed me to get out of the truck and wash. I could have spread the disease, he sternly informed me.

In class the next day I was drowsy and partially asleep while Dr. Kingrey continued his lecture on TGE. The professor ended by asking, "And the last thing you do before leaving the farm is what,

Mr. Lucas?" All I heard was Lucas. Since I hadn't heard the question, I didn't know the answer. After a long silence a classmate whispered to me, "Wash your boots, dumb ass." I almost said, "Wash your boots, dumb ass" but fortunately came to my senses before I repeated the last two words. I never knew if Dr. Kingrey knew I was sleeping and set me up with the question to embarrass me or if he had asked it because of the previous day's experience. My classmates much enjoyed my being on the spot.

We finished with the little pigs and Matt was still gloating over the great job he had done. He really swelled up when Chuck gave him a 50-cent piece.

"While you're here," Chuck said to me, "I wish you'd walk out here to the barn to look at a lame boar." I said I would and instructed, "Matt, you stay on the cement by the watering tank." I didn't want to drag him through the muddy lot. The cement was dry and was adjacent to a hog swill.

Chuck walked out through the sows talking to them all the way. He kept saying, "Unchikanada, unchikanada." I finally asked him what that word meant. He told me that unchikanada translated as "Please get out of the road nice piggy."

I thought *"Get the hell out of here you S.O.B.!"* was a better definition but didn't say so. I looked over the lame male hog, gave him some medicine and started walking back toward Matt.

Somehow Chuck and I had spooked some of the hogs and they gallantly barked and ran swiftly around the lot. Six of them headed straight toward the watchful Matt and that had spooked him. The pigs were too close for his comfort. Matt panicked and ran right off the cement. The ground's surface looked dry but underneath was two feet of watery, muddy, hog swill. As Matt tried to run on the surface, he fell in and very quickly became submerged. I hurried as fast as I could to rescue my son. Before I got there, he shot up out of the swill and stood. He was all right but what a funny sight he was. All I could see through the mud was the white of his eyes. Matt didn't even cry. I walked him over to my mobile veterinary hospital, took off his clothes and scrubbed. I dressed him in a clean sweatshirt I happened to have along, for his ride back to town. Matt seemed to enjoy the whole affair. I guess he figured it was all part of the job.

I wondered how Dr. Kingrey would have disinfected Matt before we left that farm.

As I recalled, my mobile veterinary truck and its water carrier came in very handy at another crucial time. Our family had just returned home from a vacation down in Arkansas. We had barely been in the driveway when my farm tenant drove in to inform me that I had a dead calf at the south farm. I changed my clothes and started up the vet truck. Even though we all had just gotten out of the car, all the kids wanted to ride along.

We drove through the farm gate and had no trouble spotting the dead animal. All four of its legs were sticking straight up in the air. It appeared that the calf had died from bloat. The calf's abdomen and paunch were tight as a drum.

I wanted to check the contents of the calf's abdomen to try to determine what had caused the bloat. Jamie, my daughter, was standing 15 feet away, curiously watching the post mortem. I stuck my knife in the rumen but did not make a big incision. When I pulled the knife out I had left a two-inch cut. That small cut was beginning to swell from the enormous pressure it was under when out squirted a rope-like mass of rumen contents. The contents headed straight for Jamie. She was first struck in the face, became hysterical and tried to move out of its path. It seemed no matter where she moved, the geyser followed. She turned her back only to get a dose in her hair and on her rump. The few seconds it took for the contents to empty seemed like hours. I hurried to her and tried to keep her calm. I then walked her to the vet truck and hosed her off.

On the way back to town I said, "Jamie, you have just witnessed a frothy bloat. The green stuff was foam caused by eating too much alfalfa hay. That poor little calf died from overeating."

Jamie wasn't thinking of the vet lesson as she whimpered, "I don't care, just get me back to town."

10
THE COW THAT COULDN'T GET UP

There were three notions when it came to cows in the pasture. The pasture, and how the cow acted in it, depended upon whether you were the cow, the cow's owner or the vet.

Cow-in-the-pasture calls usually began this way. The owner would say, "She's out in the pasture, Doc, but don't worry about catching her 'cause she can't even stand. I just walked up to her to try to prod her up and she didn't even move." As a vet, I knew that about 95% of those cows would get up and run off at the sight of me.

Marge Lock, widowed when her husband suddenly died, was spry for a lady of 80 years. Her husband had raised Simmental cattle and Marge continued the operation after his death. Simmentals were wild and woolly and Marge had no business working around the breed. One day Marge called to ask for assistance with a pastured cow that was down. The cow was calving.

Ray, my lay assistant, went with me on the call. On the way to the farm, Ray, who had a great way with words and was familiar with the Simmental disposition said, "I'll bet this will be one gentle son-of-a-bitch!"

Marge was waiting in her pickup alongside the road. We stopped to get directions to the downed cow. Marge said to Ray and me, "She's been trying since early this morning and nothing has shown. That's her, lying down at the top of the hill in the pasture. We can't get her in because she won't get up. She must be paralyzed. You won't have any trouble catching her."

I snickered over how many thousands of times I had heard that. It was wishful thinking that the cow could easily be caught. "Let's see what happens," I reassuringly told her.

Ray and I idled up to a "Missouri" gate about 100 yards down wind from the cow. It took both of us to open the gate with its five barbed wires. The wires were attached to posts and then were stretched between two more posts. Missouri gates were hard to get a hold of without taking a barb in the hand or arm. The minute we walked through, the cow's head went up. I immediately saw a crazed look in her buggy eyes and I knew we were in for some fun.

"Get behind the steering wheel, Ray," I told him.

In order to help this cow, we would have to try to get her tied to something. I took out my lariat rope and tied one end to the bumper hitch.

I explained my plan to Ray. "I'll ride on the back. You drive close by and I'll try to get my rope on her, before she gets up."

Ray did as he was instructed. We were getting pretty close to her and momentarily my hope soared.

That cow shot up on her feet and came at us like a fighting bull out of the stocks. I threw my lariat loop at the moving target and missed. I pulled the rope around the truck and got ready for another throw. Out of the corner of my eye, I saw the cow coming. She was definitely looking for me. I dove for the truck bed but wasn't fast enough. The cow's head pitched me forward. Still wanting another piece of me, the cow banged away at the side of my new truck and left a dent every time she connected. I grabbed for my rope. At that point, I couldn't tell who was chasing whom. The cow was chasing me and Ray was chasing the cow. On a run around, she nearly got both front feet over the side of the pickup bed. Only by throttling the truck did Ray and I escape.

The cow was coy. She knew we'd be back around for her. She stood there, waiting. That gave me the chance to lay the loop over her head. I yelled at Ray, "Go ahead, string her out and choke her down."

The cow kept up with the truck and she would not go down. We drove her up by a fence to try to close her in. I quickly threw another lariat rope over her head and tried to get it tied to a fence post. Before I did, she took off on a dead run and got ahead of the truck. Ray and I were in pursuit when we reached a corner. Coming around on the arc, the cow had us trapped. Ray took a quick left turn and drove us out of there. By happenstance, the quick left had wrapped the rope around the cow's legs. She tripped and fell to the ground near a post.

"Stretch her out, Ray!" I yelled.

We now had the cow tied and stretched out between two ropes. To be extra sure she was staying with us, I put a halter on her head and tied it to yet another post.

Unwillingly, she was ready to see the vet. Upon examination, I saw that the calf was coming breech (butt first) with its legs down and pointing forward. It was difficult to get the feet coming first, but after some manipulation the delivery was complete. The calf was dead.

"I guess I should have checked her last night," Marge said.

"I guess so," I replied.

As unbelievable as it may sound, when I am in the proper mood, cowboying is a certain amount of fun. The challenge is in conquering the wild beast. It is so much easier, though, on animal and man alike, to work with a cow already penned.

Doc Anderson was right when he would say, "We're 1/3 veterinarian, 2/3 cowboy."

11

KAY LAUNCHES THE B FARMALL

Doc Anderson's portfolio was full of quips. He used to say that Southern Iowa, as far as weather is concerned, is the hottest, the coldest, the wettest and the driest place on earth. We got it all and all in between.

Northern Iowans expected cold winters with lots of snow and they seemed to love it. In Southern Iowa, we enjoyed, on the average, mostly milder winters. Still, blasts of cold from the North did not escape us entirely. Winter could blow in bitter cold and beautiful scenic snow. Early mornings of extremely cold temperatures presented a rapture of sparkling frost and atmospheric sundogs could light up a daytime sky.

This was a frigid winter that followed the summer of heat and drought in the early 70's. It was amazing that a few months earlier it had been scorching hot. The crops had burned up in the field. Now it was colder than a penguin's behind.

The ground water level was at an all-time low and many wells had dried up. The well I used to water the cattle herd was dry and I had to devise a method to winter water them. I put a pump on the power take-off of my little B Farmall tractor. Then, I drove the tractor down to the pond, chopped a hole in the ice, stuck a hose down in the pond and pumped water up. It was an interesting operation.

My cows needed five to ten gallons of water a day to keep nutritional balance in their huge paunches. That winter they'd drink by licking the layer of ice and snow covering the ground. It was nowhere near the amount of water they required. When the supplemental water I pumped came flowing from the hose, the cows would crowd in to be first at the fresh supply. The more aggressive cows would push their way in. The more timid creatures would slink back and wait their turn.

It was a very frigid morning. I had gone to pump water for my cows but my faithful little B Farmall refused to start. I woke my wife, Kay, to ask for her help. I knew that we could start the tractor by pulling it with another vehicle. A short, sharp tug should do the trick. Kay was more than willing to assist.

Kay jumped out of bed, dressed, got a cup of coffee and away we went. We spoke on the way of the winter's dazzling beauty. Alongside the road, a cock rooster pheasant strutted in the sun. His beautifully colored feathers and long tail gleamed brightly against the sparkling frost on the fences and shrubs. Amazing, I thought, how Mother Nature equipped pheasants with the ability to withstand cold temperatures when they had only shrubs and overlaying frozen grass for protection.

The little tractor was sitting in a shed. I backed my 4-wheel-drive veterinary truck into the building until I was about three feet from the tractor's front wheels. I got out of the truck and attached one end of a 15-foot heavy log chain to the front spindle of the tractor. The other end I attached to the back of the truck. I stood back and looked the situation over. The driveway to the shed was covered with ice and snow. To pull start a vehicle, dry ground was required. Traction was needed to turn the tractor's wheels, to subsequently turn the piston over for the start. The little tractor needed to turn over before we hit the ice and snow I had concluded.

Kay's job was to drive the vet truck. I said to her, "We'll try to pull start it right in the shed where the traction is good. So, when I tell you to go, give it hell, so it'll turn over quickly while on dry footing."

Kay got behind the wheel of the truck. I got on the B Farmall with its triangle front end. I turned on the ignition, put it in the proper gear to start, and said to her, "OK, give it hell!"

What I had forgotten to say was, "Be sure to tighten the chain first."

When I heard Kay put the truck in gear and stomp on the

accelerator, I knew I was in deep trouble. When the slack came out of the chain, the tractor (with me holding on pale-faced and frozen to the seat) ejected from the building like a rocket from a launch pad. Kay headed for the road and took a sharp left. I followed on the tractor, swinging at a 90 to 180 degree pendulum, sliding on the ice. Kay never looked back. She continued toward the road at a galloping pace. When she got to the road she hesitated while she checked for oncoming traffic. The hesitation put slack back in the chain and the tractor rolled up on it.

Kay cautiously looked in both directions but didn't see anything coming on the highway. She floor boarded the truck. The chain's slack quickly dwindled as she jerked and pulled me along. Kay picked up speed. There was one last lurch before the front end of the tractor completely broke away. I came to an abrupt halt.

Kay looked back after hearing the terrible noise. She stopped the truck and sheepishly walked back to see the tractor in two pieces. She said, "Oh, oh, did I do something wrong?"

"Oh, hell no," I said, feeling slightly upset. I was too relieved to be alive to be angry. "This happens all the time," I added. It was a story I would tell our grandchildren.

During the ride back to town I reminded Kay of another time her driving about did us in. We were chasing a cow in my veterinary truck at Dwight Lovitt's. Kay was about nine months pregnant. I was holding on to the back of the truck with one hand, trying to throw the lariat with the other. The cow was fast, but Kay was faster. She must have had a lapse in memory, forgetting I was in the back. Kay drove off lickety-split into a mud seep and became stuck. This time, her poor driving actually saved me from toppling out. This was a story I would tell at the coffee shop. Amazingly enough, the whole episode didn't even start Kay in labor.

12

RALPH AND THE ANT HILLS

Everyone has a good side. In some people, the good is buried deep within. Our vet clinic's clients imitated life. Just to stay agreeable with some of them took a big shovel.

Ralph Weller was a survivor. He could squeeze a penny so hard it would choke poor old Abe. Ralph had a funny little voice as if his vocal chords were located at the bridge of his nose. At the clinic we found humor in mimicking his speech.

"I have some calves to work," Ralph said. "Could you do them Thursday after 5:00 p.m.? That's when my grandson gets home from school."

"Any chance of doing them before closing hours?" I asked.

"Oh," Ralph replied, "there is lots of daylight left after 5:00."

"OK. How many calves are you talking about and what needs to be done?" I asked.

"There are seven. Three need sevenway, two need castrating and two heifers need calfhood vaccination. And, oh yes, bring the chute," Ralph informed me.

Later that same fall, Ralph called about a cow having trouble calving. After peppering me with questions, Ralph decided he might as well have me come out. He could handle the birth, he thought, but he needed help catching the cow. The cow was still in the pasture and there wasn't a corral or building anywhere near. I had Ray and Donnie for the day so I thought we just as well head out to Ralph's. 'Lo and behold, when we arrived at the pasture gate, we could see that Ralph had sneaked up on the cow and had a rope on the unborn calf's leg. Ralph was hanging on to the other end of the rope and the cow was dragging him around the pasture. Ralph released the rope when he saw us at the gate. His attempt at saving a vet bill had failed.

It was muddy in the pasture so I locked in the four-wheel drive. We spun the truck through a grass waterway and kept it edged around a terrace to avoid falling off into a small canyon. The pasture also contained scads of five-gallon-bucket-sized anthills. We bounced over them and drove around a pond to make it to the cow.

I jumped out of the truck and grabbed my lariat. I hazed the calving cow a little and wow! I roped her the first time. I set my heels in an attempt to hold the 1400-pound animal. I kept my balance and remained standing on the muddy and wet ground as the cow began dragging me. Ralph's ten-year-old granddaughter was watching and she yelled, "It looks like he's water skiing!"

I lost my balance when I hit a huge anthill and went down, headfirst. I let loose of the burning rope and let the cow get away. I got up and headed back around the cow. She was faster than I was, but when she slowed; I got a hold on the rope again. I followed her slower pace, looking for something to tie the rope to. She was moving around an old water spring that was filled with posts and small trees. I sped up my pace in an attempt to wrap the rope on a post. Once again I tripped over an anthill and fell. The cow got away.

I was out of breath. I yelled at Ray to bring my truck. I got behind the wheel and followed the cow until I could get a tire stopped on the rope. That's a hell of a good way to wipe out a truck but the cow had exhausted most of the other options. When I had her stopped, I tied the rope to my bumper hitch and told Ray to get under the steering wheel.

"OK, Ray," I said. "Give the truck hell until you choke her down." Ray applied some torque until there was enough pressure on the rope to drop the cow. Donnie got my OB equipment. I had the pull chains on the calf and we were about to make the delivery when the cow exploded forward. She ran off with my equipment, still attached to the rope.

"Choke her down!" I yelled at Ray. Ray tried but the cow would not choke. Around and around they went, bouncing over the damned anthills. All of a sudden, the cow was running faster than the truck. She had Ray and the truck against a fence and he was cornered. Ray could not get ahead of her. All of a sudden, the cow stopped again. The wheel of the truck had gone over the rope and I told Ray to back onto it. At the same time the cow bolted. The rope caught on the lug of the tire and went to the top of the wheel. I happened to be standing on the rope as well. When the cow hit the end of it, I was thrown up in the air. I somehow forgot to somersault to land on my feet. When I came down I made a three-point landing, back, head and butt. I heard every joint and bone crack. Ray later said he swore he saw me fly by the truck window. Ralph's observing granddaughter was learning new words.

Ralph's neighbor's son had arrived to help. He tied the rope end to a four-wheel all terrain vehicle that he had brought along. Then we got yet another rope tied to my truck. Once again, the cow lunged forward. She pulled the four-wheeler over on its side. None of us were hurt and the downed four-wheeler held the cow. At last! I got my OB equipment and examined the cow. One foot and leg of the calf was back. I easily pulled the stuck foot and leg out. The wet calf emerged and fell to the ground. The calf had taken quite a ride but was still alive. We drug the calf to the cow's head so she might claim it. She smelled it and bawled and licked at it. All appeared well and all we had to do was get the ropes off.

Both of the ropes had quick release hondas which would help. I unsnapped the rope tied to the four-wheeler. Before I could get to the other one, the cow threw another fit. This time she tried to pull my truck over. Ray was ready and with my prodding, knew what to do.

I yelled, "Choke the S.O.B.—give it hell!" And Ray did, bouncing over the anthills. Around and around Ray and the cow went at a high rate of speed. The cow was gaining on the truck. Ralph, wanting to help, got in between the cow and the truck but the rope was gaining on him. The old man could run pretty fast but we watched, with eyes closed, imaging that he soon would be knocked head over heels. The cow stopped and Ralph ran to safety. His diversion allowed us to sneak up on the cow and release the rope.

A neighbor of Ralph's drug the calf near the cow but she jumped up and left it. We all hoped she would come back later when the pasture strangers had left.

Ralph, his granddaughter, and my crew all jumped in the back of the truck for a ride to the road. On the way Ralph yelled, "Watch out—there are some big anthills in this pasture."

I looked at Ray. Ray looked at me and said, "No shit, Dick Tracy!"

When we arrived at the road Ralph asked, "How much will that be, doctor?"

"Thirty-five dollars," I replied.

"Well, I guess it's worth it for a live calf!" Ralph said.

Later I checked with Ralph and the cow and calf were doing fine.

13
DOC AND THE BARKING DOGS

1989

I had a bad side. There was nothing that exposed it any faster than barking dogs. They set me off.

Early one morning, around 3:30, I had been having an excellent beauty rest when the noise of a loudly barking dog awakened me. I was a light sleeper anyway, but I was surprised the whole neighborhood wasn't up. I got out of bed and fought off the noise by moving from room to room hoping I could find a quiet spot. All I wanted was to get back to sleep. It was two hours later when I finally did.

A couple of nights after, slightly after midnight, the same dog started up again. I wasn't sure I was totally awake but I was conscious enough to know I did not want to spend another sleepless night. I went to the garage and got the shotgun down from its rack. My plan was to scare the damn dog and if that didn't stop the yelping, I was sure I'd kill it.

I sneaked down through the pasture, letting the noise guide me. I had at first thought the offending dog belonged to a neighbor I didn't like. That would make the job easy. As I got closer, I discovered the dog belonged to George Pfander. George was a bachelor who was a long-time friend and acquaintance. Old George was about 70 and his dog was his only companion. I had to rethink my plan.

At first I thought, "I can't take the chance of getting off even one shot. I can't kill George's dog. I'll just go back home, tough it out, and call George in the morning." About that time, the dog let out a series of bellows and barks. I was reasonable no more.

I aimed that shotgun through the trees and got the doghouse in sight. I figured on just scaring the dog. Within the town limits, the blast from that 20-gauge shotgun sounded like a cannon in a gymnasium. The noise even frightened me. That dog never even whimpered and we were engulfed in silence.

I was nervous and I hurried back to the house. I was hoping no one had seen me and that the cops weren't nearby. I had made a clean break, except from my conscience, which was beginning to bother me. Did I kill the dog? I never heard a thing after I fired and I hadn't since returning home. "That's just great," I told myself. "George will go out and find that his dog is dead, his only close relative and friend. The whole neighborhood will be trying to find out who the bastard was that shot it. I would have to lie, even though I'm the world's worst at it. I could never confess to such an awful deed. Lying would work! There was no one to prove that I was the bastard."

"Oh hell! I left the shell casing in the gun. I'd better go remove the casing so it won't look like the gun was used recently." Out to the garage I went. "Oh shit! I ejected the casing out in my pasture. Now they'll have evidence. I'll have to get that casing when it gets light."

I tried to sleep but was haunted by my ghastly act. Just maybe the dog is OK, I kept thinking. I listened for barking. I could hear other dogs in the neighborhood, but not the one I desperately wanted to hear howling.

When I could no longer stand the suspense, I decided to sneak down to see if I could find the dog. Out the back door of the house I went, stepping over fallen acorns on the patio. With each step I took, acorns crunched under me. I was convinced I'd wake the whole neighborhood and I just couldn't risk being discovered. My son, Joe, was not home yet either and I feared having him catch me scavenging in the dark. I went back to bed to tough out the night, or what was left of it.

I slept until daybreak. I quickly dressed, jumped in the truck and drove by George's house. My heart fell when I didn't see the dog. I drove down around town, came back, and to my joy, there stood the quiet dog! The dog and I had both learned a lesson from the previous night. The dog kept quiet and I vowed to stop my night raids.

1992
THEY KEEP BARKING AND BARKING AND. . .

In 1992, it was my same bad side, with the same neighbor and the same dog. Three nights of barking in a row had really set me off. I thought about my shotgun but decided not to put myself through that again. But, a couple of buckets of water might do the trick!

It was dark when I loaded water in the pickup and drove to George's. I knew George was hard of hearing and he would never hear me dumping water on the offensive dog. I threw the first bucket with great success and soaked the dog. What I didn't know was that George kept another dog that slept inside the house. That dog began having a fit, and woke George up.

I was ready to throw the second bucket of water. I pitched the bucket back and here came George's house-dog, running straight for me. That scared the shit out of me. I stood frozen in the truck lights just watching the dog. When it got close enough to my foot, I kicked at it. I watched the dog run back toward the house and then I looked up. There stood George in his pajamas. He was mad as hell.

I said, "All I'm doing is throwing water on your f——— dog to stop his barking. I hope that's OK."

"I 'spose so," George angrily said as he slammed the door in my face.

Huh! It didn't bother me. The dog had quit barking and I could get some sleep.

14
WALSTON
ROUNDUP

The main calving season begins in January and lingers on until June or July. The majority of new calves come in cold weather. Many farmers have a calving pasture, small enough so that a cow can be caught if trouble is suspected. Still, there are a lot of cows that calve in a timber or big pasture. If trouble comes, a wide-open area is the worst place to be for all concerned.

A cow will lie down when calving time is near. The farmer discovers her and will pound and kick at her trying to get her back on her feet so he can take her to the barn. The cow usually continues to lie there as she has a familiarity with the owner and disregards the physical plea. If a stranger appears in the pasture, it's a whole different ballgame. I believe animals can smell a vet coming and they go berserk. Some doctors refuse to attend a cow until she is in a barn or a catch pen. I sort of like the excitement that goes along with a good chase, if I'm in the proper mood that is.

It was a beautiful morning when Dave Walston phoned. He had a big cow calving. The fetus was only part of the way out and the cow was in trouble.

"Is the cow in the barn?" I asked when he called.

"No, Doc, she cannot get up. She is paralyzed," he answered. I told him I would be right out.

Frost covered everything. It had been a foggy night and the frost had flocked the countryside. The spectacular glowing sun was just peaking over the hill. The air was calm and fresh and I thought it was a great day to be alive. School was out for winter break. I stopped at home to pick up my son, Joe, who would assist me on the call.

When Joe and I arrived at the farm, we could see two pickups parked just behind the downed cow. I eased my truck down toward them. Just as soon as the paralyzed cow smelled me coming, she jumped up and took off running. I let Joe get behind the wheel of my truck so he could pace the cow. I got in the back of Dave's truck with my lariat. Dave drove alongside the cow and, safari style, I got the rope on her with the first throw. I wasn't fast enough to get the rope tied to anything, though, and away the cow went—with my rope. Dave stopped the truck for an instant and I relaxed. Not knowing Dave's plan, his next acceleration threw me out of the back of his truck. Dave stopped the truck again to find a badly shaken but not seriously hurt cowboy, lying on the ground.

Dave took off on foot after the cow. When she stopped for a breather, Dave got close enough to grab the rope and he held on to one end. I got in my truck with Joe and we watched Dave pull. The cow wasn't pulling back and instead, she charged at him. Dave, with the aid of the cow's head, was booted into the back of his truck and he let go of the rope. The cow took off. The foot chase was over as far as we were concerned. From the safety of our pickups, we decided to head the cow toward a big old barn. Dave's dad, Vane, arrived in the third pickup and joined in.

By this time the calf had fallen back inside the cow. The cow was still wearing my rope and she wanted to eat us for breakfast.

With our ever-so-gentle prodding, the cow found the barn door and she ran inside. We closed the gate behind her. Joe walked around to the opposite door and sneaked into a haymow. From his overhead position, he reached down to the cow and grabbed the rope. Like a flash the cow charged his hand and with her head, pinned Joe's arm to the manger. The cow kept her pressure as Joe began to yell. The cow would not release. The force of her head against the manger broke a board and Joe was free. He had bravely kept a hold of the rope. He quickly tied the rope around a post and had the cow securely snubbed. Just in case, I added another rope to her and delivered a healthy calf.

From a cow that couldn't get up, I had a sore back and Joe had a sore arm. But I wasn't ready to become one of those doctors who insisted the cow be penned. I wanted to be my own boss, just like I told Dr. Borkmam at the vet school entrance interview.

15

AS THE
STOMACH TURNS

At the clinic, Ron Davison was waiting for me. Ron was the clinic's lay assistant; hired to help us vets get through our daily routine. I was running a little behind because of a meeting that ran late the night before. Ron had beaten me to work.

I was on the City Council and during the previous night's meeting we had to deal with yet another dog problem. Dog problems probably occupied half of the City Council's meeting time. Max O'Neil, who lived across the block from me, had on hand 29 coonhounds that were quiet during the day but barked all night. The dogs lived just south of the City's only multiple housing complex. Complaints were coming in by the score from the residents, and I had my own to add. The City did have an ordinance on the books that allowed only two dogs per household. Max felt he was exempt from the law because the dogs were a business of his. At his legal hearing, Mr. O'Neil represented himself and presented the judge with 24 hours of blank tape to prove his dogs did not bark. Max lost the case and I often wondered how much of the tape the judge listened to. The judge ruled in the City's favor. Max had to remove the dogs.

The first thing Ron said to me was that Savannah Wilson had a sick cow to attend to. He said the cow was lethargic, lame and had a two-week-old calf that was also doing poorly.

"Probably a toxic mastitis," I blurted out.

Savannah Wilson was a former businessman who had turned to farming. He was a big man and carried extra weight on his massive frame. He was hard working and kind and he loved his purebred Polled Hereford cows. Savannah had a son who was supposed to help him with the farm work. Unfortunately, the son never got out of bed much before noon and was mostly helpless after he had gotten up. Ron and I knew we would need Savannah's help on the call.

Savannah had a nickname. At the clinic, we called him "Wimpy" after a character in the Popeye cartoons. Savannah, like Popeye's Wimpy, could eat more hamburgers in one sitting than anyone in town. I had seen Savannah order two burgers for "here" and "four to go". Eating like that led us to believe "Wimpy" had a cast iron stomach. We found out differently.

It was a beautiful spring morning. There had been an inch of rain that forced the green grass to reach upward toward the sky. The trees were heavy and water dripped from their leaves. Just outside the edge of town a doe deer and two speckled fawns were out for a casual early morning feed. "Isn't that something, the natural beauty we have in good old Southern Iowa?" I asked Ron.

"Yes," he answered, "you have to take time to see it, and smell the roses."

We arrived at the Wilson farm where Savannah was waiting for us.

"Morning," he grunted.

"Morning, Savannah," I replied. "Nice rain but it looks muddy up to the barn."

"Yep, we'll have to walk," he said. The barn was about 150 yards from the road.

"Ron," I said, "we'd better take everything we'll need now, to avoid too many trips to the truck." We loaded all we could think of and started on foot toward the barn.

"I think she's got grass tetany," Savannah said.

"I doubt it," I answered, "but I'm prepared for that also."

"What else could it be?" he asked.

"Let's take a look first," I said. Savannah wasn't unlike other farmers who delighted in making a diagnosis and then arguing about it if you differed.

As we walked toward the barn, the lethargic wide-eyed cow

stood up. She swung her head wildly and looked at us. Without much trouble, we got a rope on her and she settled down. She was not as wild as she was toxic. I immediately noticed a swollen quarter of her bag that was making her appear lame. She was running an elevated temperature that indicated an infection was to be found somewhere.

"I'm afraid she has a toxic mastitis, Savannah," I said.

"What?" he asked. "She's never had it before. Are you sure it's not grass tetany?"

"I am sure," I replied. "I'll show you where the trouble is."

Ron knew what to do as he pressed the cow against the barn wall and held her tail up. Holding a cow's tail up reduced the chance that I'd get kicked. I took my scalpel and quickly cut off one third of the cow's teat. A gallon of yellow puss emptied on the ground.

"Well, I'll be," Savannah said.

Ag-ag-ag-ag was the reverberating noise that Savannah then began to make. After about the sixth "ag", up came his breakfast. He walked, stooped over, to a corner of the barn and continued to upchuck. The upchucking turned into the dry heaves. Ron and I, trying not to laugh hysterically, continued to doctor the cow. When we had finished I asked Savannah if we could help him in any way.

He said, "No, I'll be all right in a bit, aaauugh," and he heaved again.

Ron and I bid Savannah goodbye and walked back to the truck. Just as we were getting in, we heard yet another "aauugh" coming from the barn. Ron and I finally broke out laughing. Was this the man we knew with a cast iron stomach, "Wimpy"?

I had not been in vet practice very long when I had the chance to see if I had the stomach for it. Sometimes a vet can run into some pretty terrible messes.

I had been called to Billie Hatfield's place to look at an enlargement on a cow. I took a look and said, "I believe it's a big abscess but to be sure I'll stick a needle in it to see what comes out."

I had heard stories of vets who would hurry and cut abscesses and then drop the animal's guts on the ground. I got a needle syringe from my truck and aspirated the basketball-sized abscess. The

syringe filled with puss from the swelling. For the incision, I deadened the area and put on my rubber boots. I was hurrying and quickly cut a four-inch incision. The incision allowed about two gallons of puss to run out. I then gave the cow a lavage with antiseptic and a shot of penicillin. I told Billie to watch the cow. I didn't want the incision to seal shut before it had finished draining. I was all business as I left the farm and headed home for lunch.

My wife had prepared one of my favorite meals of dried beef gravy and biscuits. I ate it as if nothing had happened. I had passed the test. I had the stomach to be a vet.

A young fellow chose to watch while I spayed his female Labrador. He began with a rapid-fire enthusiasm by asking me a lot of questions. Then, all of a sudden, he became very quiet. I looked up, but not in time to catch him. He flew over backwards and hit his head on the concrete floor and passed out. He came to quickly, and I ushered him out for fresh air then finished the surgery alone. The young man was very apologetic. I reassured his ego and stressed how frequently I had seen stomachs turn.

16
IOWA SAFARI

It was a hot July 4th holiday. Bedford was hosting its annual parade and celebration. After the parade, I had planned to attend the horse races. The two-way radio cackled with a call from Joe Everhart. He had a cow calving and she was in trouble.

I asked my usual question, "Have you got her in?"

"Yep, Doc, I have her in the corral," he answered. "She is in the east pasture."

Joe made me uneasy. He had a decent sense of humor, but from experience, I knew anything could happen. Between the two of us, we usually found a way to make fun out of work. As I was driving, I wondered what lay ahead.

As I pulled in, I could see the cow was in the corral. It surprised me that Joe had not pulled my leg. I got my equipment ready and Joe grabbed my lariat.

"Can you rope her?" I jokingly asked.

"Hell, yes, I can," he retorted, as he twisted the lariat into a massive knot. The lariat loop he fixed would have never fit over the cow's head.

Joe threw the tangled rope, the only effect of which was to rile the cow. She was nervous and started looking over the top rung of the corral. Joe threw the rope again. I figured I knew what would happen next. The cow turned toward Joe, forcing him to scramble up the corral. The cow then fired up her energy thrusters and jumped on top of the corral. She wiggled on over, running for the open pasture.

"Have you got a tranquilizer gun?" Joe next asked.

"All I have is a five foot pole syringe," I answered him.

"Well, get it, and we'll drive up alongside her and you can poke her with that," was Joe's solution.

"Joe, they only do that in Africa or on the TV," I said.

"Well, we're going to do it in Taylor County too," Joe excitedly responded.

Oh, why not, I thought as I got out my pole syringe. By now, Joe's neighbor had come along to help. I climbed into the back of his pickup bed. Joe drove his John Deere tractor, hoping to haze the cow with it. The team herded the cow toward flat ground where we could run her on a straight course.

"A little faster," I yelled to the pickup driver. He accelerated until I was right on top of the cow. I drove the syringe into her hip. "I got her injected," I squealed.

The cow was running slower and slower until she finally came to a stop. I dropped the rope over her head and secured her to the pickup. Joe gave me a lift back to my vet truck to get my equipment. When I returned to the cow, she was down and asleep. Her calf was sedated as well and it was coming breech. The tranquilizer made it an easy delivery for me. The calf was born a little sluggish, but was healthy.

"We'll need your stock trailer to load the cow and calf," I told Joe. I wanted the cow and calf to recover together. When the sedation had worn off, I hoped the cow would claim the baby.

"I may need help. You'll have to meet me back at the house," Joe told me.

Joe steered the John Deere, with its big bale carrier on the front, toward the house. As we got closer to Joe's house, I could see his neighbor's wife, mowing her yard. She was wearing short-shorts and a tank top. As she mowed, she bounced. Joe took a long look and could barely keep his eyes off of her. He made the turn into his driveway and twisted around in his seat, taking another long gander. Smack! Joe ran the John Deere's bale carrier square into the radiator of his Chevy truck.

Joe's wife had been watching the whole affair as well. Through her laughter, she told Joe, "Serves you right, old man, for not looking where you were going."

The chase was over. We loaded the cow and calf and they took to one another. All was well, with the exception of one punctured radiator in a Chevy pickup truck.

17
DONNIE RONNIE BLAKE

My life and veterinary practice would not be complete without describing the notably uncanny Donnie Ronnie Blake.

Donnie was the fourth of five children born to Ike and Lucinda Blake of Bedford. The Blake's were uneducated and extremely poor. Yet Ike was proud of his family name and worked hard at any job in order to bring home a few dollars to feed his kids. He labored at painting all over the county and beyond. He even mopped floors. Ike refused welfare. Oftentimes, balanced meals were not to be had around the Blake household. His kids would be seen scavenging garbage cans in the park and at the school.

My first encounter with Donnie and his younger brother, Eddie, was when I was in seventh grade. I had come to school early for Junior High basketball practice. Out of the dark and fog of the early morning I heard some noise in the vicinity of the garbage cans. It was Donnie and Eddie rummaging through the scraps for something to eat. I had a dime in my pocket and gave it to them. I had no idea that twelve years later I would be looking after Donnie more regularly. His humor made life interesting and with Donnie at my side, I never knew what would happen next.

Donnie was educated through the third grade. At that point his teacher gave up on his ability to learn. Before I took Donnie under my wing, he could barely talk. His words were few and those that he knew were mispronounced.

Donnie began working for me when I took the responsibility of being the sale barn veterinarian. He was thin and weak and the first time I had him wrestle and hold a pig, he nearly fainted. I could see he needed nourishment. I sent him to the sale barn café and told them to fill him up. Donnie ate and ate until he got sick. He didn't know enough to stop. Cleanliness was not part of his life either. Donnie would hang his dirty clothes to air and wear them again. Bathing and washing clothes were like a foreign language.

Donnie soon began to learn new words and his vocabulary became advanced. His thin skeleton filled out with very developed muscles, partly due to his selected method of travel. Donnie biked everywhere. The exercise filled his frame with strong calves, thighs and shoulders. He was about six feet tall and 200 meaty pounds. He had long arms and big strong hands. He was fortunate that he didn't know how strong he was.

Donnie had a way of being anywhere in the community at any given time. He could not read but he never missed a sale in town, a fire or a construction site. Donnie would always be there, with his bicycle bearing the load of the junk he collected as currency.

He had no sense of money. In time, Donnie disassembled scores of refrigerators to save the small copper wire found within. Donnie was famous locally for his bike loading. If Donnie found something salvageable, it was loaded on his bike and he would pedal for miles to haul it home. Junk was his bountiful treasure.

Donnie's real specialty was bicycles. His love for them was greater than that for junk. He knew bikes from one end to the other and if asked, would hardly ever sell one. One time Harold Cross was, in a kidding manner, trying to buy Donnie's bike. Harold laid out $150 cash and said, "You take the money and I'm taking the bike."

Donnie replied, "Like hell" and took off pedaling.

There was no doubt Donnie had a sixth sense about direction as well as some other natural abilities. Sometimes I thought that he was just a little dumb, but not stupid. Other times, he seemed stupid but not dumb. His disposition was his greatest asset. He loved to help people but cared not for money in return. If you did a little bragging on him or told him "no one can do that," was when Donnie would show you how it's done. He forgot nothing and somehow filed thoughts neatly. From his mammoth junk pile, inventory could be pulled in a blink.

One day, my fellow vet, Jim Johnson, wanted to borrow an old bike. I took the liberty of going to Donnie's place and pulled one out of a row of about 100. I told Johnson that Donnie would never miss it. The next day, Donnie said, "Someone took one of my bikes!" Donnie couldn't count, but he had no trouble missing one bicycle.

Donnie liked to keep conversation going even if he knew nothing about the topic. Strangers would visit with him for quite some time before they realized the talk was going nowhere. He was often mistaken for the sale barn vet and people would ask him technical questions. I would stand back and laugh to myself while Donnie answered them.

Donnie's disposition was smooth. If anything went wrong for him or me, his comment was always the same ... "Don't worry about it." I would get angry at him on occasion and he'd say, "Don't worry about it, I wasn't listening anyway." That would force me to apologize. I'd always have to watch myself with the temper I had inherited. Donnie's natural coolness and serenity kept me in tow.

An old acquaintance of mine, Frank Norris, was having breakfast with Donnie at the local café one morning. Frank got up to leave and fell over on the floor, dead from a heart attack. When I got there, Donnie was still sitting there, eating his breakfast and looking down at his friend. I assume Donnie thought there was no sense letting his breakfast get cold. He couldn't do anything for Frank anyway.

It got so my clients and I depended on Donnie to do jobs no one else would do. Donnie could always be found across the street from the vet clinic. Across the way was a vacant lot where a weekly junk sale was held. People of all walks of life would bring their junk there hoping to sell it as treasures. The sale was of much interest to Donnie. One Saturday, a load of lumber was brought in. One person was looking at it and commented, "That lumber is quite crooked."

Donnie looked him in the eye and replied, "Don't matter if you build a crooked house." A puzzled look came across the face of the man. He grunted and then walked off.

Donnie became quite famous. The folklore traveled from those who lived in Taylor County to their friends and relatives across the country. Unfortunately, some people would take advantage. They used to get him by selling him a bicycle for $20 and then buy it back for $5.

One spring morning, the mayor of Des Moines, Pat Drake called. He had heard about Donnie and his hundreds of bicycles. Pat bought and restored antique bikes for a hobby. "Why don't you come on down, Pat?" I invited. "I can show you around and see if there's anything that catches your eye."

"I'll be down in two hours," Pat excitedly answered. I looked forward to his arrival, as I was mayor of Bedford at the time and I figured we had something in common.

Mayor Drake was a nice man. We enjoyed each other's company and discovered we had a lot in common. A lot of city problems are the same if you overlooked the difference in population size between Bedford and Des Moines.

I was even surprised at the maze of junk and bikes that Donnie had accumulated by day and by night. "By golly," the mayor said, "I don't think Des Moines has anything like this!"

"I suppose not," I meekly remarked.

Donnie was walking along, not saying anything. He was watching and listening very closely though.

While we two mayors strolled through Donnie's property, we picked up two old bikes and a small broken-down child's wagon.

"I believe this is all for now," Pat said to Donnie. "How much do you want for these?" I had warned Pat that Donnie might not sell anything.

"First, what are you offering to Donnie," I asked in his behalf.

"I'll give him $150 for the outfit," Pat said.

I walked over to Donnie and said, "Donnie, Mr. Drake has offered you $150 for these junkers. They aren't worth $20." Donnie was poised as though he was thinking it over while he inspected the pile. I was getting the feeling that if Pat had offered $1,000 it would not be enough. I noticed Donnie roll up his lower lip and out it came.

"Those bikes are not for sale," said Donnie.

I expected as much. I told the mayor to give me some time. I thought I could eventually talk Donnie into making the sale.

"OK," the mayor said, "just give me a call and I'll come back down." I later called, the mayor came back, picked out an additional item, and paid Donnie $200 on the spot. Donnie made out better on the deal, after all.

Old Doc Anderson and I were sitting out on the worn deck discussing politics and weather one day. Doc leaned over and said, "What's Donnie doing up at the lumber yard?"

"I don't know," I said, "but I'll find out."

I walked up to the lumberyard and I could see the proprietor tearing out some old boards. Donnie had asked for the scrap boards and the store's owner had told him he could have them.

I sauntered back to the clinic and told Doc what I had found out.

"How the hell will he carry them away?" Doc asked.

"Probably somehow on his bike," I answered confidently.

Sure enough. It wasn't long before Donnie had loaded his bike with six boards, each being one foot wide and 12 feet long. Donnie had balanced the boards across the handlebars of his bike and then tied them securely with rope. His bike looked like it had wings.

"Oh, no," I said. "Donnie is heading off down the hill."

By then, Donnie was astride his bike/plane and was pedaling. The bike began to take off on him, with the weight of the lumber, and was going from side to side and wobbling all over the street. The bike built more speed and was headed straight for a parked Volkswagon Beetle. As Donnie rapidly approached, he lifted the "left wing" up and over the top of the car. He clipped off the radio antenna in passing but avoided further damage.

By then, Donnie was getting the bike under control. When he made the wide turn, he let out a big yell making the sound of a semi truck shifting gears. Away he went.

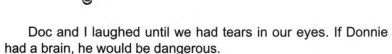

Doc and I laughed until we had tears in our eyes. If Donnie had a brain, he would be dangerous.

It was actually amazing how the community sort of looked after Donnie and Donnie looked after the community. If someone needed help with anything Donnie was willing to help. He is the subject of many of my stories.

18

REX'S COW, OL' CRAZY

Dr. Jim Johnson, my former partner, once said, "Being a veterinarian brings a new experience every day. Things happen for the good, for the bad or for the in between." One thing I learned to trust is that things happened when I least expected or needed them.

It had been a typical busy early spring day in the middle of calving season. I already had a full day of prolapsed uteri and calf deliveries when the phone rang at 6 p.m. It was Violet Holste. "We have a heifer trying to calve and we need you right away," she commanded.

"I'll be there in a few minutes," I tiredly answered.

The Holste's, Dick and Violet lived at the outer edge of my furthest western territory. It was a pleasure to work for Dick and Violet who were always ready for me when I arrived. The couple worked the farm together, as most farm couples did. They amused me with their bantering. Violet constantly gave unsolicited advice to Dick that he did not take. When I drove my truck down to the barn, Dick had the young cow locked in an old milking stantion, ready to go.

"I'm afraid Dick let the cow go too long," Violet shrieked.

"It wasn't my fault—you were the one watching her," he told Violet.

I got my obstetrical equipment ready and gave the heifer an exam. The calf was coming breech but it was still alive. I retrieved one leg and then the other, hooked on with my calf jack and easily delivered the calf.

"Oh, thank heavens it's alive!" Violet exclaimed. We all settled down. The heifer turned toward the calf and, like an old pro, she began licking it. The calf was up wobbling on its legs before we had the equipment cleaned up.

"We did it again," Dick said confidently. "I knew we would be OK when you said you would come, Doc." This gave me a big lift after a hard day's work. I was not often on the other end of a compliment.

As I drove my truck out of the driveway, we said our good-byes. Before I steered onto the road, I glanced to see if any traffic was coming. What caught my eye was Rex Laub, who was also a client and friend of mine. Rex lived across the road from the Holstes. He was sitting outside, on a stump, playing with his cats. At that moment I wasn't in a rush. Rex had recently lost his wife to cancer and he was still missing her. I drove in to say hello and Rex acted surprised to see me.

"Hi, Doc, am I ever glad to see you," Rex blurted out. "I was just going to call. I didn't realize you were just across the road."

"Oh," I replied, "what is going on?"

"I have a cow in the barn that I thought was calving yesterday but she still hasn't done anything. I thought maybe we should check her," Rex told me matter-of-factly.

"Yeah, maybe so," I answered. I pulled my OB equipment from the truck and headed for the barn. It was at the dusk of the day. The red sun was just setting over the horizon. We walked into the half-dark barn where I saw an animal resembling a cow. She was enough of a cow to know she had a stranger in her midst.

"I call this cow Ol' Crazy," Rex said. I stood at attention as I wondered what that meant.

"Oh, is she wild?" I timidly asked.

"Naw, not wild, why, we raised her on a bucket," he said, "but she is kind of blind."

The cow's eyes bulged out of her skull and I could see the whites of them. Perhaps she had a little vision in the left eye but her right eye was sightless. Her head tilted to the right when she moved from side to side. When she walked forward her head tilted one way, and for balance, her body swerved the opposite direction. Now I could see why Rex called her Ol' Crazy.

The cow was trying to decide if I was friend or foe. She walked slowly around the pen attempting to locate me. I stood myself in an old hay manger for safety and quickly gave my lariat rope a toss. Her unorthodox movements made it difficult to know where to throw. My first launch missed her, and the rope floated down, hitting her across the neck and back. She had decided at that moment I was the enemy. She blindly lunged. Her uncoordinated motion threw her against the side of the barn. It sounded like falling timber when she hit. The noise frightened Ol' Crazy even more. She lunged again, moving from side to side, bumping and running. I scurried up a pole into the hayloft for safety. I did not want to be in the manger with her any longer.

The cow followed the circular path of the pen until she found the door. She threw her weight against it and snapped the latch. Out of the barn she weaved, straight into a barnyard pen. Again Ol' Crazy walked in circles until she accidentally ran right back through the barn's open door. I was still in the loft and had my rope right above her. As she ran under me, I dropped the lasso over her head. I quickly got a double, then triple wrap around a barn pole. Crazy knew I was there and tried to get to me, but I was safe above her. She then, simply put, went a little more mad. She bucked and bellowed until she wrapped herself up in the rope. Fighting the rope, she fell to her side and was unable to get up. I quickly got my equipment for the exam. Her calf had a front leg back. After I presented the foot properly, I used the calf jack to deliver a healthy baby. I then tranquilized the cow. The sedative would give me plenty of time to disappear before Ol' Crazy got up again.

I laughed when I said to Rex, "I'll be darned if I ever stop to visit you again!"

Rex followed with "I don't blame you. But do you know what I think? I think you are the best vet in the world." Bad things could happen for the good. Also, it was two back-to-back compliments the same evening.

19

BEING ADMITTED TO VETERINARY COLLEGE THE HONOR SYSTEM

Admission to veterinary college was euphoria. Getting there was a dream with nightmares mingled in. The Board of Acceptance was one of the horrors. The Board would mail acceptance letters in three drafts. They were fond of keeping their applicants in suspense as long as possible.

I did not receive my letter in the first round. My agony was intensified as many of my friends had their admission papers. One of my best friends, Bob Bashara, got his letter in the initial mailing. He kept asking me, "Did you hear today?" and then he would laugh. My college grades were not as high as others were, yet I still felt I was better qualified. I was from a rural area and had an animal orientation. I had the dream. Then my day finally came. I had become a member of the delegated few who were to become veterinarians.

Little did I know that acceptance was but a baby step. The courses and the instructors were difficult. The standard was high. Many instructors were principled and felt they should flunk at least ten percent of their students. Those professors instilled fear in us. During the first two years, there was a strict dress code. Students were required to wear a white shirt with black bow tie. Two recruits found the situation unbearable and quit within the first two weeks.

You could never let your guard down during class. Midterms and finals were the only announced exams. A good case of the jitters and a frenzy of note cramming would ensue with one whisper, "Oh, oh, I hear we're having an exam today." Sometimes the whisper was nothing but a rumor, started just to see whose face would drop the furthest.

For the announced exams, veterinary college had a Code of Honor. The instructor would hand out the test and promptly leave the room. It was a student's duty not to cheat. If you saw a rogue classmate, it was your duty to turn him in to the instructor. For the infraction, the student would then be expelled from veterinary school.

It was during an anatomy test when Mike McGraw yelled, "Someone is cheating and it had better stop!" That humorous interjection served to wake everyone up.

When my classmates and I were sophomores, a meeting of the four class years was held in Beardshear Hall. The seating arrangement was for each class to sit together. All of the instructors, including the Dean, sat in the back. The president of the senior class conducted the meeting. The agenda included several items of business and in parliamentary fashion, the items were acted upon. We were almost through the agenda when, out of the blue, a senior, Jack Berg, walked to center stage and said, "I hate to bring this up, but one of my classmates has been cheating all the way through school. I am sick and tired of it. At this time, it is my duty to expose him."

The senior class president responded, "I don't think this is the time and place for exposure. A committee of all the officers of all the classes should be formed to handle the situation."

Berg replied, "Hell no, I want to take care of this matter right now!"

Other class officers jumped in on the discussion. The tension was building and the place began to rumble as arguments ensued. As emotions escalated, you could feel the electricity in the air. I excitedly tried to get the floor to voice an opinion but could not. I had strong sentiments but I was later grateful that I'd kept quiet.

Berg yelled, "I have had enough—that cheater is — ———!"

Tom Wilton jumped up from his seat, pointed a gun at Jack, and yelled, "You son-of-a-bitch, I told you to keep your mouth shut." Three shots were fired. Bang! Bang! Bang! Jack slumped to the floor.

The lights went out in the hall. Everyone was panicked. Some of us took cover as best we could, some hid. Ron Iverson, a classmate of mine, literally dove under the seats. Dick Waney, the brave, crawled out the back door, ran to the next building and called the police. I was bewildered and wasn't sure what to do. I just stood there, smelling a rat. The next thing we knew, the cops had surrounded the place. Sirens were blowing and ambulances arrived at the front door.

All four classes reveled in the authenticity of the perfect skit. The only group not amused was the police unit. The displeasure of the authorities ended the traditional burlesque for a period of time. The skit's revival occurred a few years later, with the same end result. The tradition was then halted for good.

20
THE
ROLLING B

Ross Township is nestled in the rolling hills of southern Taylor County, Iowa. Its south border runs adjacent to the Iowa-Missouri state line. Around here, this portion of God's green earth is called Lapland. It is called this because Missouri's border once lapped north into Iowa for some 13 miles. The Honey War was fought over this boundary.

In 1816 a United States survey set out to mark the Osage Indian land along the southern border of the Iowa Territory. The surveyor used mounds of earth for markers. The markers were soon washed away by the elements. In 1837, Missouri commissioned a land survey of its own, determined to mark its northern boundary. Due to a misinterpretation, Missouri's surveyor marked a line about 13 miles north of the original United States line. Approximately twenty-six hundred square miles of land was added to the Missouri State coffers. A year later, Missouri officially declared the new line its northern border.

Then the trouble began. A fellow living in Missouri came into the disputed territory and chopped down three trees filled with honey. The action created turmoil. As far as Iowa settlers were concerned, the honey trees belonged to them. Not so, according to Missouri, the boundary lines were well marked. To add fuel to the fire, Missouri officials attempted to collect taxes in the area from settlers who considered themselves Iowans.

The Iowa militia was called to action for the first time in 1839 to settle the conflict. Without firing a shot, the militiamen, cold and lonely for home, decided to let the state legislators work out the problem. The militia left and the Honey War was over. Ten years later the matter was put to rest when the Supreme Court ruled the original 1816 line would be the official boundary between Iowa and Missouri. A solid iron marker was installed in the middle of a dirt road to mark the dispute. The iron marker stands today, just east of Ross Township, in Lapland.

Paul Brummett purchased a large tract of land in Ross Township. The Brummetts were Swedes and were the subject of many stories and the blunt of jokes. Paul farmed during the years of the Depression and, as most people did, survived by living lean. He instilled his conservative life-style in both of his children, particularly his son, Roger. When he was of age, Roger went off to the service and then to Iowa State University. After graduating, Roger came back home to farm his father's acreage.

Roger was a good athlete in high school and excelled in track as a sprinter. He was competitive and his adrenaline ran high. His spirit showed in his family life, on the farm, and at the ISU Extension office where he worked. He was in the public's eye and became the blunt of many jokes himself. He learned to answer to his nicknames of Ol' Clomp-Clomp, Cannon Ball, and The Senator.

Roger would never have a cow penned when he called for vet service.

I'd always ask him, "Where is she?"

Roger would invariably answer, "In the pasture."

"Can we catch her?" I'd ask.

"Hell yes, Lucas, did you ever see a cow I could not run down afoot?" the sprinter answered.

"Oh, hell no!" I'd reply in a disbelieving tone.

I pulled in Roger's farm one day and found that he had gotten his old "black bomb" ready for the cow chase that we were about to embark upon. The black bomb was about the oldest truck I had ever seen. Not one part of it was road legal. It was held together with baling wire instead of bolts. "Follow me!" he yelled.

I wouldn't have missed it for anything as we headed toward the pasture.

The back of his truck held a student, Ronnie, who was working for Roger that summer. As I followed them in my vet truck, we bounced over plowed ground until, out of a deep ditch, the patient showed herself. The cow had horns with a four-foot spread, the points of which glittered in the setting sun. Her eyes were as big as apples and fire was blowing out her nose and she was trying to have a calf. All we had to do to help her was to catch her.

Roger bolted out of the truck and yelled at Ronnie, "Stay with the truck!"

Roger had a wound-up lariat in his hand that he kept tripping over. All of a sudden, the cow was chasing Roger instead of the other way around. Roger did have bragging rights. He was a hell of a good runner. The cow was in a race to keep up with him. Roger kept his feet over the plowed field but the cow tripped herself up and Roger had momentarily escaped the charge.

He yelled at Ronnie, "Bring the truck!"

But Ronnie had gotten out of the truck to go help Roger. They both had their feet planted on the ground. That confused the cow and she couldn't decide which one to chase. She spun around two or three times and gave Ronnie time to make it to a tree. Roger sprinted to the truck and got inside. The cow picked Roger as the target and she rammed the rear of the truck with her head. She nearly knocked herself out. Roger got the rope over her horns and tied her to the black bomb.

The cow came alive like a wild cat. She tried to tear herself away from the rope. As she did, the truck clanged, bounced and collected more dents. The baling wire somehow held together.

I drove my truck to within a safe distance and roped her again around the neck. We had her between the two trucks where she choked herself down. We delivered the live calf and after releasing the ropes, hurried out of there. As the cow revived from the choking, she was more interested in her calf than killing us.

We were about as far out of the pasture as we could be when Roger said, "See Lucas, no problem at all."

"A piece of cake," I replied. At least I wasn't the one who had been chased this time.

Incidentally, in later years, I refused to tie a cow to my truck. I had both doors smashed in, the grill knocked out, and the rear fenders crushed, among other things. On a call at the Leo Waldier farm, I had roped a cow from the back of my truck and secured her with 15-feet of rope. The rope acted like a rubber band. When the cow pulled back, the rope became taut and stretched her forward, driving her, head first, into the back of my truck. Every time she pulled, the rope sprung her back until my tailgate and both brake lights were smashed. I'd watched all I could. I jumped back into the truck and with full throttle force, literally dragged the cow until she choked herself down. If she got up, I gunned the truck again. If I were writing a veterinarian guidebook I would put that in. Never tie a cow to your truck. Use the farmer's.

It was late spring when Roger phoned for an OB call. Naturally, when I arrived, the cow was in the pasture and Roger was no where in sight. Betty, Roger's wife, came out of the house to greet me. We exchanged pleasantries and she said, "Shhhh, I think I hear Roger now."

Both of us became quiet in the already still evening. Clomp, clomp; clomp, clomp—sometimes slow, other times fast—broke the silence. Then through the trees and brush came a roar of obscenities.

"You old sour bitch. You son-of-a-bitch, god-damn you!" Then Roger yelled out, "OK, I got her."

Betty and I drove around the section tracking the voice we'd heard. My headlights caught a human form in their beam. It was a hatless Roger, with a torn jacket and scratches on his face, hands and belly. As though it was nothing, he said, "The bitch gave me a bit of trouble but I got her!" The cow had drug him through the brush.

The calf delivery was uneventful. Roger had earned his Ol' Clomp-Clomp nickname from me. I can still hear his big feet hitting the ground.

I was forever gullible when it came to Brummett. He had called about a Charlois bull that was lame with foot rot and needed me to take a look. The bull was in the pasture. Roger had learned to answer me before I could even ask the obvious. "Oh, we can throw a lariat on him and tie him to a post," he said.

I said, "We could try."

We drove back through the hills, timber, and pasture and found the huge animal. The drive had been beautiful. The sun was red and was setting over the treetops. A large pond reflected the image back. The cows were lazily grazing and acted unaware of our presence. My peacefulness was interrupted when I caught sight of an all-too-familiar tremble in the bull's ears. The Charlois was most certainly aware that we were in his pasture.

"Are you sure he won't take us?" I asked Roger.

"Oh, hell no. We showed him in 4-H when he was a calf," he said. "He won't do a thing."

I really did know better. I was the stranger in the animal's domain and that spelled berserk to me.

I prepared my lariat and sidled up along the fence to get close enough to reach the bull, hoping that just once, things would be normal at the Rolling B ranch. I carefully started twirling my rope getting ready to release the loop. Even if I missed, I had decided, the startled bull would probably run on down the fence line. I threw the first time and the bull charged at full blast. The rope had barely left my hand. The only advantage I had was that the rope was 35-feet long. This was exactly the distance between the bull and me. Even then, I had to run at right angles as fast as I could toward some trees. An old posted sign I had seen earlier flashed through my mind. The sign read, "It's 100 yards to the fishing pond. If you're a fast runner, you can make it in 10 seconds. The bull can do it in 6.5."

I was proud of my sprinting ability at that moment. My speed increased every time I looked back to see where the bull was. I did not have to look far. The closer he got, the bigger he looked. He was breathing down my butt. The biggest tree I could see to grab was a two-inch across sapling. I lunged for it. The bull smacked me, hitting me in the ass. The forceful hit increased my speed but it wasn't enough. I fell to the ground. The bull rolled me over and over with its head. Roger came yelling down through the timber to chase off the bull. I had a bruise on my butt the size of a dinner plate and I never tried to rope a bull again.

Jokingly, Roger said, "You sure give up easy, Luke."

I'm sure I didn't answer him.

OLD CANNON BALL

As Roger grew older and wiser, he realized he wasn't keeping up on foot with the cows like he used to.

It was on a hot summer day when Roger borrowed a 3-wheeler from his neighbor so he could chase in his cows. He had most of the herd headed in the right direction except for one old wild Hereford. She bolted for the get away at top speed. Roger turned the 3-wheeler on a dime in pursuit. He hit full throttle through the tall grass and was closing in when he accidentally ran over an old hidden fence. The fence stopped the vehicle in its tracks. Roger flew through the air as if he had been shot out of a circus cannon. He hit the ground, landed in a pile, and did not move. In slow motion, Old Cannon Ball picked himself up and the pieces of his broken glasses. He just wasn't sure where he was. The Cannon Ball got a lot of support from his friends and he made a quick recovery.

Showing even greater wisdom, Roger built a state-of-the-art corral system to sort and handle his cows and calves. The facility met with my immediate approval. It still stands on the Rolling B.

TRUE FRIENDS ARE FRIENDS FOREVER, SUCH AS THE BRUMMETTS

It was working for people like the Brummett family, which made the veterinary profession a very interesting career. Each day or each call at the Rolling B could bring excitement, humor, sadness or euphoria. The euphoria of a rodeo man waiting to ride the next bull.

One evening my wife and I were to play cards at the Brummetts. I was on call at the clinic so I left a message on my answering machine giving out the Brummett telephone number. My message read, "If you have an emergency, call 1-278-3592 and Dr. Lucas will respond." Their phone system was out of Missouri but it lapped over into 'Lapland', leaving many Iowa customers with a different area code number. Usually even the operator couldn't find their number. Later, when I listened for my messages, I heard "Oh, shit, he's to hell and gone. I never heard of 278—I'll call Clearfield's vet." ——Click.

Roger and I served voluntarily at the same organization and community meetings. As I was a vet, it was not unusual for me to get called away before the gathering was over. Roger began to notice that I would get 'my call' right after the steak supper but before the program commenced, but he never said anything. Other people were impressed with my importance when over the speaker they'd hear "Dr. Lucas is needed out front on the phone." They felt sorry for me, for getting called out again.

You can fool all the people some of the time, some of the people all of the time, but you can't fool all the people all the time. My pattern was repeated once too often, and Brummett finally caught on. "Lucas, you S.O.B., you're having Joe (my youngest son) call you after supper aren't you? And home you go! Huh, am I right?" he inquired.

"Why Brummett, how could you accuse me of such a thing!" I answered with a laugh.

PICKING UP WISDOM AS YOU GO

A young veterinarian was bound to make some mistakes. As the years pass, you made even more. One error I made at the Brummett farm was to dehorn twenty big Holstein steers before all the seasonal flies were dead and gone.

Few veterinarians ever learned to enjoy dehorning. It was a

brutal procedure, both on the cattle and the vet. Removing horns leaves big, open sinus caverns where horns used to be. What could happen, if you dehorned early, was that a fly could crawl in the hole and lay its eggs. The eggs hatched into maggots and the maggots started crawling. This about drove the cattle crazy. They would run in a frenzy, shaking their heads, trying to rid themselves of the pests. That's what I had done to the Brummett steers.

The cure was to run the cattle through a chute and spray their sinuses with chemical which killed the maggots. It was a sickening job, to say the least. After the spraying, puss and maggots literally boiled out of the cow's head. Roger, with only occasional grumbling and gagging, was kind enough to help me doctor his cows. The cows recovered without complication. Roger didn't. There was one steer I failed to watch closely. I had hit the release on my headgate to let her go and the handle, under great pressure, flew up. It struck Ol' Clomp-Clomp in the chin and cheek. Roger had a chipped tooth and scar to prove wisdom can sometimes be tardy. He told everyone he swore he could hear me laughing while he was knocked out cold. I told him it was the tweet, tweet from his head's singing birds he'd heard.

Roger will find a way to get even and I am still waiting for that day.

21
CLIENT
APPRECIATION

Each and every year there were clients I went the extra mile for. In return, those customers showed great faithfulness and appreciation. I guided and advised them and we would make decisions as a team. To pay them back, I sponsored an annual meeting supper, entertainment included. The event became very popular among my clients. I provided my guests one drink of their choice, the meal, a brief vet science update, and to top off the evening, a musical group would perform. The evening began with my thanks and I would introduce the honored guests. I had kept notes all year to be able to tell a joke or rat on them.

The first year I held the appreciation night I had only invited men. That was my mistake. One woman was very upset she had not been invited. After all, she informed me, women worked hand in hand with their spouses and were as responsible for the success of their operation as any one person. I phoned everyone on the guest list back and extended an open invitation. I had already prepared my program and it included joke telling of questionable appropriateness for a mixed crowd. Due to a time constraint, I went with the format and hoped no ears would burn in the Bible Belt that night.

This joke I told as if it had really happened. I began:

"Norman Williams called me and complained I had insulted his wife over the phone. I asked him to let me explain what had happened. Early that morning David Brown from Oxford, Missouri called. He had a cow with a difficult prolapse. I was 30 minutes late getting to the office and when I arrived the street was lined with clients. I walked in to the office to a ringing phone. Marvin Sleep, better know as Nervous Marvin, asked for a dose of 'commonbiotics'. As I was getting that, Frank Jones barged in yelling at the top of his lungs. I told Frank to sit down. The phone was still ringing. Sissy Whittier came in with two nervous cats. Frank paid no attention to my telling him to sit down and be quiet. He said all he wanted was 25 cents worth of spray and handed me a 50-cent piece. The phone was still ringing. I pulled out the cash drawer for Frank's change and it spilled all over the floor. Keith O'Dell came in with his big St. Bernard dog. The dog started chasing Sissy's cats. The cats knocked over a bottle of medicine and it broke on the floor. The phone rang again. I slipped on the mess but made my way to the phone. It was your wife. She wanted to know how to use a rectal thermometer. And by God, I told her!"

My partner, Jim Johnson, and I had a routine we'd perform. It involved fielding written questions from the guests. Jim would sort through, then hand me the same question, year after year. I asked, "If a pig drinks a quart of buttermilk before it starts and runs a mile before it farts and the further it runs the faster it gets, how far can it run before it shits?"

Only Jim knew the answer to the perplexing question and he practiced it to perfection. Jim would rejoin, "In order for me to make that bet you must take me to where the fart was let. A farmer by the road saw the pig pass with a stream of gas flowing from the pig's ass. The farmer was about a mile from where the pig started. The pig passed the farmer just as it farted—it was so funny that the farmer had to laugh, while that pig ran another mile and a half. Now if that pig can hold its gas and run a mile with a puckered ass, it seems to me if it keeps its wits, it will run five miles before it shits." The guests roared with laughter.

Everyone involved certainly enjoyed the annual dinner, including myself. It put my work at a personal level. For every customer I ratted on, they good-naturedly flogged me in return. Wilbur Rowe had the whole year to get one back on me. And he did.

I was intensely pregnancy testing cows at the sale barn

and running them through as fast as I could. On purpose, Wilbur ran a big steer through the chute. I pushed my arm inside the animal and couldn't feel anything that was normal. I was puzzled. I withdrew and stuck my arm inside again. I came up with nothing.

I yelled, "I guess this one is open."

"I could have told you that," Wilbur said. "What's the matter Lucas, can't you tell a steer from a cow?"

The best I could come up with in a hurry was, "At least I didn't call him pregnant."

22
HAROLD HILTON
OF HOPKINS

Iowa summers can be a mixture of weather. With summer heat comes high humidity and that's what makes Iowa's corn grow. With adequate rainfall, a bumper crop could be harvested in the fall.

In the late 50's and early 60's few people had air conditioning. Hot and humid days were toughed out with fans and open windows. You hoped for a breeze to come along. Why… you'd sweat just lifting a glass to your mouth.

July 1, 1963 was a very humid day. The phone rang at the clinic and Harold Hilton was on the other end. Harold wanted seven bull calves neutered. They were shut inside his barn.

Harold was a Missourian, living in Iowa's neighboring state to the south. Missouri was nicknamed the "Show Me State," show me being defined in the dictionary as "insistent on proof or evidence". You could interpret from the slogan that Missouri people were stubborn and bullheaded. I figured I knew a few Iowans who could be included in that headstrong category as well.

Doc Anderson made our appointment for right after noon, during the hottest time of the day. It was 100 degrees in the shade with 80 percent humidity. To make the day even more miserable, the weatherman had said we had a heat index of 120 degrees. It was hot enough to fry an egg on the hood of a truck.

For small jobs, Doc Anderson did not like taking his cattle chute to the country. He just thought it was a lot of bother hooking on and setting up a chute. He was the owner of our business and had a little of Missouri in him. We did things his way.

It was a very warm drive south. I had the truck windows down, creating a little bit of a breeze, which made the trip bearable. I noticed the corn in the fields was showing signs of heat stress. The leaves were rolled for protection and reaching to the sky, looking for moisture to relieve the thirst. Pastured cows were standing in ponds or crowded around shade trees to cool themselves.

Missouri is beautiful country and has more rolling hills than Iowa. There is more timber and pasture too, as the soil is not as rich. Missouri roads were seldom square. Early settlers must have formed the road with horse teams, pulling their goods to market by winding around the hills. Doc Anderson and I followed their path, winding our way to the Hilton farm.

Mr. Hilton had on his property a nice bungalow-style house and small, neatly kept buildings. His spread overlooked bottomland that surrounded the 102 River Valley.

Harold greeted us with, "Where is your chute?"

Doc Anderson answered, "Oh, I thought we'd just tail the bulls behind a gate."

"I have no gates in the barn," Harold replied.

"Oh, well, we'll throw a rope on them," Doc said undeterred.

We got from the truck a lariat rope and the bull clamps and headed for the barn. Bull clamps were tools used to crush a bull's testicular cord, rendering sterility.

"These bulls are wild little buggers," Harold said. "I didn't want them to get away so I've nailed all the barn doors shut. We'll have to climb through the hay loft to get inside."

We climbed up a small ladder to a door at the loft level. We crawled in and stood up. The loft covered about half the barn area. Nothing lay below us but seemingly very empty space. When the snorting, wide-eyed, 500-pound bull calves saw us they began to panic. They crashed into and ran through broken boards and old hay. Harold was right about one thing; the bulls couldn't get out of the barn.

"What's next?" I turned and asked Doc.

"Well, hell," he said, "I guess try to rope one and we'll snub him to a post." I eased down the ladder. One calf ran right at me and I laid the rope over its head. I tightened the rope and secured it to a center post. I had him. Harold held on to the rope while I tailed the calf. Doc Anderson clamped the calf's cords.

"Now, that wasn't so bad," Doc said with confidence. "Let him go and we'll catch another one." I pulled the honda release lever and, just like it said in the book, the rope released. The calf was enraged. He bellowed and ran around the barn head butting anything he could find.

"We need to get him out of the barn," I said rather emphatically.

"Oh no, we can't do that. The others will get away," Harold said back to me.

"Well, I guess we'll have to continue roping," I irritably answered.

Sweat was pouring down my face and neck. The heat was intensifying with the addition of my adrenaline burst. Not only was I scorching hot, my temper was warming up as well. I made an attempt at roping another calf, all the while trying not to get killed by the neutered beast bull.

I roped one. Old Doc was about to clamp him when the mad-as-hell bull came at our heels, and tried to knock us down. We had ended his sex life and he was looking for revenge. I muttered again, "We sure need to get him out of here."

"I just don't see how we can do that," Harold said back.

The angered calf was now marked by driving, forceful energy and was more aggressive than ever. We were working on a third calf when the aggressor charged again and nearly knocked Doc Anderson down. Once again I ordered, "We've got to get that son-of-a-bitch out of here!"

"Just can't do that," Harold replied.

I was about to rope the fourth calf when out of the blue came the maniac from across the barn, wide eyed and bellowing. I picked up a five-foot long 2x4 and stood my ground. The bull charged and I stepped to the side. I turned, and with all my might, perfectly swung the board and caught the bull smack between the eyes. Much to my relief, the steer dropped in its tracks. He lay there, wiggling.

Harold said, "I think you killed him."

"I hope so," I replied. But the steer 's head moved upward, and he was trying to get back on his feet. When he did, I swung and connected again. The bull dropped.

Harold yelled, "We have to get that son-of-a-bitch out of here!" Harold pried the nails out of the barn door and let the calf run out.

He must have seen the look in my eyes and was convinced I would have killed the calf. The door sure wasn't opened for my safety. In the absence of the lunatic calf, we were able to finish the job.

In those days, we did not charge a trip fee but Doc charged Harold an extra seven dollars.

"I've never paid over 50 cents for cutting a bull in my life," Harold said, "but that's OK, you fellows did a nice job."

Doc and I just looked at each other. We were covered with dirt, hay and cobwebs. At point, I was tempted to put a 2x4 over Harold's head.

23
CRAZY
SISSY

Will Rogers once said, "I never met a man I didn't like." Well, during the 35 years I practiced veterinarian medicine, I met plenty of them I wouldn't invite home for Sunday dinner, not that they didn't have a good side. After all, that was what I looked for in order to create a happy working atmosphere when it came to dealing with some people and their animal problems.

The Whittiers, Joe and his daughter, Sissy, loved animals. Their pet population grew to enormity over time when every stray in town discovered that the Whittiers were a soft touch. In fact, Joe and Sissy made one of the many houses they owned into a pet dormitory. Sissy treated her dogs and cats as if they were her children and as she pampered and looked out for them over the years, I became her house vet. The Whittiers thought I was an animal doctor sent from heaven. I was kind and always tried my best to work with them. They called me 'Doctor Lucas' with emphasis placed on the word doctor.

Sissy had a funny little soft voice. She spoke rapidly with it and hardly stopped for a breath. She ended each conversation with deafening raspy laughter. My daughter, Shelly, was my reserve after-hours secretary during her school years. She answered the phone and performed miscellaneous duties. Shelly took many calls from Sissy and learned to mimic her to perfection. Shelly would say in imitation, "Shelly, your dad, DOCTOR Lucas, is the nicest man in the world. He is so kind and listens to my problems with my animals. I know God has a place for him in heaven. Heh! Heh! Heh!" My family would burst into laughter at Shelly's performance.

On a Saturday evening in July, Sissy was on the phone

uncontrollably crying and wailing. Through her sobs she said to me, "DOCTOR Lucas, my dog Poopsy just got run over by a car. I think she is dead. She's still in the road. Would you come over and get rid of her if she's dead? I can't bear to look at her."

"Of course," I answered soothingly, "I'll be right over."

When I got there, two city workers had stopped and were standing over the dog. I joined them, made my examination and sure enough, Poopsy was gone. The city boys offered to haul the dog away for Sissy who agreed to the proposal. First, Sissy insisted, she would offer a prayer for her beloved pet. We waited for her words. The boys picked Poopsy up and gently laid her in the truck. Sissy watched them leave for the city dump, the planned site of Poopsy's internment and then ran, sobbing, into her house. Her grief poured out in buckets and was so loud I felt the whole town would hear her.

Later the same evening, Sissy decided she could not bear the thought of Poopsy lying in the dirt of the cold and anonymous dump. She felt her disposal decision was inappropriate and extraordinarily harsh in light of how much she loved her dog. She beckoned her father to go find Poopsy, to dig her up and return her to their backyard. Joe immediately left on his mission. On the way, he picked up Donnie Blake who could help him dig. The two of them found Poopsy's shallow grave, dug her up and transported the body back home.

Sissy cried for two hours over the dog's cold bones. Still in mourning, she then asked her dad to find a nice box. Poopsy needed a casket. The box was found and once again, Joe asked Donnie to help him dig. Together, they put Poopsy in the covered wooden box and after the formality of a proper funeral the dog was laid to rest.

It was 2 a.m. and Sissy still could not bear the thought of her dog lying in the ground and wanted to see her one last time. She awakened Joe and asked him to reopen Poopsy's grave. Joe, alone and tired, reluctantly dug the hole. When he opened the grave he found the dog laid out in the dirt. The casket had disappeared.

Now, Donnie Blake hated to see anything go to waste and he thought it a great injustice to bury such a fine box. It seemed as soon as Joe had fallen asleep, Donnie went back to the grave, dug up the dog and took the box. He had reburied Poopsy in the dirt. Sissy slept little that night. Now that Poopsy's body was soiled, it had to be bathed.

In the wee small hours of the morning, Sissy made a final decision. She waited for business hours before she called a mortician friend who lived in St. Joseph, Missouri. Between them, they made arrangements to have the dog embalmed. The dog would be placed in a nice casket and laid to rest in the pet cemetery. So it was. The funeral bill came to $300.

I did a little accounting on my own. All in all, I figured, the dog had been buried five times that night. A great amen must have been proclaimed when Poopsy crossed over into puppy heaven.

I was deep in sleep when, on another occasion, Sissy's phone call tossed me out of bed. "Oh, DOCTOR Lucas," she said, "I so hate to bother you at this hour, but I have a problem and I just don't know what to do."

"What's the problem?" I asked in a disinterested voice.

"Well, I have this little Rat Terrier named Sammie and he was breeding this big Black Labrador and now he can't get away from her and she is dragging him around by his ———. You know what I mean."

"Yes, Sissy, I know what you mean. It's his penis, right?" I said. "Just give them some time and they will separate. That's a normal thing for dogs and it's called tying-up. Go to bed and when you wake up, everything will be OK."

"OK, DOCTOR Lucas, I'll try not to worry," she responded.

But worry she did. I found out that after Sissy had spoken with me, she called another vet for a second opinion. That DOCTOR was not as kind. He told Sissy to throw a bucket of cold water on the dogs and go to bed.

24
KEEPING UP
WITH THE JONES'

"Dad, I'm so cold," Winston Jones said in a small voice. It was January and a skift of snow covered the ground. It was 10 degrees above zero with an east wind. The wind-chill index was at 20 degrees below. Winston was the grandson of Grandpa Jones and the son of Paul.

Grandpa Frank Jones homesteaded the land and changed it over to a family farm after Paul graduated from law school. The farm was Paul's life-long ambition. Law was an occupation, being a landowner and livestock producer was his life's calling. In his spare time away from his legal practice, Paul ran cows.

"Tell yourself you are not cold and you won't be cold," answered Paul with a military type command.

"But, Dad, I am cold," Winston chattered from his shivering body.

"Just shut up and do your job," replied Paul. To Paul the day was a learning experience for Winston. Paul believed you had to work hard in life to get ahead, and not let small adversities get in your way. Sensible people would not be outside on such a frigid day. Veterinarians and Paul answered to the beck and call of work. That was the farm ethic.

Donnie, my helper, and I answered Paul's call and went to his farm, prepared to suffer in the cold. Paul had cows that needed pregnancy testing. I took along a heating device to keep my syringes from freezing.

Winston's job was to record the stage of pregnancy of each cow and he was expected to keep the records in tip-top shape. For record-keeping purposes, most cow operators used ear identification tags to mark their herd. Paul did not like to use the tags, complaining they were often lost. For I.D., Paul had Winston write a brief description of each cow—such as 'red, white faced with spot on her side.' I couldn't imagine keeping track of 150 cows that way.

Donnie was trying to help Winston with the sorting. Winston would fall behind and Donnie would bellow, "What's the matter kid, can't you take the cold?" Donnie was raised in an old house heated by a wood-burning stove and he was a survivalist. I told Donnie to keep quiet.

Frank had built a corral for the cows. It was one of the few in existence in my practice area and I much appreciated a good corral but I did not like Frank's. It was built with hedge posts and hog wire and was lined with cottonwood poles tied with bailing wire.

Frank was not a big help to us on this wintry day. He mostly paraded around the chute and shouted orders. None of us paid any attention to him. As I watched him walking aimlessly around, I remembered a summer day I had spent with Frank. He had a big bull in the wired-together corral that he wanted me to examine. That bull was huge and he majestically held his head high.

"What's the matter with the bull, Frank?" I asked.

"Why, he's lame," Frank answered.

I climbed on the pen and as the bull measured me up, I said, "He looks mean to me. I would hate to put a rope on him. He'd tear the place up."

"Oh, no," Frank said as he walked over to the gate, "he's gentle as a kitten."

"What are you doing, Frank?" I asked.

"I'll get in there and turn him around so you can see his leg," he answered.

"No! Stay out," I yelled.

Frank hobbled in through the gate. At first, the bull just stared at Frank, taking a moment to think. I could see what was going to happen. When the bull decided there wasn't enough room for two in the corral, he shoved Frank into a corner. With brute strength, the bull threw Frank up in the air. On the descent, Frank landed on the bull's head and was thrown back up again.

Frank was yelling and swearing. "I'm going to be killed! Damn, I'm going to be killed!" The bull kept at the game. Frank was the yo-yo and the bull held the string. I leaped on the fence where I could reach the bull. From there, I kicked him in the rear. The bull turned his attention my way and went after me. I had a height advantage and was unreachable. My maneuver gave Frank enough time to climb out of the pen to safety. I remember him saying, "I should have listened to you. You saved my life."

Winston was still on the back of my truck, identifying cows. He was trying to write but his hands were as cold as blocks of ice. I felt sorry for him. Perched as he was, Winston couldn't even move around to combat the cold. Paul scoffed at me when I instructed Winston to get into the heated cab of my truck to warm up. Winston did not have to be told twice.

Paul was meticulous with his farm operation. He carried a legal pad containing a cow's history and a checklist of questions for each animal. When he would call me, Paul was able to cover a lot of ground in one conversation with those notes.

Paul worked at his law practice Monday through Friday. On the weekends, his kids were out of school and Paul would plan any veterinarian work that needed to be done. Paul or I would find a job for each one of his children. While some of the jobs seemed insignificant, the siblings would dutifully handle their assigned parts. Of course, Grandpa Jones would make the rounds with us. His job was accounting. Frank would ask the cost of each procedure, complaining all the while about how high my prices were.

One time, Frank had thirty bred heifers in a sheep shed that were ready to calve. The shed had no electricity and was built low to the ground. Only a midget could have walked under the crosspieces. Frank had decided he couldn't afford a veterinarian to deliver the calves. He played doctor and lost the first seven. After that experience Frank reluctantly began calling Dr. Jim Johnson or me. Frank never lost another calf although we suffered through many hair-raising experiences in that dark shed. Imagine a wild heifer banging around those crosspieces, attached to the end of a rope, with Frank moaning and yelling in the background, making sure he could be heard above the racket.

One night a very aggressive cow got loose in the shed and got Frank down. From out of the dark I heard Frank screaming, "I'm going to die, this is it!"

I had to guide myself to Frank by following his hysterics. Somehow I got the cow off and let her out in the lot. I told Frank the only thing that saved him was the blackness of the shed—the cow couldn't tell what she had a hold of. That shed could have done any of us in. Jim Johnson told Frank that he himself would wire the shed with electricity as a Christmas present, but he never did.

Being more or less gentlemen farmers, if a way could be found to do something wrong, the Jones' would discover it. One Saturday, Paul and Frank borrowed my sprayer in order to treat their cows for lice. I had left two gallons of spray and the directions for its use. The directions instructed to use one gallon of spray for each tank full of water. When the Jones' came back to town for more spray, I knew something was amiss. I asked them where the spray had gone. The Jones' had doubled the dose, and put both gallons of treatment in one tank of water. I immediately called ISU's poison center and spoke to the toxicologist. The toxicologist informed me the cattle would die from the overdose, unless preventative steps were taken. After the treatment, Frank and Paul had turned the cows out to pasture. There was little hope of recapturing them in time. I considered calling out the fire department. I could wash the cattle off with the department's hoses and portable supply of pressurized water. Night had fallen and I abandoned that idea. There was nothing, within reason, we could do.

I couldn't sleep all night. At 3:00 a.m., I drove out to the pasture to see if anything abnormal was going on. It was a beautiful night with a full moon that lit up the sky. There were stars galore and they added to the serenity. The cows were spread out, laying and standing about the pasture. Having a stranger amidst them left them unconcerned. Some were lying down, chewing their cud, while others milled about nibbling grass. None were sick from the spray and not one of them died as a result. The toxicologist had thankfully been off the mark on that one.

It was summer. The clinic practice was a little slow. Most cows had their calves by then, with the exception of a few late stragglers. It was then that I tried to plan some pleasurable activities. It was also a special time for Frank Jones to call. Frank's voice over the phone would temporarily deafen you. He thought you still had to yell into the receiver, much like when phones first came out.

"I have a cow calving and wonder if you could check her out," he yelled.

"Do you have her in?" I asked.

"Nope, she is in the pasture but we can walk right up to her," he replied.

I was as gullible as ever. I answered, "OK, Frank, I'll be right down." I knew that cow would never let me walk right up to her. There was no sense screaming with Frank about it over the phone.

It was a two-mile drive to Frank's farm and I was prompt as ever. Frank greeted me with, "I suppose this will cost me more since she is in the pasture."

"Of course it will," I shot back.

I have been wrong before and this was one of those occasions. I walked right up to the cow and laid the rope over her head. Before I could tie the rope to a tree, the cow had a dose of reality. She thought she might be snared and in one swift motion, she came to her feet and ran. I gripped the rope with all my might but I was no match for her. She ran away with my rope. Frank and I made a gallant chase as we tried to grab the rope end. The cow was wise and ran for the deep ditches for protection.

"We are going to have to find someone with a horse to catch her now," I yelled at Frank.

"Oh, gee haw," Frank wailed. "Who in the world can we get?" he wondered out loud.

"Try your neighbors," I said.

We had a name for those neighbors of Frank's, the Fearless Foursome. All of them were farmers who kept horses and they were known to chase anything, usually with great success. The group was made up of Wilbur Rowe, Henry Russell, Buddy Ross and Monte Churchill.

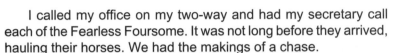
I called my office on my two-way and had my secretary call each of the Fearless Foursome. It was not long before they arrived, hauling their horses. We had the makings of a chase.

Frank's cow was smart as a whip. She stuck her head in brush and ran us through some rough areas. The horses followed and it was not long before our posse had another rope on her. She did not give up easily. The cow bolted at a right angle and nearly toppled a horse. The rider had to let go of the rope, and away we went, around the pasture again. It was an exciting chase. The cow was running out of options when she jumped into a good-sized pond and swam across the middle. When she reached the other side, she stopped. She was in deep water about 20 feet from us. The boys threw two ropes on her and tied them to the saddle horns. With each pull, they attempted to tug her out of the pond. The cow pulled back, burying her feet in the muddy bottom. They could not budge her.

It was a hot day and the chase had heated me up even more. I took my clothes off and jumped in the pond with the cow. I had decided I would first cool off and then come in behind the cow to drive her out to a point where the horses could hold her. When I swam up behind her, she whirled around and tried to get at me. The saddle-held ropes kept her at bay. I could not drive her out. I tried twisting her tail but had no success. In a moment of nonsense, the thought struck me, why not examine her on the spot? I reached in her vagina and found a set of immature twins. The calves were dead. I untangled the mess and delivered the set right into the pond. I loosened the ropes on the cow and left her standing in the water and I swam out. When word got around at the sale barn the next day, everyone wondered if I had learned underwater delivery in vet school.

When Paul's oldest kids graduated from high school and went away to college, Paul was left with his youngest daughter, Jennifer.

It was up to Jennifer to pick up the slack and do what the three boys had. She reluctantly accepted the challenge. With Paul, there wasn't an option. Jennifer was a little frail and in the winter she would dress in layers in an attempt at keeping warm. Once she was outfitted, my helper, Donnie couldn't tell if she was a boy or a girl.

On a very chilly day, Jennifer was helping us push cattle to the chute. We were waiting for the next calf when Donnie blurted out, "Come on boy! Get us more cattle!" With the exception of Jennifer, we all chuckled at Donnie's blunder.

Working cattle was a dangerous proposition, no matter whose farm you're working. I have witnessed many accidents caused by pushing cattle up a chute. If the pusher got too close, the animal could land a kick, and it hurt. The animal could kick straight back and hit you on the shinbone, the hip, the groin or stomach. They could kick with both feet, like they were kicking for the moon, and catch you with an uppercut to the jaw.

On one occasion Paul's son, Dan, was helping us push cattle up a chute and was handling the end gate. Dan swung the gate around on a cow and when it hit her in the butt, she kicked. The gate flew back at Dan, hitting him square in the nose. I heard Grandpa Jones holler, "Oh my gosh, Dan is hurt bad!"

I ran toward Dan as fast as I could. He was laying on the ground in a great deal of pain. He rolled over and I reached down to help him to his feet. Blood was pouring out of his nose. His nose was out of joint, and obviously broken. Dan was still a little groggy when I reached for his nose and snapped it back into place. Grandpa Jones thought I was a miracle man for making his grandson look normal again. Dan was taken to the doctor and eventually healed from the gate wound.

Paul and Frank appreciated my prompt service. There was a phone across the road from the farm at the City Airport. Paul would call me from there and oftentimes I would beat him back to the barn. It was a game we played and was one of the fun experiences of doctoring their animals.

The experiences were not all amusement. One time Frank had a cow down with a uterine prolapse. I replaced it and as I was suturing the last stitch, the cow let out a big moan and died.

"Well, gosh darn," Frank yelled. "She's deader than a hammer."

"Yes, she is," I replied.

"Will I have to pay for this one?" Frank yelled.

I didn't answer.

In later years, Paul wrote a testimonial to my service, from a cow's point of view. With the help of Mother Nature, I had helped deliver a calf from a mother who was too small. The editorial follows.

I was just fifteen months and three days of age and experiencing intense but fruitless labor pains as my owner hung around looking helpless and fidgeting, when Dr. Lucas quietly approached, calf jack in hand and with a gentle but firm touch pulled my son from me with such skill that within seconds he was holding his head up and I was able to walk to him unassisted and without wobble.

I heartily recommend the Bedford Vet Clinic to any of you ladies who fool around when you're too young or with someone too big. Thanks again.

From: The Red Blaze Heifer out
of the stylish wide belt,
Paul Jones, owner

25

OL' FIDO
WON'T BITE

Animals and people dictated what happened every day that I was a veterinarian. Simple calls could turn complex once the potion of human personality was added to the mix.

Blaine Shupe was a special person. He was Bedford High School's football coach and many a young man played under his leadership, including myself. Later in life, Blaine and I became friends and we quail hunted together. Blaine called one day concerned about his pet dog, a St. Bernard. The St. Bernard breed was popular back then and I found most of them to be docile. I did notice, however, with the onset of age the breed became very protective of their masters and the premises they were meant to defend.

"My St. Bernard is sick, Doc," Blaine had said when he called.

"What is he doing?" I asked.

"Oh, he is really lethargic and won't eat. He just lies around. He's laying on the front porch now," Blaine explained.

"I will be right over," I said as I happily agreed to make a house call.

I parked the vet truck on the street and casually walked toward the front porch. I paid little attention to anything except for the neighbor's garden I was admiring. Out of the quiet, my preoccupation was shockingly altered with the tremendous bang radiated from a just-burst-open porch door. A barking, lion-looking beast was in full charge toward me. I felt I would be killed. The beast hit the end of his chain and fell with a thump at my backpedaling feet. The St. Bernard kept right on barking at my frozen-in-place statue. Blaine stepped out on the porch.

"Is that the sick dog?" I yelled at Blaine.

"Well, ah, yes. I thought so," Blaine responded between peals of laughter.

"I could have died here, you know, from a heart attack or fright. That dog doesn't look sick to me," I said.

Then I remembered a truism from the veterinarian's Bible. If an animal's owner ever spoke these words to you, 'Don't worry, Doc, Ol' Fido wouldn't hurt a flea,' look out. You were about to get bitten.

It never ceased to amaze me how some farmers were so nonchalant about their dogs, particularly when their dogs were working livestock. Virgil Kirby had a beautiful, but brainless, Springer Spaniel. Virgil would be working his calves and the stupid dog would literally chase each and every calf through the lot fence. Virgil would laugh and merely say, "Look at that."

He never disciplined the dog even though, year after year, Virgil had to rebuild fence. Every time I helped Virgil, the same thing would happen. "Look at that," Virgil would say.

Animals are unpredictable, despite their owner's judgement of the pet. A veterinarian was examining a cat when the cat clamped its teeth on the vet's hand and wouldn't let go. With the cat attached, the veterinarian instinctively threw his arm in the air. On the downward arc, the vet slammed the cat down to the floor. Being in an unconscious state, the cat released its grip. The vet, without thinking, then stomped on the cat's head and killed it. The vet said, "Oh, hell, I shouldn't have done that!" Fortunately, the vet's contriteness produced sympathy from the cat's owner.

The 'Ol' Fido wouldn't hurt a flea' line always reminded me of the required vet course that covered the autonomic nervous system. The fight or flight impulse was part of that system. I learned some species had no fight in them. When they were threatened they ran as fast as they could. Other species stood their ground and fought. I found over and over my impulses lay with the species that instinctively preferred flight.

One evening back in my ISU days, I had gone alone to an

Iowa State basketball game. I was walking through Pammel Court when an old car spun around the corner. The car came so close to me I was forced to leap out of its way to avoid getting hit. As I jumped, I yelled at the top of my lungs, "Slow that SOB down!"

The car came to a screeching halt and from it an Iowa State jock emerged. He was big and he was wearing an Iowa State football letter jacket. He mumbled something about what he was going to do to me when I said, "Settle down and we can work this out."

The letter winner was in no mood to make friends. I took advantage of a head start and ran a 100-yard dash in ten seconds or less. As the cinders were kicking up under my feet, I heard him yell, "Chicken s—t." Better to be a live coward than a dead hero.

In my case, flight was not as much of an instinct as it was learned behavior. Ol' Fido wouldn't hurt a flea if he was never given the chance.

26

SHE'S A
TAME COW, DOC

When a call came into the office, our vet secretary was instructed to ask, "Is the cow where you can catch her?"

The responses were varied. "Don't worry, Doc, the cow ain't goin' nowhere. She's a tame cow. The cow is paralyzed. She's too sick to run. It's so lame, it can't walk." For every cow that just lay there, there were the other 95% that got up and ran off. Then the chase would begin. The vet sometimes chased the cow. The cow sometimes chased the vet. It was strange how I could look a cow in the eye and have a good idea whether she would charge or run the other way.

I would say, "That cow is getting ready to take us."

The farmer would reply, "Oh, no, not old bossy. I raised her on a bucket." That made me worry every time.

On the Vern and Donna Paxson place, an old cow was trying to have a calf. When I walked in the pen her eyes were as big as saucers. I said, "She looks kinda' goosey, will she take us?"

"Oh, no, she's just an old pet!" Donna said. About that time, here came the cow. I sidestepped her head and she missed me but her big stomach rolled me along her backside. A water bucket flew in the air and threw water over everyone. My OB bag went flying and spread instruments all over the barn. Before I could move out of the way, the cow turned on me and caught me in the butt with her head. She lifted me up and threw me in an old horse manger. At least I was then in a safe place.

After we eventually roped her, we delivered the calf. Donna

and Vern apologized over and over again. They just couldn't believe it. Donna said, "I'll never say an old pet again!"

When I would return thereafter to the Paxson place, I would always ask, "Will this animal take me?"

Donna would answer, "I'm not saying."

I've had farmers walk and prod a cow to the barn from clear in the back of 160 acres with no problem. The minute the cow spotted me, a stranger, she would go ballistic.

About daybreak one morning in June the phone rang. It was Glen Gamel. Glen had a cow calving. I asked if he had her in the barn lot.

"Yes," he answered. "I have her tied to a tree." I thought, oh good, as I climbed into my coveralls.

Glen lived down by Hoover Timber. As I was driving, the sun was just peaking over the treetops and lighting up the rolling hills. I imagined the notorious Jesse and Frank James when they rode their horses over this territory. There was a story that Mrs. Hoover was about to lose her farm to the banker. Jesse heard about it and gave her the cash to pay off the land. When the banker came and got the money, Jesse robbed him and stole the money back.

I arrived at the Gamel farm. I could see the cow's head when I drove in the driveway but could not see a rope attached to her. I thought to myself, Glen said she was tied up. I got closer and could see that Glen had the rope attached to the backwards-coming calf's rear legs. The other end of the rope was tied to the tree. Glen had been whipping the cow to try to get her to pull her own calf. I had never seen that tried before but I suppose if it worked, it would have saved a vet bill.

I tied the cow's head to the tree and with the calf jack easily delivered the calf. It was very important to pull at the correct angle to deliver a safe calf and save the cow. Pulling at an odd angle could kill both animals.

One quiet evening, Doc Anderson called me to assist him on a call. John Frazier was a quiet older gentleman who kept a few cows for something to do. He had a beautiful place and he kept it as clean as any golf course. As Doc and I walked up to the beautiful old barn, John opened the door and said, "There she is." We carefully walked on in and John shut the barn door behind us. Doc surveyed the situation and I could tell he did not like what he saw.

"Is that cow a little mean?" he asked.

"Naw, she is like an old kitten," John said.

"Looks like a wild cat to me and I don't see any exit for us," Doc responded. Doc was right. There were no stalls and the middle of the barn had sides about 8 feet high with little toe holders for climbing. To make matters worse, the cow had huge horns.

"Oh, hell," John said. "Throw a rope on her and snub her up."

I had the rope so I said, "I'll try, but Doc, you first see if you can climb that 8 foot panel." I had no more than said that when here the cow came. Doc moved really well and climbed that panel like a chimpanzee, only spilling a bucket of water on his way. I climbed up also and threw the rope over both horns. The cow whirled and fought the rope but I managed to hold on. Soon, the cow settled down a little and I threw my rope end around a big post. Each time the cow jumped back and forth, I would shorten the rope until I had her snubbed.

Doc slid down the wall to watch me deliver my first calf. The calf was coming backwards and its butt was visible with its rear feet and legs pointed forward. If a calf is still alive, this kind of delivery isn't too difficult. It was necessary to get the feet coming first, however.

"Old Doc Mayberry would just turn the calf around and bring him out head first," remarked John. I didn't want to comment as this was my first delivery, but headfirst sounded totally impossible to me. Doc Anderson came to my defense and told John like it was.

"That's bullshit, John, old Doc Mayberry was a drunk and a liar so he wouldn't know which end was which," Doc blurted.

That ended the conversation. I had one foot out and the other was soon to follow. "Now," I said, "let's every one gently pull."

As we applied more tension, the cow began to push and out popped the wet little calf. I was ecstatic to see the little live calf that I had helped rescue. Down through the years, I never lost the feeling of that first delivery.

Ol' John thanked us with enthusiasm. Some things just never

ceased to amaze me but I was proud to have lived up to the likes of Doc Mayberry.

27

DON'T WISH FOR CALLS

It was a beautiful day, perhaps the one that signaled the end of a long old winter. The changing of seasons in Southwest Iowa is indescribable. A hard rain had just blanketed the Midwest setting the stage for dark green grass to explode against a bright blue sky. The buds on the trees were swollen in expectation of bloom.

It was a slow afternoon at the clinic. I had taken time to organize my thoughts and make a game plan for the remainder of the day. I was the on call vet for the night but I was hoping for a quiet finish and the enjoyment of spending time with my wife, Kay.

The phone rang. Floyd Bunn had a new calf born with its intestines hanging from the umbilicus. Kay accompanied me on the call so we could indeed spend some time together. We drove on winding roads, just before an orange sundown. A rooster pheasant jumped in the six-inch tall alfalfa. His bright red head feathers glistened in the sun. He fluttered his wings at us to let us know he was the cock of the walk.

Mr. Bunn was waiting for us on his 4-wheeler. He would lead us to the calf. Floyd was surely not a mechanic. His place was filled with run-down tractors and machinery seemingly left in place at the time they quit working. He drove us through this maze of junk to the newborn calf.

It was a mystery how intestines wiggle out from a calf's navel when the opening is no larger than your finger. They sure won't go back in the same way. I enlarged the opening and reinserted the intestines. As I was suturing the wound I had made, the calf's mother seemed grateful I was about to finish. She licked and nurtured the calf.

I loaded up my equipment and found my way through the junk pile, heading home. On the way, another junked up farm came into view. That farm owner had owed me money for three years or more. Veterinarians could file a lien if work was performed and not paid for within 60 days. The thought crossed my mind that I wished the guy would call or consult with me about his bill. If he did the process could begin, and then there was hope I could collect the full amount. After three years, I didn't feel lucky about the prospect of collecting any part of the bill nor receiving a call.

Kay and I had just arrived home when the phone rang again. It was Don Wood, a hard-working, good client of mine. He had a first calf heifer that he could not deliver himself. I had driven up the road about two miles from home when my car phone rang. It was the farmer who had the three-year old bill! He also had a heifer calving that needed help. It seemed my luck had changed. The call came that I had wished for.

I joyfully answered to the debtor, "Of course, I'll be right there. I have one stop to make and then I'll come out." A big smile came over my face as I thought I had hit a collection home run.

Things went well at the Woods' farm. I had to snare the calf's head to bring it through the pelvis. After bringing the head and feet out together, and with a good pull the calf delivered alive. The mother nursed the calf and was anxious to clean it up.

It was just getting dark when I finished at Don's. By the time I got to the Ed Garson farm it was very dark. Ed motioned for me to drive in the barn lot. I drove in and my truck slipped into a mud hole. I put the truck in 4-wheel drive and ran over a hidden concrete chunk. The truck lurched but it didn't seem damaged.

I pulled up to the dark barn. Ed had no electricity but he did have a flashlight. With my portable lantern, we had two dim lights. At the least, Ed had the heifer in a homemade chute. Wild was not a strong enough word for this cow. The creature was absolutely crazy, kicking and throwing her head at us. I reached immediately for the tranquilizer to settle her down.

"This is her second calf," Garson said.

I looked at him, unbelieving. The cow wouldn't weigh 500 pounds I decided. Her calf was already dead. Its front feet were showing, but not a head. When I explored the uterus I found the head that had been forced back the other way. After some difficulty, I was able to get the head snared and headed out with the feet. Ed's boy, Terry, came to help. I let him run the calf jack while the heifer fought us both all the way.

I had been stumbling over something the whole time. During a couple of crucial maneuvers, I had pulled the calf jack around to produce pressure and both times, I stumbled and fell. The jack flew back against the barn. "What the hell tripped me," I had yelled.

"It's a dead sow," Ed said. I had been wallowing in the stinking remains of the busted carcass.

Terry and I jerked and pulled over and over. We had moved the calf to its hips and then it locked. I had to cut the calf in two at the hip. Then I used OB wire to cut the calf's pelvis in two. In pieces, I pulled out the rest of the calf. I was totally spent. A caesarean section would have been easier to perform had I known the calf was that big.

Now it came to settling up. I asked Ed about the old bill. He said he didn't remember and hadn't received an invoice. I wasn't sure that he had and said I would check into it. Ed paid me for this night's work. Later, after a reminder, Ed remembered the old bill and he paid it. I felt like I had earned it all in that one evening.

Before I got into the truck, I took a deep breath. I looked up to the sky to drink in the warm and beautiful night. The moon was smiling at me, watching me in my misery.

"I love it, I love it, I love it," I kept saying to myself. Then I decided I'd think twice about wishing for a call.

28

ABOVE AND BEYOND THE CALL OF DUTY

My wife used to tell me, "You chose this profession. It did not choose you."

On a cold and muddy day, Richard Fitzgerald chose me to assist with a calving cow. When I arrived at the call, the cow had been tied to the back of a John Deere tractor. Richard had driven the cow to the gate but she refused to go any further and the cow was in mud clear to her hocks.

The calf was presented with its head sticking out and both front feet back. It was so cold; I left my coveralls on while I used the plastic sleeves. I shoved the calf's head back in to make room for the feet. When I did this, the cow gave up and rolled over into the mud. It made my working room very tight. I somehow managed to get the calf's feet coming normal, but the head would not come through the pelvis. After groaning and cussing, I got a head snare around the calf and managed to get everything coming through.

"Hold your breath," I said to Richard. "Maybe the calf will come out in one piece."

The calf was out to the hips when it became hip locked. By that time, I was a big mud ball. I groaned and cussed some more and jacked out the dead calf. The cow then gave a great big strain and threw out her uterus. This was a veterinarian's nightmare, especially after working so hard on a delivery. I got down in the mud and started to replace the massive organ.

Richard had his tractor radio on for entertainment. John Denver

came on and sang, "Thank God I'm a Country Boy." I wished John Denver was with me, there in the mud.

I got the uterus lined up and eventually it found its place back inside the cow. I was cold and muddy and still did not feel like singing along with Denver.

Down east and south of Bedford the twins Dale and Dean Newkirk had grown up. Dale and Dean worked and played hard. They would do anything for work and built fence all over the country. One day I had stopped by to visit a neighbor of theirs. The twins were at the farm, stretching a barbed wire fence for him. They stretched one section of that fence too taut and broke a wire. The wire snapped back at them and one barb cut the bottom of Dale's ear lobe. He never even stopped working. By the time I left, the blood clot was about as big as a hen's egg.

On another occasion, the twins called late one evening. "Doc, this is Dale Newkirk, and I have a real sick calf. Can you come see about it?" he asked.

"I suppose I can, if you don't think it can wait until morning," I said.

"I don't think he'll make it that long," Dale replied.

"And, say Doc, do you suppose you could bring a six-pack of beer along?" Dale asked. Wearily, I told him I supposed I could.

I sleepily pulled into the farm drive and headed for the house. Dale met me at the door. "Come on in, Doc," he said.

"Where is the calf?" I asked in a most business-like way.

"Well, Doc, I'll tell you. I made up that story so you'd bring me the beer. There is no sick calf. I lost my driver's license and the taxicab refused to make the run, so I called you. But I aim to pay you for the call."

That night's duty was way above and beyond the call.

29

MOSQUITO RIDGE

It was mid-June and ordinarily the corn would be knee high. This year happened to be one of rain and more rain. Some farmers had beaten the relentless downpours and planted their row crops in early April. Those who hadn't taken advantage had virtually no planting done. Farmer's moods were grim in confirmation of the universal notion that nobody can change the weather.

Foliage farmers, those with grass and hay, had themselves an abundance of crop. In turn, cattle producers, who were next up in the food chain link, had ample feed and water. The excessive rain made ponds of water where none had existed before. The largest bumper crop of all was that of the mosquito.

I had made an early evening call to attend a calf that had hair growing in its third eyelid. The calf was born with irritated eyes as the hair constantly rubbed its cornea. How uncomfortable that must have been, I thought. Surgical removal of the hair would solve the problem but I elected to wait for full daylight to perform the procedure.

My drive home was unquestionably beautiful. The trees were in full foliage. A late flock of geese flew over honking which announced their northern flight. A turkey buzzard was lazily eating at a dead rabbit along the side of the road. A rooster pheasant strutted across the road, just ahead of a hen and seven babies. The air was clear, cool, and invigorating. I felt lucky to be alive and luckier still to drink in the natural beauty surrounding me.

When I arrived home, I greeted my wife, Kay, and told her I

was going to take a bath and settle down for the night. The awaiting tub was full of steamy water when the phone rang.

Steve Kernen, on the other end of the phone line, said, "I'm in real trouble, Jimmie."

"What's going on?" I asked.

"I have a mare foaling and a mass of something is coming out and I know it's not the foal."

"Try to hold her down, and I'll be right out," I told him.

Mares rarely had difficulty foaling. When a call like Steve's came in, it meant the client was overly excited or was really in trouble. This mare was in trouble.

The pasture was as muddy as it could be without having turned into a lake. I drove through a weed patch and nearly got stuck going downhill. When I made it to the mare's side, I found that she had birthed the foal's head and front feet out. Three of us attempted to pull the foal but we could not. I got my calf jack and jacked the foal out but it did not survive the long labor. The mare's intestines were hanging out her rectum and were wound around her legs. The intestine had been severed and there was no hope in saving the mare either.

"We'll just have to put her down," I said to Steve.

"Do what you have to do to stop her misery," Steve answered with resignation.

The mare rolled up on her belly, nibbled at the grass and nickered. Tears rolled down from my eyes as I looked into hers. The mare was much relieved that the foal was out. She did not understand the condition she was left in.

Mosquitoes were in swarms all around us. In the heat of the battle, we hadn't noticed their presence. Now they were drilling us.

"I'll have to run back to the clinic," I said, "I'm out of my euthanasia solution."

I gave the mare a big dose of sedative to keep her quiet and took off for the road. I was in four-wheel drive through the mud holes and it was still difficult going.

I made it back to the clinic and was trying to think of what I could use to repel the mosquitoes that awaited my return to the pasture. The only thing I could think of was a cattle pour-on used to repel flies and insects. I was desperate. I poured the repellent on my hands and rubbed them together. Then I rubbed some on the back of my neck and on my cap.

Back in the pasture, the little dive-bombers were working overtime.

It was necessary to drip a quart of euthanasia solution intravenously to put the mare down. In order to do so, one of us had to remain motionless to hold the needle in the mare's vein. I hit the vein once and started the IV. I was trying to keep the needle still when I felt the punctures from hundreds of the little devil mosquitoes on my back. The mare lunged and I lost the IV. Her sudden movement gave me an instant to walk away from the mosquito attack. The mare then rolled over and I was able to hit the vein again. The bottle slowly emptied and the poor mare gave a desperation breath and died.

I threw everything in the back of my truck and started to drive out. Twice I buried the truck in mud and in order to exit the pasture, I had to back down the hill. I could still hear the mosquitoes buzzing in my ears. I swatted at the phantoms flying inside the truck cab.

Back home, Kay greeted me as I ran another tub of bath water. When I climbed out, Kay counted nearly 50 mosquito bites on my legs, arms, back and butt. In sympathy, she rubbed me down with calamine lotion. In 33 years of veterinarian practice, I had never experienced such an onslaught of mosquitoes, nor had I ever been so pink.

30
T.E. ANDERSON AND SON

I decided by the age of sixteen I wanted to become a vet. Before I was of college age, I worked for Don Anderson, DVM, who was one witty, intelligent guy. Don had followed in his father's footsteps, T.E., who graduated from Chicago Veterinary College in 1908. It was with great interest I listened to the stories told by T.E. who made his calls driving a horse and buggy.

In the days of T.E. there were few paved roads. The county was scattered with small farm parcels of 20 to 40 acres. T.E. practiced his trade by combining his book learning with certain quackery medicines. My Grandpa Lucas did the same thing although he had no title or license. Grandpa sold his own version of a horse salve used to treat sores. The salve contained carbolic acid, jimson weed and lard. Even T.E. would have had to agree with the medicinal value of the concoction.

T.E. suffered from senility in his later years, and, although he was absent-minded about current affairs, he was very keen on things that happened long ago. T.E. was currently of the opinion my services were no longer needed at his family's vet clinic.

I was out of the office the day my dad, the late Max Lucas, stopped by. Old Doc was sitting in the rocking chair by the bay window. He was looking out at the huge pin oak tree he had planted when he was a young professional - the same days when he wore a white shirt, tie, vest and suit to work.

My dad asked Doc, "Have you seen Jim?"

Doc was not putting things together well that day. He knew

who my dad was but it didn't once cross Doc's mind dad and I were in any way related.

"No," Doc said, "and I wonder whose boy that is."

"By golly, I do not know," Dad replied.

"Well, I know one thing," T.E. said, "he's not worth a shit for anything around here."

For some reason, my dad found that to be humorous and told everyone of Doc's opinion.

I spent a lot of years in their family vet clinic, five in partnership with Doc Anderson. I learned rapidly that clients who had no respect for Doc's time heavily taxed his patience. With his wit and fury, he could cut anyone to the quick.

At five o'clock one morning, Doc's doorbell rang. He begrudgingly got out of bed and answered the door. Standing before him on the step was a perfect stranger. The man was holding a dead chicken by the neck.

"Sorry to wake you, Doc, but I have been losing some chicks and I thought I'd better get this one posted," the man said.

"Get your ass off my porch and never darken my door again," Doc yelled. I assumed the man never did.

Claude, a client from Missouri, came to the office one morning to ask Doc and myself to work his cattle. We set up an appointment for the next day. Claude had the cattle penned in an old roofless barn that had no gates when Doc and I arrived. The cattle were wild. The mud and manure that covered the barn's floor took a good churning from their hooves. I entered the barn to help Claude drive the cattle up to the chute where Doc could do his work. In a cartoon-like fashion, Claude and I chased the cows and the cows chased us. Back and forth we went until Claude advanced around a wooden partition and stepped into a pile of the blended mire. The mud sucked him in right up to his knees. A big calf ran by him, he dodged, and fell over backwards with his legs lodged in position.

"Oh, oh, Claude, you fell in the shit," I said mockingly.

Still on his back, Claude said, "That is not shit, Jimmie, it is just mud."

I helped Claude back to his feet and ushered him out of the barn. A few months later Claude walked up the street toward our office. Doc saw him coming, locked the doors and escaped out the back. No wit of Doc's was as quick as the mud in Claude's barn.

On the day Doc and I went to work cattle for Dwight Davidson, Doc had left his truck parked alongside the paved road. When we finished with the cattle, I jacked my chute up, hooked on to my truck and with a good-bye, took off. At a fair rate of speed, I drove down the gravel road and onto the highway. When I glanced in my side mirror I thought I saw something whipping in the wind on the back of my chute. I stopped the truck. There was Doc Anderson, hanging on to the chute for dear life. Without my knowledge, Doc had jumped on in order to ride the short distance to his pickup. I had given him a good one.

The world for T.E. Anderson revolved around horses. The animals were his veterinarian specialty. He also trained and raced horses in harness, both pacers and trotters. Doc followed suit and he too became a well-known equine vet, breeder, trainer and harness racer. Horses seemed to run in their blood.

It was November 22, 1963. Doc Anderson was to attend to a thoroughbred racehorse at the stable. The horse was lame with bowed tendons. Doc was going to 'fire' the horse's leg and I wanted the experience of assisting him with this surgery. To 'fire' meant a vet would first block the nerves of the affected leg and then apply a design of pinpoint burns. The burns created an inflammation and as the inflammation healed, the injured tendon would heal along with it. Once a horse's leg was 'fired' the horse was required to take an eight-week rest. No one was certain if it was the rest from racing or the 'firing' which helped the most.

My mind was excited about the opportunity to assist with this procedure. My car radio was on when the program was interrupted with this disheartening announcement: "President John F. Kennedy has been shot by a sniper's bullet and is presumed dead." I was in shock when my car coasted into the curb. At first I remained in the car in disbelief to what I was hearing. Slowly I slid off the car seat and walked to the stable.

Doc Anderson was inspecting the affected leg when I told him the news. He suddenly lost interest in the horse as he reeled back in a chair. It was hard for us to believe this had happened. We were both near tears when I repeated the announcement to Abe Smyzer, the horse owner. "Well, I'll be damned," he replied and tried to get our attention back to his horse apparently unconcerned about JFK's assassination. It is something how a lot of people live in their own little shell. I'll bet Abe didn't even know JFK was our President.

We listened to the news for awhile and after regaining our composure continued with the surgery.

Life goes on.

T.E. MAKES DIAGNOSIS

John Arnts and his wife had opposing personalities. John was subdued (henpecked) and the Mrs. could talk a blue streak. When she finished a sentence, it was with a long sustained giggle. Early one morning, the Arnts' were waiting on the clinic doorstep for us to open. With them, they had their little crossbred dog, Suzie. Old T.E. and I walked all three of them into the exam room. There I asked Mrs. Arnts, "What's the problem?"

"That's why we brought her to you, Dr.," Mrs. Arnts said belligerently. Then she giggled.

"It would be nice to have some history of what brought you here," I tried to explain.

"Go ahead and tell him," her husband said.

Mrs. Arnts began and ended her sentence with a giggle. "Well, ha, ha, the dog was sleeping under our bed when the bed fell down on top of her. She was real wobbly at first but seemed to get better. We thought we should have you check her to make sure she is OK, tee hee."

Old Doc had been standing quietly in the background. He casually walked by Mrs. Arnts and said, "And what were you doing to make the bed fall?"

T.E. waited briefly for a reply, lit his pipe and walked out. Mr. Arnts was more than a little embarrassed. His wife broke the silence with one long, continuous giggle. Suzie jumped off the exam table and was fine.

31

A SALE BARN VET'S TRIALS AND TRIBULATIONS

A sale barn veterinarian is a policeman, sworn to uphold the law and keep the peace for buyers, sellers and sale barn owners. Prior to selling, all livestock had to be inspected. Protection was written in by State and Federal laws, healthy or diseased animals were not permitted to change ownership. Part of the problem was if all animals of questionable health were turned away, there would not have been much of a sale. It was up to me to decide which animals were the least problematic. With each head of livestock sold through the barn, veterinarian-signed health papers were required to complete the transfer. Breeding animals were tested for pregnancy, blood tested for brucellosis and identified. The vet needed to be at the unloading dock, the testing chute, the auctioneer's box and the sale barn office all at the same time. In the middle of it all, a business client invariably needed you back at the clinic.

The sale barn was a gathering place. Spectators, buyers, sellers and characters known as traders assembled there. Traders were known for buying sick animals at one sale barn and then passing them off at another for profit. When 'traders' brought in stock, I tried to find a reason to turn them away. The traders and I often argued, face-to-face. It was like being the umpire at a baseball game who made a questionable call. One time I even took a closed-fisted swing at a trader. I missed.

A cattle trader brought in a calf that did not look right. My gut feeling was it suffered from thoracic adhesions of chronic pneumonia and its health would hardly improve. When the trader came back to discover I had rejected his fine calf, he carried on and on about my poor inspections. He would not listen to my line of reasoning.

"I'll tell you what I'll do," I told him, "just to show you how nice of a guy I am. I'll sell your calf through the ring but I will announce that I think the calf has chronic pneumonia and will probably die."

The trader was set off. He kicked gravel, cussed and yelled. "If you did that," he said, "the calf won't bring anything. Well, shit, if he's worth nothing, I just as well turn him out in the street and forget him." The man did just that. He opened the gate and out the calf ran. The fracas entertained the good-sized crowd that had gathered to watch. Later I enjoyed watching the trader round-up his calf and load it alone for the next unsuspecting buyer.

One Saturday, a load of hogs had come into the sale barn. The hogs carried rhinitis and I had to turn them away. Rhinitis is an insidious disease of swine that affects the sinus cavities of the snout. Even though mortality is low, the greater loss is from poor performance of rate of gain.

The owner asked me to prove to him that his hogs were infected. In front of his very eyes, I killed one of the hogs with an axe, sawed off its snout and showed it to him. He still did not believe me. I sent the snout off to the Iowa State Diagnostic Lab and they confirmed my diagnosis. The man did not believe the lab either and much to my disbelief, he threatened to sue me. The lawsuit threat ended at the slaughterhouse when the diagnosis was, for the last time, upheld.

When it came to Saturday sale day, I needed a lot of able-bodied help. I often hired high school kids, including my own children. At first, the teenagers were eager and wanted to do a good job. When it came to swine, the enthusiasm halted. Whether there were 1500 or three hogs, the animals all had to be individually identified with metal tags. It was a stinking, dirty job. After a few Saturdays of work, the most commonly asked question was "How many pigs are coming today?" I never had any idea of the numbers that would show, still the question never stopped being asked. There were some teenaged boys who looked at the lighter side of tagging.

One time, two pigs came in the sale ring tagged together at the ear. Another time one pig had one tag holding its ears together. I chewed the boys out for their orneriness. To avoid tagging altogether, my hires would oftentimes find an unsuspecting spectator and pay them a dollar to do their work.

Donnie Blake had a brother named Eddie who helped us out as well. One Saturday, Eddie had really angered me. I said to him, "Ed, you are fired. Get your butt out of here and never return!"

Ed's response stunned me. "You can not fire me," he said.

"Just what the hell makes you think I can't fire you, Ed?" I asked.

"Cause I will work for nothing," he answered.

I shrugged my shoulders, shook my head and walked off. Hard for me to give that up, I thought.

There was truly one thing I hated about being the sale barn vet. Without fail, when I was about to leave for the day, a sale barn patron would ask for just one more little thing. The patrons were sitting in the café drinking coffee trying to beat the last liar's story when one would say, "Oh, yeah, Doc, I forgot I wanted you to fix a ruptured pig I bought."

I would go out to my truck, get instruments and medication, and act as if I was enjoying myself. Bitching made it all the worse.

On one rainy day, I was hiding out in the Boar's Nest—the most descriptive name for the vet's sale barn office. The sale was over and I was preparing to exit the dump. Donnie was standing by the chute watching a few farmers load their purchases. From my nest I saw an older gentleman coming my way. The old guy sort of walked between Donnie and me and asked, "Is the sale barn vet here?"

I pointed at Donnie and said, "There he is."

The elderly man turned toward Donnie and asked, "I bought me a couple of calves with horns. Could you dehorn them for me?"

Donnie didn't blink an eye and answered, "It's too late in the spring. If you dehorn them now they will get maggots."

"Well, I never thought about that," the old man said.

I didn't say a word. What I did do was laugh, I hadn't wanted the job in the first place and I hadn't realized Donnie could cover for me so well. Come to think of it Donnie was quite an authority when he wanted to be.

On my way out, the rain clouds had broken. I leaned on the fence to absorb a few rays of sunshine. I noticed a client heading my direction. He had purchased a boar hog which weighed about 175 pounds. that needed some work. Donnie slammed the filthy rascal down and pounced on it to hold it for me. I was fumbling through my surgery box for instruments when I realized I had no suture. Brooke Turner also worked for me part time and was somewhat familiar with the layout of my vet truck. "Brooke," I yelled, "run to my truck and bring me back some suture."

"Sure will," Brooke replied. It wasn't just a little bit that Brooke was back bearing the wrong suture. Donnie was starting to wear down and was disgusted after holding the hog for so long. Donnie looked up at Brooke and implored, "What's the problem, boy, can't you read?" Although Donnie couldn't read himself, it was no excuse as far as he was concerned.

Another time, a client backed his trailer to unload a bunch of hogs at the sale barn. As far as I could tell, there were about 100 pigs on the load. Donnie stood by the gate and while pointing at each pig, began counting. Donnie knew we'd have to count to sell the pigs off but I knew Donnie couldn't count. Finally the last pig went by and the farmer yelled at Donnie, "How many did you get?" With authority, Donnie yelled back, "seventeen!" The farmer stopped in his tracks, turned and shook his head with disbelief. He obviously didn't agree with the count.

At the auction, Donnie customarily sat in the bleachers with the farmer buyers. The auctioneer got excited fielding bids from all over the arena. Donnie got excited too and would coyly raise his hand. The bid takers continued until they realized it was Donnie that was creating the action. The bidding would then have to stop and start all over again.

Donnie's eagle eyes would at times put me to shame. It was my job to inspect the pigs prior to sale and make a statement on their condition. While the hogs were selling, I often saw Donnie lean over the ring's fence and point out a blemish or a bad pig.

Just the fact he could point them out was reward enough for Donnie. It was embarrassment for me.

One sale day, a truck had been parked and left in front of the unloading dock. The pickup was nosed up at the side of the barn. A farmer needed to unload and when he saw Donnie standing there he asked, "Can you move that truck out of the way so I can unload?"

Donnie told him, "Sure can," although Donnie had never driven before.

The truck was a four-speed manual and had been parked in low gear. Donnie jumped in the pickup and without taking it out of gear, stepped on the gas pedal and turned the key. The engine ignited and both Donnie and the truck lurched forward until they rammed into the sale barn. There the truck's engine stalled. Donnie again turned the key and the truck lurched further yet into the sale barn, making its way through the new entrance. Then, Donnie found the clutch. He pushed on it with one foot and the truck rolled back. With the other foot, he had the gas pedal to the floor. His foot came flying off the clutch and the truck tore out a board section of the barn's side. Donnie took his foot off the accelerator and the engine died.

Sheriff Marven Weed was called because of the damage to the barn and the fact that Donnie had no driver's license. As he began to reprimand Donnie, Donnie shot back with his favorite saying, "Don't worry about it." That was the end of Donnie's driving.

A sale barn owner had to be ambitious and persuasive in order to make a go of it. His job was that of a ringmaster. He directed the buyers, the sellers and the veterinarian. Duane Simmons, the sale barn owner and I were getting ready for one Saturday auction. On the top row of seats a poor soul sat and continuously rolled his tongue. "Who is that poor fella?" the owner asked me.

"Oh, he used to run a sale barn!" I sarcastically remarked.

"Probably so," the owner muttered in resignation.

The sale barn was a magnet for merry pranksters.

"Lucas, you old quack, I'll bet you $5 that woman in the lunch room has a tattoo on her breast," Dean Combs once yelled at the top of his lungs to me.

"How do you know?" I asked, "maybe I should ask your wife. You've probably checked with her, heh?"

"Oh, hell no, don't ask her," he mumbled under his breath.

The lunch room attendee had evidently overheard our conversation. She coolly walked by us with her tank top down far enough to expose her ... tattoo. "Have a nice day, fellas," she said.

In our practice, the veterinarians carried a two-way radio at all times in case of emergency. For convenience, I preferred the belt clip kind. I was standing in the sale barn office one day with my radio belted on. "Doc," an unknown lady said, "why in the hell do you always carry that contraption with you?"

"Well, it's like this," I answered. "My wife comes into heat every six months and by golly, I sure don't want to miss it." The woman quickly exited, wearing a red face.

Harmon Sleep was a sale barn regular who spent his days off there. Harmon was a big but gentle guy. He had a soft voice and when he spoke, an impediment slowed his speech. He told stories that would put you to sleep. Harmon also was athletic. He could put the milk bottle booth at the county fair out of business.

Harmon and I were together in the sale barn office. Sellers that had small things to sell, like eggs, produce, puppies or kittens, brought them to the sale and they would be sold out of the office. A lady in a very tight fitting sweater had just brought in two really cute kittens that day.

Harmon was watching the kittens and said to the lady, "Those are sure nice titties you have!"

The lady slapped Harmon and said, "You'd better get your butt out of here."

Harmon turned to me and said, "I knew I should have said tats," and out he walked.

32
OL'
COLOSSAL

I once owned a big Black Angus bull named Colossal. He was not mean by nature, but Colossal pretty much did what he wanted. If I tried to drive him, he might have allowed it or he might just as well have pawed the ground and dared me to come closer.

I had one rule I always followed. Never put your trust in a bull or a boar. In the case of Colossal, the rule was golden. If Colossal took a notion, he would walk up to the gate, put his head against the middle of it and push. The gate would snap in two. I finally placed a hot wire in front of the gate. The shock Colossal took from the wire kept him away.

It was not unusual for my kids to tag along when I made vet calls. I found it was a good education for them and it gave my wife, Kay, a break. The kids would help me and I enjoyed their company. It was also not uncommon, when we caught up with the work, to unpack the fishing rod and reel from the truck. A nearby fishing pond was not hard to find in the country.

It was a beautiful spring morning. The sun's rays were beaming through the trees and the air was beginning to warm. The frogs were singing their clickety clickety tune. The season was sure at hand. Matthew, Shelly and I had finished our chores. We had no further business at hand.

"How about trying to catch some fish?" I asked.

"Oh yes, yes, yes," they answered with enthusiasm.

"The east pond is just over the hill in the pasture. We'll buzz over there," I told them.

As I was helping them set their fishing poles, I remembered Ol' Colossal was pastured here. I didn't think he would cause a problem. Nonetheless, I warned Matt and Shelly that we were in the domain of Ol' Colossal.

"Ol' Colossal is out here," I said to them. "If he should scare or chase you, just jump in the pond and swim to the other side."

Matt and Shelly were both good swimmers. I laughed at myself for being such an old woman. I was confident the bull was content in the pasture and we were not in harm's way.

Matt had tired of fishing and slipped around the pond. He was throwing rocks at the frogs. A pool of minnows swam in shallow water below him.

Ever much to my surprise, Ol' Colossal popped up over the bank. He was right above Matt. The bull was huge and with Matt looking up at him, Ol' Colossal must have looked like a locomotive. The bull stood his ground and surveyed the landscape.

Matt was startled at first, but he stood his ground as well. He yelled, "Get out of here," to the bull and threw a rock at him. Ol' Colossal casually shook his head and walked on over the bank towards the pond.

Matt remembered my instructions. He jumped in the pond and swam across to the other side. Ol' Colossal took a good long drink from the pond, turned and went back to the cows. Matt's swim had dampened him and our enthusiasm for fishing.

On the drive back to town, I told the kids the tale about a man named Bramble, a client of mine who worked for the electric-power company.

Bramble and his crew were doing some work on the power lines at my farm when Mother Nature made an urgent call. Bramble ran into a bull shed and dropped his drawers. Ol' Colossal walked up to the shed's door and peered in.

With his pants below his knees, Bramble picked up a club, yelled, and threw it at Colossal. The bull shook off the stick and walked into the shed. Bramble, waddling as fast as he could, made it to a gate which he attempted to climb for safety. Ol' Colossal looked Bramble over and decided he wasn't worth the effort. The bull turned and quietly walked out.

"He scared the shit out of me," Bramble told me.

I, of course, retold the tale at the coffee shop the next day to anyone who would listen.

The bottom line was to never trust a bull or a boar. The same could be said for animal mothers with newborn babies. Protection was a natural instinct in the female species.

My daughter, Jamie, had a calf named Baby Black that she had raised on a bucket. We kept Baby Black to be a member of our herd, bred her and she had a calf. Up to that time, she would let you walk up to her, pet her, and she would let Jamie sit on her back.

I had Jamie's cow penned in the barn. Baby Black had calved and I walked in to see if all was well. Suddenly, Blackey blew her nose and charged me. I was close to the manger when Blackey's charge caught me in the butt. Her head on my rear toppled me to safety. I felt lucky I had not sent Jamie to check on the new mom. A few hours later, the cow had settled down and acted proud of her newborn calf.

I was always aware of the lurking danger surrounding new animal moms. I had a client named Galen Keats. He had sent his wife to check on a calving cow. The cow had horns and in a rage, gored the poor lady to death.

Having my kids work with me in the practice gave them an education most children would never be exposed to. There were many times they received an ear and eye full of wild animals and inconsiderate clients.

At home one evening, I was in the bathroom washing off a hog manure smell when I heard a ruckus in the next room. We owned a big white German Shepherd dog. I peeked through the partially opened door to check on the noise. There was my 4 year-old son, Matt and the dog. My son had a plastic puppet on his hand and had a hold of the dog's tail. It appeared my child was attempting to test the dog for pregnancy like he had seen me do a hundred times with cattle. My son yelled in a gruff voice, "Come here you c— s——!"

I couldn't believe my ears and wondered where he had ever heard such language.

It was rewarding to teach the kids the work ethic that being a veterinarian required. They learned to save money, to appreciate long hours and hard work. The older kids, Jamie and Matt, used to argue over which one would operate the calf puller. I would have both of them pull at the same time. There was such pride when a live baby calf arrived. The girls, Jamie and Shelly, did the same work as the boys. They held pigs, tailed calves, were office secretaries, and ran the cow chute under my supervision. The girls even tagged pig's ears at the sale barn.

Only my 100 pound Jamie wanted to follow in my footsteps. I discouraged her as I thought she was too small framed to do the demanding work. I overlooked the other veterinarian opportunities and I should have encouraged her to go for it! On the other hand, if she had pursued the commitment and time required of a veterinarian, the birth of my two grandchildren would have been much delayed.

Both of my sons worked hard as my assistants even though they had more of an affinity for ornery pranks and disappearing from work.

Once I had purchased a big office cooler with sliding glass doors. The cooler was something I had wanted for a long, long time. A feed store in New Market had advertised the cooler for sale. It was a good price at $700.

Every Saturday, we had the sale barn to work. It was the day I always needed extra help. I hired my son, Matt, along with Billy and Jay Murphy as my regular Saturday workers. They were a good team and usually had the work caught up by noon.

"Matt, will you and the boys take your old pickup truck to New Market and pick up a cooler I bought?" I asked.

"Sure," Matt answered. "Where is it?"

I gave directions and handed them some ropes. "Tie the cooler to the pickup bed so the cooler won't slide out or blow over. I spent $700. Handle it with care," I cautioned.

Away the boys went to New Market. I was doing paperwork in the office and lining up calls when my son Joe dropped by. "Dad, Matt's looking for you," he said.

"OK, I'll be right there," I answered.

As I was walking across the street, Matt came out to meet me. "Well, Dad, we lost the son-of-a-bitch," Matt confessed.

"YOU WHAT?" I screamed. I had a feeling this was not a joke.

"Yep, we lost the son-of-a-bitch," he repeated.

"What in the hell happened?" I demanded to know.

"We were going around the curve near the Ingram place when a gust of wind blew the cooler out onto the highway," Matt told me.

"Did you tie it in with the ropes?" I implored.

"Nope, we thought it was so heavy it could not possibly fall out. We were wrong," Matt explained.

"Where the hell is it?" I steamed.

"Behind the clinic," was Matt's reply.

We quietly walked in the alley behind the clinic. There stood the cooler. One of its double glass doors was broken, one corner was bent inward, the cooling unit was precariously hanging from the bottom, and trays were everywhere. I couldn't look anymore. My blood pressure escalated and I let loose with profanities. I accused the boys of never doing anything right and worthlessness. I stomped and kicked gravel. The boys were too big to whip so I kept on ranting and raving about my lost $700 and the piece of equipment I had wanted so badly. The boys had their backs to me and I couldn't see the smirk on their faces.

A cousin of mine, Dr. Tim Lucas, had come walking along. He found humor in the situation, much to my disappointment. He helped smooth me out by noting that the boys had not caused an accident on the highway nor had they been hurt. "It could have been worse," he reminded me. I agreed.

The following week a plumber repaired the cooler and made it nearly as good as new. The cooler was still working the last I knew. And the boys were still reminding me of the show I put on for their benefit that day.

Some things I preferred not to remember.

33

HERE KITTY, KITTY, KITTY

Behind my city residence, over on the next block, lived two good neighbors who were both a little eccentric. The men were known to frequent the bars for an occasional nip. One of the neighbors was known as Doc D and he dealt in parakeets. The other was Harold and together they made up the merry prankster team.

Doc owned several birds and he'd always pick out one to keep in a special cage. If Doc had a customer, the gilded caged bird was the last to be shown. For all the others, he asked $5 apiece. Curiosity always got the best of Doc's customers and they would inevitably ask about the special bird in the special cage. Doc would tell them, "Oh, that's a very special bird indeed. I would have to have $15 for it."

The customer, without fail, asked to buy that bird. With the remorse and drama of an opera singer, Doc sure hated to sell but he guessed he could. After the customer left, Doc put another bird in the cage.

On my property sat a little barn that held tack and feed for my horses and was adjacent to Doc's property. One day I walked down to the barn and as I rounded the corner, I found a dead possum lying in a pool of blood. Doc and Harold were there as well, leaning on their clubs discussing the kill. I sauntered up to them and asked, "You fellas haven't seen my kid's pet possum, have you?" Harold and Doc glanced at each other with their mouths open. Harold stuttered, "D—d—d—did your kids have a pet possum?"

"Oh, yes," I quickly told them, "didn't you know?"

"Oh, my God!" Doc wailed in his deepest voice. I waited to retract the story until after I'd had one good hearty belly laugh.

Harold had a couple of town cats that he was getting tired of having under his feet. He asked if I minded if he took them out to my farm. He said he'd take food out to them periodically and make sure they had plenty to eat. I told him that would be fine with me. The cats would help keep the mice and rat population under control. Shortly after Harold had moved his cats, my farm tenant Jerry and I were calving some cows in the barn lot. One of the cows was a Charolais and she was mean all the time. After she had a calf, she was doubly nasty. Jerry called me one evening to warn me that the Charolais had delivered. What Jerry told me was "She'll eat your shorts. Don't go walking up in the lot."

The very next morning after Jerry's call, Harold went out to the farm to feed his cats. He climbed the lot fence and yelled, "Here kitty, kitty, kitty."

Out of the barn roared the old cow, running straight for Harold. She had red in her eyes and fire blowing from her nose. With a little help from the cow's lowered head, Harold leaped back over the fence. His eyes still bugged out when he told me of the encounter. As far as I was concerned, it was just another warning to be leery of domestic livestock.

Sheep, however, were as quiet and loving and docile as animals could be. I was called to the country to doctor some calves and as I performed my service, I noticed a big buck sheep standing back of me. He stared intently and stomped his front feet. "I don't think your buck likes me," I told the farmer whose livestock I was attending.

"Oh, don't worry about him. My little son, Bobby, raised him with a nipple on a pop bottle. Bucky wouldn't hurt anyone," the farmer replied. "But, if he continues stomping and does charge you, just hold your hands out and he will stop," the farmer directed.

I finished treating the calves and as I walked back through the lot, Bucky measured me up with his eyeballs. All of a sudden he made a charge. I remembered what the farmer had told me and I dropped my vet instruments and held out my hands. When old

Bucky's head reached my outstretched palms, he stopped. Then he turned around and trotted back to his original spot. How cute, I thought. When I heard the stomping begin again, I turned just in time to face Bucky's second charge. I stuck out my hands but that time, Bucky didn't stop. With his hard head, he hit me in the stomach and knocked me-ass-over appetite. I got up with a loose temper and grabbed a two-by-four. With it, I hit Bucky right on top of the head. He shook that off and walked away, proving what an extremely hard skull sheep have.

The farmer moved Bucky to another pen so I could exit the farm lot. Whether the farmer was protecting me from Bucky or Bucky from me had yet to be decided. I was still holding on to the two-by-four.

34
DE-SCENTING
SKUNKS

My brother Donovan joined the Air Force for a four-year stint. By the time he finished his service, I had completed two years of pre-vet school. Donovan decided he too would become a vet. I would be a junior when he was a freshman. It was the first time I would be ahead in the order with my older brother. It was an exciting time for the both of us.

It was during one of our summer breaks when two little skunks waddled out of the hay field. They were about the size of a small rat, but Donovan and I thought they were cute. We decided to capture them, de-scent them and keep them for pets. Several people kept skunks back then, until it was discovered they harbored the rabies virus. The domesticated skunk fad waned considerably after the finding.

Donovan and I picked up the babies by their tails as we had been told that skunks would not spray if picked up in that manner. With all the skills of the amateur vets we were, we calculated the dosage of anesthetic required for de-scenting and put the skunks to sleep. I was appointed to squeeze the little skunk glands while Donovan surgically removed them. Our methods worked magnificently on the first skunk. With the second skunk, Donovan latched a hold of the neck of the gland and I squeezed below his grip. The forceps I was holding somehow slipped off but I never adjusted my squeeze. A terrible smell permeated the air as the gland released spray that landed on Donovan's face and in his hair. Donovan cussed and ranted and ranted and raved just like

Yosemite Sam. I could not keep from laughing and he could not keep from cussing. I knew then and there, I had inherited my swearing proficiency.

When we got home, Mom would not let Donovan in the house. She got the old Saturday night tub out, filled it with hot soapy water and tomato juice and put Don in it. Donovan rinsed until he smelled no more. One of our skunks ended up dying from the anesthetic and the second we gave away to an Ames classmate. Donovan and I never again looked at skunks with the same light heartedness.

35
SINGING
DOGS

Ralph and Vadonna Price brought their small Rat Terrier dog, Spot, in to the vet clinic. Spot was white with black markings.

"Spot wants to sing you a tune, Doc," said Ralph.

"Can he do it?" I asked.

"You see what you think," Ralph responded. "OK, sing for the good doctor, Spot."

The dog acted a little embarrassed but he stiffened up and in a high note sang, "rhi rove ree, rhi rove ree."

"Did you get what he sang, Doc?" Ralph asked.

"Not exactly," I answered.

"He said 'I love you' in dog Latin," Ralph said.

Steve and Patty Paxson owned an English Shepherd that put Spot's singing to shame. Steve claimed their dog could talk and would answer every question.

"Oh," I said, "he could be famous."

"Go ahead," Steve requested, "ask him anything."

I played along. "What is the name of your dog food, Jack?" I asked.

The dog sat back, looked at me and mouthed, "rhi ront rowe." (I don't know.) The dog answered each question the same way. I decided I could have used Jack around the clinic to field all the dumb questions I was ever asked.

36
BELLY
SURFING

There was something about a cow chase that attracted amateur cowboys. I have to admit I thought it was a crazy, wild thing to do but I joined right in. I was pretty fair with a rope. I roped from my feet, from horseback, from the back of a pickup truck and even from the truck's hood. I'd get the rope around the cow's neck and hand the rope off to whoever happened to be closest to me. Then I would say, "Here she is, now tie her to something."

Lanny DeMott kept his cows and calves in a big pasture and he had one having trouble calving. In my usual manner, I roped her from my truck and handed the rope over to Lanny. Now DeMott was a good-sized man, but even after digging in his heels, the cow overpowered him. The cow pulled Lanny over on his belly and dragged him across the hard ground. I had to give Lanny credit for hanging on while he belly surfed. The cow dragged him through a ditch, through some buck burr and finally stopped after running through the trees. When I caught up with the surfer I found him to be in pretty good shape, suffering only from minor scratches and skin abrasions. I enjoyed watching Lanny's new sport and delivering a live calf.

When Dr. Greg Young was still a student and working for me part-time, he took a call at the Gerald Garner place. Gerald had a cow calving in the pasture.

"You can handle this one yourself. Just do what you have to do," I told him as I sent him off.

The Garner pasture was filled with musk thistles that grew anywhere from six to eight feet tall. Greg and Gerald drove the cow through the pasture and the thistles until she became hot and tired and jumped in a cool-looking pond. Greg, not to be outdone by my swimming finesse, tore off his clothes leaving only his undershorts on and dove in too. He took the lariat out into the water with him, sneaked in behind the cow, and tied the rope to the undelivered calf's feet. He was cinching the rope when the cow took off swimming. Greg held on tightly to the rope and surfed, belly down, over the water. When the cow reached the dry ground of the pond's bank she was running. Greg, too, hit the ground on his feet and hung on to the rope for dear life. The cow ran him right through the thistles. When the tired cow stopped for a moment to rest, Greg quickly tied his end of the rope to a tree. Gerald ran over and got another rope on the cow and with some effort, the calf was delivered alive. When Greg returned to the office he told me the story of the thistles, the pond and his tattered underwear and then swore me to secrecy.

Somehow the story leaked out and over and around the town.

37
JIM JOHNSON, DVM

I made a lot of effort on a daily basis to follow my cousin Basil Lucas' favorite Biblical passage—*This is the day the Lord hath made, let us be glad and rejoice in it.*

Rejoicing was easy if I happened to be in the country and had a little time. I loved to sit back on a fallen log and examine the serenity and beauty which surrounded me; the wild flowers, tree blossoms, croaking frogs and sawing locusts. But work had a way of interfering with my gladness. When that was the case, I'd try to smile at least once when forced to do something I really hated. If the smile failed to produce joy, there was nothing better than a good practical joke.

In 1970, I asked Dr. Jim Johnson to join me in my practice. Johnson and I had been classmates in veterinary school. We knew each other very well, both personally and professionally. I liked the man and we lived by the same rule: a laugh a day in all that you do.

Jim was a full-blooded, good-natured Swede. He was both the giver and receiver of tomfoolery. Townspeople were quite aware of Jim's notion of a good time. They would pick at him and he would pick back, until someone ended up at the butt end of a joke. I used to call Jim 'Conan the Barbarian.' An old client of Jim's had seen him get mad at a cow. The client swore to me Jim had beaten the cow unconscious with his fists. Somehow I doubted the feat but my suspicions were raised when every time I mentioned Conan, Jim got defensive.

A MAN AND HIS TOOLS

On a summer day, Jim and I went on a call to a farm owned by widow Myrtle Risser. Mrs. Risser was a great gal, she was tons of fun, and told it like it was. Her farm lay in a Missouri sector with rough and rolling ground. Myrtle knew me from way back. She used to hold barn dances and my Grandpa Lucas was an invited guest. He was a fun-lover, too, and I imagined how well they must have gotten along.

Jim and I were herding the calves into a little shed. Suddenly, one of the calves ran right by Jim, kicked sideways, and with its foot, caught Jim in the groin. Jim dropped like he had been shot. We showed no sympathy. I kept asking Jim, as he was doubled over, "Does it hurt?"

Myrtle had a little smirk on her face when she commented, "oh my, and such a young man, too!" Jim was pale as a ghost but he soon sat up and took normal breaths.

"Thanks one hell-a-va lot!" he said. "It's sure nice to have concerned and caring friends."

Myrtle was not a grieving widow. I would see the neighbor and her holding hands. I innocently asked him what relation he was to Myrtle. "Oh hell, none, we are just friends," he told me.

That wasn't exactly the answer I was looking for, but instead of sticking my foot in my mouth, I dropped the inquiry. It was fun just thinking about it.

One evening Jim arrived home, carrying his electric prod with him into the house. His intention was to make some minor repairs to it. His wife, Kay, was getting the table ready for supper. As she carried a plate of spaghetti across the room she pointed to the prod and asked, "What in the devil is that thing?"

"Oh here, I'll show you," Jim answered.

Jim was not all that familiar with the inner workings of an animal prod. He knew if he pushed the activator button, the prod would deliver a jolt of electricity to whatever it touched. It was just what he needed, at times, to get an animal moving in the right direction. The prod also stored one jolt of electricity in its contact pins, just in case of emergency. Jim believed he was on safe ground, he hadn't pushed the activator button. He turned to Kay and prodded her on the buttocks and the reserve jolt released. The spaghetti supper ended up on the kitchen ceiling, and just hung there. While he offered an apology, it was not good enough. Jim ate out that night.

MISTAKES CAN BRING JOY

Late one mid-summer evening the phone rang. The callers were Harold and Noah Johnson. Noah was elderly and Harold lacked ambition and brains. They had a huge sow pigging that needed my assistance farrowing. This sow could weigh up to 700 pounds making it tough for me to handle alone. I gave Dr. Johnson a call as I expected no help from Noah and Harold.

We enjoyed the ride to the farm as the beauty of the night engulfed us. The moon was full, there was a theater of stars, and the countryside shone like a stage. The frogs were in competition, trying to out croak one another. Harold was at the gate waiting for our arrival.

"Where is the sow?" I asked him.

Harold answered, "As the old saying goes, she is down in the barn."

Jim and I laughed at one another. We headed for the illumination of the barn's single, dim bulb. The sow was huge but she appeared to be gentle. She had delivered one pig by herself and she stood up when we entered the barn. She nosed her baby and talked to it in sow talk. She was proud and showed off to us. The sow's belly dragged on the ground and her mammary glands leaked milk.

Jim asked Harold, "Is this one pig all the pigs that she has had?"

"As the old saying goes, that's it," Harold answered.

I removed my shirt and put on a plastic arm sleeve. I gently reached in the sow's vagina and extended my arm to its length. I couldn't feel anything, no more babies and no afterbirth either. I said to Jim, "I can't feel a thing. She surely has to have more pigs in her as big as she is."

Dr. Johnson agreed with me. I gave the sow a shot of oxytocin, a drug that would contract her uterus and let her milk down. The drug was designed to work within 5 to 15 minutes and the pigging process should have begun all over again. We waited and waited. I reexamined the sow and felt nothing.

"We just as well do a cesarean and get it over with," Jim concluded. I agreed.

Dr. Johnson was a good surgeon. He gave the sow an anesthetic, cleaned and disinfected the surgical area, and made his incision. The uterus was comprised of two horns, each approximately three feet long. Jim ran the horns out through the incision and searched for the babies. He went from one end to the other but found nothing. We were stunned. A sow that size should have had a litter of ten to twenty pigs, and for certain, more than the one she gloated over. We apologized to Harold for the unnecessary expense we had gone to. Jim sutured the sow back up and she rested comfortably, no worse for the wear.

"As the old saying goes, you did what you thought was best," Harold replied. And again as we left the barn, "As the old saying goes, thanks a lot."

As the old saying goes, Jim and I decided we'd never do a cesarean again based on what appeared to be the obvious when the obvious had failed the physical exam.

On the way back to town, Jim said, "That sort of reminds me of the time we were asked to spay a cat. I anesthetized it, prepped it for surgery and proceeded with the operation. I got in there and couldn't find the uterus or ovaries."

I continued, "Oh, yeah. So, I prepped myself, and poked and looked in the incision as well. I couldn't find anything either. That's about the time you raised the surgery cape and found two testicles staring you in the face."

Our client had asked us to spay his pet and we had forgotten to double-check its sex. Sex was a difficult thing to determine in a young cat. Mistaken gender was something that happened to every veterinarian at least once and now Jim and I had found out how difficult it was to spay a tomcat.

JOHNSON ON FOOT

Bill Cruth, from up north of Gravity, called with a calving cow. Buckets of rain had fallen that day. The pastures were muddy and the ditches were filled with water. Bill's farm had a lot of timber and was full of hills and ravines. Bill met us and yelled at us from his yard, "That's as far as you can go! The cow's in the pasture and it's either walk or go horseback from here."

"Don't you have a tractor?" I asked him.

"The tractor's not running," Bill answered back.

Horseback it was. The Swede clumsily climbed on the back of a dapple-gray gelding and was mounted like he'd never been on a horse before. He hung the calf jack across the saddle. Bill and I both doubled up on a big sorrel. The horses were climbing up a ravine which put an angle on the calf jack and made it spin around, spooking Johnson's gelding. The horse pitched and Jim slid off the back of it. He landed square in a mud puddle with the calf jack resting on his stomach. A string of moans and profanities echoed from the dltch.

Johnson walked the rest of the way, leading the horse, until we reached the tree where Bill had tied the cow. The rope looked secure but I put another halter on her to make sure she couldn't run. I plastic sleeved myself and reached inside the cow. I felt three feet. Ah, twins, I said to myself. I untangled the feet and made sure I had a hold of only two. With one pull, the first calf slid right out. I reached back in and found the second set of front feet. Twins were smaller at birth as a rule, and I didn't have any trouble pulling the second calf. With a little encouragement, the calves got on their feet and had begun to nurse. "Well, I'll be damned, twins!" exclaimed Jim, "That was worth a ride in the mud puddle." He must have been joking. I never saw Jim on horseback again.

FUN IS A SERIOUS BUSINESS

North of Bedford was the Bedford Country Club, a splendid 9-

hole golf course. It covered 40 acres groomed with rolling hills, flowing streams and ponds. The entire community was proud of the facility and it drew people from miles around. Dr. Johnson was an accomplished golfer and he won many local tournaments on that course. One year, he even won the American Veterinary Medical Golf Tourney in Detroit, MI.

Besides his frequent course appearances, Jim served on the board as well. He helped sponsor golf tournaments and had a vote on maintenance and improvement issues. A group of lady golfers approached Jim to express their desire to add live ducks and geese as residents of the course. They could just picture the birds swimming on the ponds and nesting in the grassy areas. The setting would be much improved, the ladies had decided.

They petitioned the board. Jim was not in favor of the idea but was overruled in the vote. Twenty geese and fourteen ducks soon called the course home. Members of the club thought the gaggle was a quaint and lovely sight. The geese and ducks lumbered in the grass and swam on the ponds. Why, their antics entertained everyone, particularly those golfers who had shot a bad hole.

It did not take long for the golfers to change their minds. They noticed that spots of grass had been plucked from the putting greens and fairways. It had not escaped their attention, either, how much food was required to feed 34 birds. And then the droppings piled up, first on the fairways, then the greens and finally on the clubhouse driveway. Two camps formed. Nature lovers said the birds had to stay. The board members said the birds had to go. The debate was in full swing.

Jim and some friends were out for an early morning round. The birds were scattered everywhere, in the trees, on the fairways and on the putting greens. As the foursome stroked their way around the course, they stepped and drove through bird droppings. It stuck to their shoes and the wheels of the golf cart. On one hole, they had to drive the birds out of the way before they could swing their clubs. The golfers yelled and screamed.

"Get the hell out of here, you sons-of-bitches," Jim told six geese standing in the center of a green. He flared his arms and threw his seven-iron at the flock to drive them off. The golf club circled around like a boomerang. On its return path, it wrapped itself around one of the bird's necks and snapped it like a twig. The bird was dead. That kind of surprised the foursome but they didn't think too much of it. After all, it was a quick, painless death.

The heckling followed soon after. The nature lovers and the golfers were at each other's throats. Editorials appeared in the local newspaper and condemned the dastardly act. Rebuttal editorials would appear in the next week's edition. For every statement, there was a counter until time and loss of words cooled the controversy. The birds kept up with their annoying habits and were eventually removed from the course with little protest. The Swede kept the kettle stirred and the controversy lasted longer than the birds. It was said Dr. Johnson got a birdie on one hole and a goose on the next!

NEVER A DULL MOMENT

Early one morning I was merrily driving up the 4-lane highway which ran north and south through Bedford. I saw Jim's truck pop over the hill and he was headed my way. All of a sudden, the car ahead of me pulled clear over to the right and drove up on the right of way. I was caught off guard. Then another vehicle in another lane did the same thing. That unnerved me. I looked ahead of the cars to try and see what the problem was. It was Johnson's truck, on the loose. No one was driving it.

My perplexity caused me to drive my truck closer. I warily edged it over trying not to create an accident. I glanced into the cab of Jim's truck and then I saw him. He was lying on the seat. Jim saw me and pulled his truck over to the curb. He explained that he was merely having a little early-morning, eye-opening fun. He had the truck under control and steered it by looking through a peephole in the floorboard.

YOU CAN LEAD A HORSE TO WATER

I never had a desire for tobacco. I didn't like it and my stomach couldn't tolerate it. It was the same with alcohol. I tried to socialize but could not handle it well. Johnson was just the opposite. He loved his beer and believed everyone was the same as him. He once asked a teetotaler-client for a beer. The man was grumpy and sternly replied, "We don't keep beer around here."

One spring day we had a call west of Hopkins, Missouri. Neither Jim nor I was busy so we went together. In the truck, Jim asked me, "Have you ever tried a chew of Copenhagen?"

I answered "No."

"Well, any tough cowman or veterinarian doesn't have a hair on his butt if he can't handle a little chew," he informed me.

I told him I could live without it.

"Come on," he urged. "Just try a little pinch in your lip."

I was driving but looked over at the pinch he was holding in his fingers. It was a small enough amount it seemed, less than the size of a pencil eraser. "Well," I manly answered, "I could surely handle that." I pulled my lower lip down and told Jim to tuck it in. With my tongue, I tamped it down in my lip as far as it would go.

"There," Jim said, "That's not so bad, is it?"

The sensation of driving while dizzy is one I could never get used to. "Oh, oh," I told Jim, "I think I'm beginning to feel a little whoozie."

He told me I'd be OK, I just had to get through that first part. I hung on. The truck went slower and slower as I felt sicker and sicker. "You've almost got it made!" he yelled.

The truck coasted into the driveway. I pulled the door latch open and fell out of the truck onto the ground. I was sure my face was green. It was the worst kind of sick I had ever experienced. I was the funniest thing Jim had ever seen. He laughed until he cried. I wanted to kill him, but was too weak.

It was a cold night at midnight when I had an urge to pay Jim back. Thelbert Kendrick was a client of ours who lived on a very curvy road, further away than any of our other business. I phoned Jim and pretended Kendrick had asked for help. Jim was the vet on duty and he was obliged to take the call.

"You're shitting me," was Jim's response.

I told him I was sorry, but Kendrick had indeed called. I even offered to go for him.

"No! I'll do it," he said.

I told Jim I'd see him later. I watched the clock. I wanted to give Jim enough time to dress and be out the door. I waited until I figured he was about five miles out of town and then I called him on the two-way.

"Go ahead," Jim answered.

"I was just kidding about the call!" I told him.

"YOU WHAT?" he yelled back.

"I thought you probably needed some fresh air," I said.

"Why, you dirty SOB, what if the radio hadn't have worked?" he shot back.

"Hummm, never thought about that," I said. "See you tomorrow."

To say Johnson influenced me would be an understatement. He was already aware that I couldn't smoke or drink. My wife, Kay, didn't smoke or drink either and she bristled at Johnson's urgings.

It was Christmas Eve and Jim and I decided to have a party at the clinic. We stocked in toddy, cheese and crackers, and invited our clients who enjoyed a holiday nip or two.

The veterinary business was demanding. Jim and I were setting up when a call came in from old Tom who lived south of town. He had a bunch of sick calves. I told Jim, "I'll take care of the calves and you take care of our friends."

It was cold and nasty outside. I finished the call in three hours and headed back to the clinic. By then, the gang was feeling good and the Christmas spirit soared. I was greeted and handed a drink. Not one sip had passed my lips when the door banged open and in charged my wife.

"This is really great! It's Christmas Eve and here you are getting drunk when you should be home with your kids," she screamed at me.

"Yes, dear, but ..." I tried to explain.

"But yourself, you never do anything to get ready for Christmas," she went on and made up for past years of neglect.

"But, honey ..." I continued.

"Do not HONEY me," she said as she slammed the door in my face. She never did believe I had not even had a sip, not then and not to this day.

A FAMILY AFFAIR

Jim and I shared the same first name. Our wives were both named Kay. Our mothers were both Dorothys. It was a coincidence. Our kids were close to the same ages and participated in the same sports. Jim and I attended many of the same activities together. We also both liked yelling support for the home team and hurling insults at referees.

We were sitting in lawn chairs just outside the third base line one evening at a baseball game. The game was close and Jim was riding the umpire. Jim's voice was loud and it carried very well. The two of us were close to getting out of hand when a little girl walked directly in front of Jim. She asked, "Are YOU the coach?"

That worked for the both of us. We were put in our place and red-faced. The yelling stopped, at least for that night.

Jim Johnson and I shared a lot of things. Rejoice.

38

OXFORD, MISSOURI

My father and grandfather were born near a small community in Missouri named Parnell. Parnell was located in the northwest part of the state and lay sandwiched between rolling hills and the bottom land of the Grand River. I loved the geography and the people there a great deal. Its inhabitants were quiet, not too excitable, and they took each day as it came.

I had started early in the day so I could stop by Buddy's Café to pick up a tray of homemade cinnamon rolls and an urn of coffee. I was headed down the road past Parnell and on to the smaller community of Oxford. Oxford put me out of radio range of the office and I could not be reached. That was the best reason of all to love that part of the country.

The sun peeked over the horizon and it was too early for other people to be out. The quiet engulfed me, the only interruption being the melodious singing of birds. Rabbits hopped on the side of the road. My passing truck hadn't disturbed the six feeding deer I came upon. As I came to the top of a hill on the crooked road, the Grand River bottom lay out like a great plain. The background hills held trees with changing leaves. There was low hanging fog that began in the pastures and knifed up into the trees. Beauty surrounded me.

As I turned by the old Oxford country school and church, I neared the farmstead where the cattle and my work awaited. I heard the clippity-clomp of horse hooves. Further in the background a couple of four-wheeler engines bellowed.

My client had a corral already set up to drive the cows into. In almost every herd, there were one or two cows that served as ringleaders. If you found and led them, the others would follow. I spotted an old wild-eyed Hereford with her head held high in the air and knew she was the rabble rouser. The farmer and his help had not picked her out and they screamed and yelled at random hoping to scare the herd into the corral. As quick as lightning, the lead Hereford turned, and with the herd trailing behind her, ran straight at the men and beyond as if they never existed. The old cow knew what they were up to and eluding the cowboys was her main goal in life.

From my hiding spot, I eavesdropped as the cowboys cussed and yelled at each other for letting the herd through. They apologized to me for not having the cows gathered and I was sorry I didn't have my cow pony along to help. There was a cow chase brewing and to me, there was nothing like that event. I yelled to distract them from their bickering, "Come here, guys, I have something for you."

I set out the tray of warm rolls and the urn of coffee on my tailgate. It was one of the best public relations moments of my career and the boys never forgot it.

The rolls and coffee cooled the heads of the cowboys and they were ready to focus on the task at hand. "Let's go gettum," was the charge command.

I unhooked my chute and joined in the chase with my pickup. The running made the cows tired and the more worn down they became, the easier they were to herd. Around noon, we all stopped to eat lunch together at the house. A bountiful home-cooked country meal, the norm for those days, was served. We left the table bonded in the way only shared work and a community meal created.

I enjoyed working for the people from Oxford even though they constantly argued and cussed. The arguing never came to blows and I figured it was part of their job. They had a system in place and were able to work several herds a day. Some of the boys would go ahead and get cows in for me and I was able to work at a steady pace. On that day, we pregnancy tested many cows and it was pitch dark before we finished the last of them. We had worked from the light of flashlights and trucks before we called it quits. As I packed up my truck, it began to snow.

On the drive back to Bedford, a spectacular meteorite, which looked like a continuous bolt of lightning, lit up the heavens. When it hit the ground, a huge ball of fire rose into the sky. I heard sometime later that another person had seen the meteorite and called the local authorities. He was sure he had seen a plane crash as nothing but a disaster could have created an explosive light of such magnitude.

The snow had quit falling and the clouds disappeared. The moon shone brightly through the back window of my truck and reflected off the small dusting of snow that lay on the ground. As I popped over the hill east of Bedford, the little city welcomed me. The warmth from the glow of its streetlights seemed every bit as spectacular as the meteorite.

39
SURVIVAL OF THE FITTEST

In ranch country, like the terrain found in Nebraska, North Dakota, and Montana, the number of acres set aside to keep one cow ranged from 25 to 50. Ranchers had more acres than time when it came to getting around to check the herd. It was often up to the cow to forage for food and survive the onslaught of harsh weather, predators and disease. The cows were tough old critters and they bred the survival instinct into their offspring.

A veterinarian school instructor of mine, Dr. Chivers, said when it came to surviving the cold, the three toughest things in the world were Shetland ponies, Hereford cows and women's legs. Shetland ponies grew long, thick hair for protection. Hereford cows had a thick layer of extremely tough skin. Women students at ISU were required to wear skirts and during the harsh winters they surely had legs of steel, tough enough to survive walking between classes bare legged.

In the state of Iowa, there were only a handful of cattle producers I knew of who had more acres than time. Jerry Longfellow was one and he called his ranch the Brand L. His ranch mark was drafted with an upside down L and an upright L drawn on top of it. At the Brand L, though they were well fed and cared for, cattle roamed the range. If a cow became sick or needed attention it was up to me to chase it, rope it and try to hang on.

I went on a sick cow call at the Longfellow acreage with my daughter, Jamie, who was 14 at the time. I put Jamie behind my pickup's steering wheel and told her to chase the cow down and I would rope it from my perch on the truck's bed. Jamie jammed her foot down on the gas pedal and nearly threw me out the back. On the second attempt, the cow dodged right and the loop of my rope fell precisely over her head. The roping took me by surprise. The cow ducked left and took off running, dragging my end of the unsecured rope on the ground behind her.

Jerry, in his pickup, took up the chase from there. The cow ran and ran and for being ill, she tired very little. The chase ended for us on the bank of a big ditch. The cow had jumped over the ravine, the depth of which was to great for our pickups to cross. She was free and she had my rope.

Two weeks later, I saw Jerry and asked how the cow was doing. "You won't believe it," he said, "all that cow needed was a hell of a good run. She seems fine but somewhere along the way she lost your rope which, by the way, I'll pay you for."

At the Longfellow ranch we were forever chasing something. If a cow died from participating in a pursuit it was just too bad as far as Jerry was concerned. Jerry had a Dodge truck that he liked to pit against his cows, muscle for muscle. He once hit a cow with the truck's bumper, knocked her down and then drove over her to hold her to the ground. "Here she is," he beamed at me, "you can doctor her now."

For some reason, people had a tendency to get all moody and nervous when they worked their own cattle. I was that way when I worked mine and Jerry was that way to an extreme. Maybe it was because he'd pick the coldest day of the year. It must have been 0 degrees with a wind blowing out of the north the day he called. Jerry had a crew working with him and they edged the cattle toward the spot where he and I had set up. Trouble was, the crew was not working fast enough for Jerry's pleasure.

"Those guys will never get them up here," he ranted with a few cuss words thrown in for good measure. Jerry jumped in his Dodge Ram and took off toward the cattle.

Directly between the cattle and the point where Jerry left me standing was a large frozen-over pond. Jerry, with the aim of a marksman, drove his truck directly toward the ice. I wanted to close my eyes but feared missing the excitement of watching the heavy Dodge Ram sink like the Titanic. The winter had been cold just long enough and Jerry and the Dodge safely skated across the pond. Impatience had done him no harm and I leaned back and exhaled the deep breath I had been holding.

Jerry's land was adjacent to land owned by my father and I was familiar with the layout. I was still waiting for the crew to drive the cattle toward me when my mind wandered to a broken down farm that was visible from my dad's place. Nate Waldon lived there with his mentally challenged daughter, Dorothy. I was working for Dr. Anderson at the time, testing cows for tuberculosis. All of the herds in the area had to be tested in order to forestall an epidemic. Nate owned some cows and as he had no phone, I drove out to his place to set up an appointment. I eased my truck into his yard, got out and walked slowly toward the house all the while making friendly gestures toward his dog. No one was in sight and all I could see through the overgrown weeds was the boxed-in porch attached to the front of the house. Suddenly, a woman dressed in overalls with a baseball cap backwards on her head jumped up out of the porch chair. She waved her arms and sang at the top of her lungs. I didn't recognize the loud but somewhat beautiful tune. Dorothy had scared the poop out of me and I ran back to the safety of my vehicle.

I was still waiting for Jerry and the boys and the cows. It was freezing cold, just about as cold as the day I nearly broke my head out here. That time we were working with a chute and the boys held a big iron bar up against the cows so they had to go forward out of the chute instead of backing out. I happened to be leaning over when a wild calf entered the chute before the restraining bar was in place. The calf hit the bar, swung it around and it caught me square in the head. The impact knocked me out for the long count.

Longfellow told me I flounced around on the frozen ground and yelled, "I broke my head! I broke my head!"

When I came to, I bandaged the bloody wound with my handkerchief and kept right on working.

The crew finally had rounded up the cows and a space heater. The syringes and my fingers had begun to freeze. By the time we wrapped things up, a sundog had appeared in the sky. The sundog was a sure indication it was to cold to be outside. I didn't need a sign. The cold had worn a hole clear through me.

40

UP IN THE SKY ...
IT'S A BIRD ... IT'S A PLANE
... IT'S SUPERVET

My hopes disappeared. I had done all I could. Death was imminent and I had lost the cause. All of a sudden, the breath of life reappeared and I felt like a god. I had Doc Anderson and Mother Nature to thank, both of whom taught me to never give up. I was SuperVet!

A man named Orville lived at the top of Illinois Street with his big yellow tomcat, Jinx. While Jinx was well liked by Orville's neighbors, he was often involved in territory disputes with other cats. Orville and Jinx were frequent visitors at the clinic where Jinx would be treated for infected cuts and scratches. "Old Jinx was telling all the other cats what a good vet you are," Orville would proclaim, as if Jinx had been injured protecting my reputation.

One day Jinx became very ill on his own. He had not been able to eat nor could he pass waste. He was capable of only one motion and that was to stretch out. I examined him thoroughly and found what I believed to be a hairball or tumor blocking his intestinal tract. "He'll have to have exploratory surgery to see what's in there," I explained to Orville. "You'd better take him to an expert at Iowa State Veterinary College."

"Nope. Jinx wants you to do it, Doc," Orville answered firmly.

Jinx was a very nice cat and he barely moved when I hit his vein with the hypodermic needle and injected anesthetic. I made a large incision to give myself a big playing field. I followed through his intestines and gave a look at his organs. Everything appeared normal to me and I felt disappointment as I sutured the big cat back together. I injected Jinx with antibiotics and placed him in the warm recovery cage. In a few hours, he was back on his feet and playful. He arched his back and rubbed on the cage door, purring his throat out. Jinx ate and drank all the food and water I provided.

"See, Dr. Lucas, Jinx was right. He knew you could do it," Orville said.

At home, Jinx never missed a feeding. I had no idea what the problem had been. I only guessed that Jinx needed some air let in. Every time I saw Orville, he said to me, "Jinx is running up and down the street telling all the other cats that you're the best vet in the world."

I never told Orville what it was I had never found.

Even SuperVet needed help on occasion. With many calls, I enlisted the aid of my own children. The kids would run back and forth to the vet truck for me, open gates and even drive the truck, legal age or not. On one warm summer evening I was called by Ray Randerson to a pigging sow. My son, Joe, went along with me and just in case the pigging went fast, we took along our fishing poles.

The little sow had one piglet by the time we arrived. To speed up the process, I gave her a shot of oxytocin to continue the farrowing. The drug worked well but it was necessary for me to assist her with each birth. When it came time for the last of the litter, the sow's pelvis had tightened and had become too small for the insertion of a hand my size. I looked down at Joe, five years old at the time, and said, "If you'd reach in and pull that pig we'd have time to do some fishing."

"OK," he replied innocently, "if I could use a sleeve I think I could do it." Joe reached in as far as his arm would go and exclaimed, "I've got him!" I instructed Joe to gently pull the piglet through the sow's pelvis. Joe had delivered the last piglet, prompting Ray to say, "Boy, you should be a vet."

Joe never became a vet but we were fishermen together. We pulled in many hungrily biting crappies that day.

There were times when SuperVet had the strength zapped right out of him. Despite all effort, nothing seemed to work, even when the book had been followed to the letter. Never give up, I was taught, Mother Nature could play her hand.

Meredith Fluke was getting up in years but still kept a few cows around to care for. He was a Laplander farmer, living just north of the Missouri State Line. Meredith had a cow that was laying down and could not get up. She was not eating either and her bowels weren't working. I diagnosed her with atypical grass tetany, a metabolic disorder. Tetany was treatable with an IV injection of calcium, phosphorus, potassium, magnesium and dextrose. I injected two bottles of the treatment into the cow and told Meredith the medicine needed time to work. I would check with him later to see how the cow responded.

Later that same afternoon I picked up Meredith to accompany me to the pasture. On the way, Meredith and I reminisced about old-time animal medicines and practices. When we got to the cow, I wished I'd known more of the potions. The modern-day IV had not done the cow any good. I stammered and bided my time, trying to think of something else to try.

Meredith offered a suggestion, "Maybe she needs a physic to make her bowels work."

I agreed it certainly wouldn't hurt to try mysticism although my professional logic told me it would be a waste of time.

I went back to my truck and picked out an injectable laxative. I filled the syringe and jabbed it in the cow's rear hip muscle. The pain of the injection alarmed the old cow and with much effort, she got up. Once on her feet, the sick cow proceeded to defecate. As a matter of fact, she crapped with such volume I wondered if she would ever stop. Meredith's eyes widened to the size of coffee cup saucers and he said, "Well, by jing, I never saw anything work so fast in my life."

The old cow walked off and began eating grass. I never did figure out what affected the cow that way but I took all the credit.

Doc Anderson was known to take a little credit himself. Anderson had gone to Elmer Roberts' place to spray cows for lice. Doc sprayed a few of the herd at a time and let them out to pasture. Half of the herd had been released before Doc Anderson realized he'd forgotten to put the lice insecticide in with the water. He knew it was nearly impossible to get the cows back in so he continued. Without Elmer's knowledge of the flub, Doc Anderson washed the rest of the herd.

Two weeks later Elmer walked into the clinic and told Doc Anderson, "Boy, Doc, those cows really straightened up after you sprayed them. Whatever you used really made their coats slick and shiny. Thanks a lot!"

ABLE TO LEAP TALL BUILDINGS

Faye Dukes and Trixie, a little Rat Terrier dog, were inseparable. Trixie rode on the back of Faye's pickup seat and sat right next to his shoulder. Trixie was a canine with a lot of fire and even though she wouldn't bite a flea, everyone knew not to put a hand on Faye's shoulder while Trixie was perched behind him.

Faye stopped by the clinic one day to have Trixie vaccinated for rabies. I wanted to get friendly with the dog and I reached into the pickup to pet her. Trixie bared her teeth and growled at me and I immediately jumped back. Faye explained to me Trixie was not trying to bite, but I had mistakenly touched her tail. Trixie hated for her tail to be touched he told me. I had a healthy dose of curiosity and wanted to test Faye's hypothesis. I reached in and just grazed Trixie's tail. She went wild and turned round and round in an attempt to catch it.

I, of course, was amused. I said, "My, Trixie, what a nice tail you have."

She looked at her tail and growled. I had never seen a dog that hated its tail as much as that one. Faye scolded me and asked me to quit teasing his dog. "Get on with the vaccination," he demanded.

It was June in Iowa. The trees were in full foliage, the grass was forest green, and the drab winter was covered with fresh carpet. It was time for the first hay cutting which would be stored for the next winter's feed and Faye was ready to mow. Trixie was in her position near the tractor seat, right next to Faye.

The mowing was going as planned when the lowered mower

bar chased a half-grown rabbit out of its hiding place. Trixie instantly jumped down from the tractor and began chasing the ball of fur. Trixie overran the mower and then changed direction. When she did, the mower blade caught her front leg and in a rapid repeat motion, nearly cut it off. Faye shut the tractor down and picked up his best friend. He held Trixie in his arms and ran for the truck and then for the veterinarian clinic.

I gave Trixie an anesthetic to examine her leg. The cut was oblique in shape and was through the carpal bones. Her foot was attached with a mere half-inch of skin and a small amount of underlying tissue. I did not think there was enough tissue remaining for the leg to heal and I believed I should amputate. I told Faye as much and he pleaded and asked if I couldn't possibly save Trixie's leg.

I looked again and said, "I don't think there is a chance in the world of this thing healing. There is one thing about chance, though, if the leg doesn't heal, I can always amputate later."

I sutured up about everything on the dog's leg that I thought would hold. There was nothing I could do about the metacarpal bones. After I finished suturing, I put Trixie's leg in a splint to hold everything in place.

A month passed before Faye brought his pal in for the verdict. As I removed the bandage and splint I was encouraged when I did not detect a bad smell or nasty discharge. Then, I couldn't believe what was in front of my very eyes. Trixie's leg had healed perfectly. Mother Nature had kept out infection and a new circulatory route had grown and fed healthy tissue. Tears ran down Faye's cheeks. He and I were in disbelief. It was a miracle that had happened.

Trixie became my favorite canine patient. Every time I saw her, I marveled at her magic leg. Nonetheless, I couldn't resist saying to her, "My Trixie, what a beautiful tail you have!"

SUPERVET TO THE RESCUE

The calving season occurred in early spring. The majority of new calves were born within weeks of each other and owners watched their herds very closely. But in every herd there were straggler cows that calved later than the rest and they were often ignored. The owner's attention was spread elsewhere as the spring progressed and the weather allowed work in the fields to begin. Veterinarians had a term for those late calving cows. They were said to suffer from "corn planting disease." A vet never knew what to expect on a call for a late calving cow. It was only a guess as to how long the cow had been in labor. If a cow had been trying to calve for over 24 hours the calf usually died inside the cow and putrefaction occurred.

It was a hot day in July when Joe Dawson called with bad news. Joe had a late calving cow and all he could see of the birth was the calf's tail. He also said his cow looked bloated. I took my helper, Donnie, with me and when we arrived we could see Joe was correct. His cow was very bloated. That could only mean a dead, swollen-up calf. I put on a sleeve and attempted to examine the cow. She was so tight I couldn't insert my hand any further than my wrist.

"Joe," I said, "the only way I can get the calf out is by cesarean and I guarantee you this cow will die."

"That's OK, Doc, " Joe remarked, "I have to leave but give it your best try to save the cow."

"All right, Joe, I'll do the best I can," I said, "that's all I can do."

Donnie and I anesthetized the cow and tied her in position for the cesarean. We didn't worry about sterilizing around the incision area as the dead calf would have contaminated the cow anyway. I made a two-foot-long cut to allow room to remove the swollen calf. When I had exposed the dead calf, Donnie put the chains on the calf's feet and we lifted the huge mass from the cow's abdomen. The enlarged dead calf came out in one piece and it looked as if it could have weighed 500 pounds. The mother cow did not look well at all. Her uterus was an infected mess and was torn every which way. The peritoneal cavity was contaminated as well. I made the decision not to suture her uterus as I was convinced the cow would die. I whipped the body wall together haphazardly and closed the incision. I gave her a shot of antibiotics and untied her. It was only a matter of time.

Three months later, while working at the sale barn someone yelled at me, "Hey Doc! Here's the old cow you did the cesarean on last summer."

I looked with utter amazement at Joe and the cow. I could see a stitch hanging from her belly. There was no mistaking her.

"Hey, did you ever have any doubt in me, Joe?" I asked.

"Nope, Doc, I knew you would save her and you did," Joe said as he beamed.

Mentally, I could not take any credit. I had violated every law of good surgery. I had given up on her life. Sheer willpower saved the old Hereford cow despite my bungling.

NEVER UNDERESTIMATE SUPERVET

One evening Mrs. Warik called and asked if I could come to examine a cow.

"Why, what seems to be the problem?" I asked her over the phone.

With a nasty air about her, she answered "Well, that is why I called you!"

I agreed to meet her husband in the pasture.

I found that the cow had just had a new calf. The cow was in a deep coma with milk fever, caused by low blood calcium.

"I hate to call the vet if the animal is going to die," Mr. Warik lamented. "She seems so near death now I hesitated to waste my money."

I didn't mention the availability of a new drug that often worked on a bad case of milk fever.

"Well, Mr. Warik," I said, "I am already here, I might as well treat her and we'll see what happens after that."

"It will be all for not," Mr. Warik said rather doubtfully.

I got my IV tube on a 500cc bottle of calcium, inserted the needle in the cow's vein and started the flow. I noticed a quivering of her skin and muscles, a good sign the medicine was working. I pulled the needle out and pushed up on the cow's neck. The cow opened her eyes and rolled up on her stomach. "Let's give her another five minutes," I told Mr. Warik who was at that moment speechless. When the five minutes were up, I slapped the cow on her butt and she stood up. She had a good and healthy bowel movement and turned to begin licking her calf.

Warik had regained his speaking ability. "I owe you an apology for doubting you, Doctor. You are truly a miracle man," he declared.

"No apology necessary," I told him. "I do what I can, the best that I can, with what I have available. Sometimes I win and sometimes I lose."

Armed with the thoughtfulness of clients and cooperation from Mother Nature, SuperVet had saved the day.

X-RAY VISION

Kay, the kids and I were savoring the rare event of having supper together. That all ended when the phone blasted off a ring. It was Richard Cabeen calling. Richard had one of his best milk cows down with the bloat. I asked Richard over the phone if he had tried rolling the cow up on her belly.

"We tried," he said, "but we couldn't move her, she is too big."

"I'll be right down, Richard. While you are waiting for me, take your tractor and move her around if you can," I advised.

I broke the speed limit getting to the farm. A bloated cow would not live long if it remained immobile. Without motion, the bloat would continue until the cow literally died.

As I turned into the farm driveway, Richard came running out to greet me. He had a smile on his face. "We did what you said," he shouted at me, "and, by golly, she belched that air right out after we got her on her stomach. Then she got up. I want to really thank you, Doc. We would have lost her if it hadn't been for your advice."

I was as tickled as Richard was about the cow. After several years of practice under the belt, a telephone diagnosis was getting easier to make.

41
OB
SEASON

It was a typical March day in Southwest Iowa. The outside temperature registered a balmy 60 degrees, which gave everyone the feeling that spring was just around the corner. The ground hog saw his shadow, foretelling the arrival of a welcomed season change. The weatherman, however, told us that a cold front was edging its way from North Dakota. Maybe it would miss us and we would be on the edge of it, we all theorized. With the weather, anything was possible in the Midwest. Just two weeks previous a thunderstorm had woken us from winter and stirred up a tornado to our south.

It was an odds and ends day at the clinic as business was slow. I was the vet on call and looked forward to a quiet evening to follow the quiet business day. That was not a logical thought for a veteran DVM, I realized, and the point was driven home when the phone rang at 4:45. It was Sharon Fletchall, a widow lady who called. Her farm stood in the boonies in Missouri. She had a cow trying to have a calf and I told her I would be there in twenty minutes.

I was in surprisingly good humor. As I walked outside to get in my truck, I noticed the air had changed and the wind was whispering from out of the north. The snow cover had melted and the ground looked utterly abandoned. The only hints of spring were some small buds on the maple trees and an occasional early-bird Robin out in search of night crawlers. I fired up the old Ford pickup and headed for Missouri, land of my heritage. My paternal grandparents lived on farms around and near the little towns of Parnell and Sheridan.

I knew instantly when I was at the Missouri State Line. The road narrowed to ten feet in width and was carved out of the hills. In that part of the state, the old county roads were nicknamed the roller coaster hills. The thrill belonged to drivers brave enough to drive them like they were interstate freeways. With enough speed, a driver could literally bounce up off the car seat and be airborne just at the point where the hill topped out and the descent began.

A couple of weeks previous I was on one of those Missouri gravel roads trailing my chute behind me. I was driving to the right in the loose gravel as the worn center track crested a hill. In a flash there appeared a big red pickup and it was pointed right at me. I was eyeball to eyeball with its driver. I guessed the speed of the red pickup to be about 50-60 m.p.h. Pure instinct told me to veer to the right as hard as I could and head for the ditch. At about the same time, the other driver veered to his right and we avoided impact by a hair and kept both trucks on the road. The thrill of that roller coaster road left me believing in divine intervention.

I was clipping along right through Sheridan looking for the widow's farm when I met another pickup south of town. The driver motioned for me to follow him. The road he led me on was nothing but a dirt track through the country. The track was rough and deeply rutted and we wound through the hills like a cold snake. The ground was frozen and as I straddled the track it felt like my teeth were beginning to loosen. As I pulled into the farmstead I saw rusted antique machinery, sitting in the same place it had been left years before.

Mrs. Fletchall's cow was standing in a makeshift corral. I roped her on the first try and got a wrap around a post to secure her. I had my OB equipment in hand and began moving toward the back end of the cow. She saw me coming and lunged with all her force stretching about 30 feet of rope out as tight as a fiddle string. She ran to the north and the rope clotheslined me at midriff and slammed me to the ground. I was laying there, flat on my back. My head had bounced off the frozen earth with such great force that it threw my glasses about ten feet across the lot. I stayed unconscious for five seconds or so. When I was able, I popped back up and drove the cow into a smaller pen where I delivered a breech live calf. Mother and baby were nursing as I left.

The weatherman's prediction was right on target for once. The temperature had dropped severely and the wind was unforgiving. I was steadily making my way back through the ruts when my portable phone rang. Judy Gamel was calling about a new calf she had that could not get up. I turned the truck to the west and cut across country to go take a look.

The evening's driving wind had chilled the calf to the bone. I measured the calf's temperature at 82 degrees, quite below the normal 101. I loaded the calf into the cab of my truck and told Judy I'd take it to the veterinary clinic where I would place it in my warm room, designed especially for chilled baby calves. I put the truck heater's fan on full blast and by the time the calf and I reached town, it was doing better already. I penned the calf in the warm room and walked through the clinic to the door. I was just stepping out when Kirby Welch phoned. Kirby lived south, across the Missouri State Line.

"I got a cow calving, Doc," he said. "Can you come help me out? There is a leg back."

"Yes, I can, Kirb," I answered. "Do you have the cow caught?" I then asked.

"Yeah, she's tied to a dead willow tree in the timber. We can walk right to her," he said.

I cheerfully told Kirby I'd be right down. I surprised myself with my pleasantness. It wasn't often I looked forward to treating a cow in the timber in the dark. I drove through mud ruts, an open gate, and across a narrow pond toward the headlight beacons of Kirby's pickup truck.

"Follow me," Kirby yelled when I was close enough to hear him. Kirby drove like a mad man across rough pasture until he stopped at the top of a very steep hill. "We'd better walk from here," he instructed.

"Where is the cow?" I asked with wonder.

"Down there, across the crick," Kirby said. I peered into the dark and discovered 'down there' was probably 100 yards, straight down. "I'm driving to the bottom," I told Kirby, "I'll take the chance my 4 wheel drive can get me out." I disliked carrying OB equipment that far. I knew that I wouldn't have any trouble driving down. So, I did. I would worry about getting back up the hill later.

Kirby and I gathered up the OB equipment and began walking toward the creek bank. The creek was approximately three to five feet wide and one foot deep. I measured it up and down and found what I thought to be a decent place to cross.

The cow was indeed tied to a dead willow tree. As soon as she saw me, she jumped up and in the dark of the night she sounded like a bulldozer pushing brush. I held my lantern and watched her as she moved the dead tree around until she tired of it.

The calf had a foot back just as Kirby said. The other foot was presented and the calf's head was large. I reached in and the foot I needed was clear back below the pelvis. I pushed the head back inside in an attempt to retrieve the out-of-position foot. Each time I got close to grabbing it, the cow would strain and push the calf's head back out. The cow's strain squeezed my arm until it was numb. Sweat had begun to trickle down my back. The cold wind blew up my shirt and cooled me down. I put my other arm inside the cow to hold the calf's head back. Between one of her strains I quickly grabbed the missing foot and leg and pulled it up, just ahead of the calf's head. Using chains and the calf jack, I finished pulling the calf. The cow seemed relieved and she quickly jumped up and began licking the calf. I relaxed, took a deep breath, and looked up at the galaxy of stars and the moon. I had feared the worst but was proud of delivering a live calf. The calf was trying to get to its wobbly feet and once it did it would be looking for a teat and its first meal. I gathered up my tools and drove in four-wheel drive back up the hill.

It was 10:00 p.m. when I arrived back to town. I went home, bathed and slept hard until Jay Lischer called at 12:30 a.m. "I've got a heifer that needs help calving," Jay informed me. I knew Jay had a good calving pen and a chute and I told him I would be right out.

I delivered the calf without a hitch. The first-time mother looked a little puzzled as she approached her newborn. Soon she licked the tenacious fluids off and nuzzled up to the calf.

"While you're here, Doc, I'd like you to check another calf of mine," Jay said in apparent ignorance of the fact it was 1:30 in the morning. I started off to the other pen but a wild cow chased me back to the barn door.

"Watch that cow!" I yelled at Jay.

"I've had no problem tying her," Jay told me and proceeded to enter the pen. The cow was instantly in his face. Her eyeballs were protruding and she shook nervously.

"You just don't know how drastically a cow's behavior can change when a stranger is in sight," I informed Jay.

"I'd never believed that before," Jay answered as the proof stood there, staring him in the face.

I finished up at Jay's and was as close to bed as my garage door when the phone rang again. It was Dale Kohler, a neighbor of Jay's. He, too, had a heifer calving. I headed back to the country and delivered the calf. As I was leaving I asked myself 'what's next?' The 'what next' came in at 5 a.m. after I had been in the sack, all of 45 minutes. Jerry Murphy had a cow calving and having already made a night of it, I figured one more delivery wouldn't ruin my schedule. I was tired and hoped for an easy delivery.

I finished at Murphy's and drove back to town. The café was open and the early-morning coffee drinkers had taken their places. As I walked in the door, a patron greeted me with, "Hi, Doc, I'm surprised to see you here so early. I figured vets had banker's hours since they make so darn much money!"

The regulars snickered with laughter.

The thought never crossed my mind to tell them about the night I had just had. Instead, I answered with "Yeah, it's an easy life."

I pledged to myself that the next time I pulled an all-nighter I'd drag the butt of that jester along with me.

Nothing truly prepared a young or old vet for the brutality of an OB season. I never knew what surprises the dawn of the day would bring. I had trouble believing how much energy was used up during a difficult delivery. I never adjusted to the loss of sleep. And the worst thing was to get called out of bed, arrive at the farm and have someone say to you, "We already got it, Doc. You can go back to bed now."

During the busy OB months, unusual presentations strained my knowledge. Paul Wolverton called and said he had a calf that was coming backwards. Paul had seen the bottoms of the calf's feet and they were up as they appeared out of the cow. That was a sure sign, all I had to do was put the OB chains on the calf's feet and pull the calf out with the jack. I jacked and the hips came, then the abdomen and the rib cage, then the shoulders and front legs. When I got to the calf's head, everything stopped. I twisted the calf, changed angles and jacked harder. Nothing gave way. Come on, I thought to myself, I've seen backwards births a million times but have never had trouble like this. I loosened the chains and went exploring with my hands. I reached in along the neck towards the calf's head and what a surprise of nature I found. The calf was two-headed. I had to decapitate the heads and take it by caesarean. The heads were not totally divided but split back to one eye in the center with the outside eyes on each side.

It was a cyclops!

42
FAMOUS
LAST WORDS

If not by law, than by social grace, public swearing was forbidden at one time, particularly if you were in the company of women and children. On television, the use of the words damn and hell got networks in serious trouble during the 1960's. Calls made to veterinarian clinics were tempered with gentle words then too. For example, if a cow had thrown her vagina out, a client often said, "The cow has something on her behind." Condition descriptions were necessary at the vet clinic. I needed to know what supplies to take along on a call.

My secretary Julie received a very composed call one morning. The voice on the other end of the line said, "I have a cow with an infected snapper."

Julie asked, as if she didn't hear correctly, "Her what?" The embarrassed caller shot back, "Oh, you know what I mean!"

After many years, Julie compiled a list of the "Top 12 Clients' Famous Last Words."

1. I'll pay you Friday.
2. She's a gentle cow, Doc.
3. The cow can't get up.
4. Can you come after hours, when I'm home?
5. What time can I talk to the Doctor on the phone? (Most frequently asked during calving season.)
6. Can you drop the medicine off at my house? My car is sick too.
7. While you're here, Doc …

8. No, you won't need a chute.
9. We can tie her to your truck.
10. In cold weather, a weak calf is never cold.
11. Oh, I forgot my checkbook.
12. It got killed by lightning, what else could it be?

In the spring of 1998, it was thirty-five years since I was the proud ISU vet graduate. I had no fear when I was 24 years old and I had no idea of the dangers and excitement that awaited me. I believed everything, until experience proved otherwise. I grew older and experience grew moldy, particularly when I heard one of the following.

1. Don't worry, Doc, old Fido wouldn't hurt a soul.
2. Why that kitty wouldn't scratch a flea.
3. You can do anything with that horse.
4. He won't kick, Doc.
5. We don't need to get the cow in the barn, why we can just lay a rope over her head in the pasture.
6. He's a tame bull.
7. We can tie the cow to the back of your truck.
8. All you gotta do is get in the back of my truck and we'll drive alongside and put a rope over her neck.

I loved my vet practice, I really did.

43
JUST WHEN I THOUGHT I'D SEEN IT ALL

Every day was a new one for me. I had decided early on, in order to take pleasure from the short time given in life, I'd find joy where I could. In veterinary medicine, some circumstances just lent themselves to mirth better than others.

Dr. Jim Johnson received a call one blustery, fall day. A ewe, owned by Wilbur Rowe, had a vaginal prolapse. A ewe is a female sheep. When ewes are heavy with lamb, they often have problems with premature straining. The straining could result in the sheep's vagina or rectum slipping out of place. That condition was far from one of my favorite calls and I was delighted that my Swedish partner had fielded the request.

In the earlier years of veterinary medicine, I would use a local anesthetic when faced with a prolapse. The local was nothing compared to the tranquilizers and total blocks commonly used today. Dr. Johnson, however, had developed his own method he learned from working with Dr. Max Pool of Mt. Ayr.

Dr. Johnson took baling twine and wrapped it around and around between the ewe's legs, applying just the right amount of pressure. The twine, when left in place for a period of time, would force the extruding organ back into position. The ewe could stand and her organs would stay inside. Wilbur watched Jim as he employed his homespun remedy and began making fun of how the ewe looked. Rowe was a person who spent a great deal of time in revelry. But once a joke was played on him, retaliation could be expected, by a power of ten.

"Laugh if you will, Rowe, you SOB, it will work!" exclaimed Johnson. "There, it's done."

Dr. Jim rolled the ewe on her feet and stood her up. The ewe took one step and fell over. She landed on her back, making her look like a turtle. Wilbur and his wife, Patty, who was also known for merriment, laughed until they cried.

Wilbur said to Patty, "If Johnson would help us put up hay, we wouldn't need hay balers. He could tie up the hay, then we could pick it up, just like we have to pick up this ewe."

Vets weren't the only ones who practiced home remedies. Farmers were ingenious when it came to saving the expense involved in calling a vet. I was once at the Vane Walston farm to look at a mare. While there I noticed a cow that had a horse collar draped around its neck. Out of curiosity, I had to take a closer look. Vane had taken baling string, tied it from the yoke of the horse collar and wrapped it back around between the cow's legs. Baling twine held that organ in as well, with just a little different twist. She looked about as hilarious as Wilbur's ewe.

I've heard meat butchers tell of other home remedies they've seen while working in the packing plant. Cows and ewes could come to slaughter with a big wine bottle sutured in their rectums. The wine bottle was holding in a prolapsed organ.

During the 50's and 60's, mutton was not a popular supper table dish. As marketable livestock, sheep weren't worth very much. There was little demand for their meat and the price per pound was low. During those years, a mature ewe might not bring more than five to ten dollars. One of my favorite stories tells of that time.

At midnight, the phone rang. "Whom may I ask is calling?" asked Dr. Mack.

"Dis is Hans from south of town," announced a voice.

"And what's your problem, Hans?" asked Mack.

Hans replied, "Me old 'yo' had her lamb and now her insides are out."

"How old is your ewe?" asked the Doc.

"She is four years old," Hans answered.

"Is her lamb alive?" the Doc queried.

"No, he is very dead," Hans said sadly.

"How much is your ewe worth?" asked Dr. Mack.

"Oh, I suppose she is worth $10," was the reply.

"I'll send the check in the mail tomorrow," said Dr. Mack and he hung up the phone.

One cold wintry night, the widowed Maybell Brigg called for assistance. She had a wild cow about to deliver a calf. Maybell was extremely poor and keeping the farm was a hardship for her. When her husband passed away, Maybell asked for help from no one. She strained doing the farm work alone but she kept her independence. If Maybell needed town supplies, she would hitch a ride or walk the distance. She had no tractor or car.

I had taken the call but because of the described unruliness of Maybell's cow, I thought I might need help. I called my partner, Dr. Johnson, and got him out of bed. When we arrived at the farm I was glad I'd taken him along.

The cow was in an old non-electrified barn. It had few doors but was well ventilated from the gaps in the aged boards. Maybell held a lantern that cast a faint light. Jim and I had decided we would need to rope the cow. From out of nowhere, as we were thinking over a plan, a sow came running through the barn. The sow ran underneath the cow and frightened the heck out of her. The cow started running and she crashed through a pen full of laying hens on their nests. The chickens instantly came to life. They flew out of their nests, loudly clucking, cackling and screaming. A few of the hens landed on the back of the cow, frightening her even more. In a chorus, the cow was bellowing, the sows were squealing and the chickens were clucking. The vets were hiding behind a safe pole.

Still scared, the cow crashed through a gate and landed in a v-shaped hay manger. There she became stuck, head first. The cow's rear was visible and from our hiding place we could see the feet and nose of the yet unborn calf. Opportunity had arrived! We hurried up to the cow and put a pulling chain on the calf's feet. One tug later, the calf was delivered alive. The frightened cow began to settle down as she got on her feet and licked the calf.

Maybell was ecstatic. In the calf, she had a new animal to sell in the fall to make her farm payment. She paid us well to boot. It was the beginning of what was to become a very long night.

The two-way radio was blaring when Jim and I arrived back at the truck. Fred Thompson, north of Gravity, had a cow with a prolapsed uterus. Don Lyons had a cow trying to calf as well.

"We just as well make a night of it," Dr. Johnson said with resignation.

We had driven from place to place and finished both calls. It was nearly 1:00 a.m. when my wife, Kay, caught up with us.

"Carl Israel has a gilt pigging and wants you to come," she said.

"We're on our way," I replied.

Carl Israel happened to be one of those guys that if anything could go wrong in his presence, it would. Still, he was an expert on cattle and swine and we were friends from way back.

Snowflakes flittered through the truck's headlight beams. The wind gusted and twisted the snow on the road in front of us. I was making conversation. "Have I ever told you about Carl's bad luck of 1977?" I asked Johnson.

"No, I guess not," Jim replied.

"Well," I began, "about a year ago, Carl was chasing some hogs out of his wife's garden. He picked up a rock about the size of a grapefruit and threw it ahead of the hogs to try to stop them. The rock sailed through the windshield of his wife's Buick. A month later, Carl was chasing some sows. His ammunition of choice that time was a stick. He similarly threw it. The stick stuck in the ground and a sow ran up on it. The stick stabbed the sow in the heart and of course, it died. A while after, he was chasing a cow that wore a neck chain I.D. This time, Carl was armed with a Pepsi bottle and he threw that at the cow hoping to change her direction. The bottle hit that cow's chain, shattered and cut her jugular. She consequently bled to death."

"Now, that is bad luck," said Johnson.

"Well, that's not all," I continued. "Carl had called me saying he had a cow calving. I was within five minutes of his place and I told him I'd be right there. I jammed my foot into the accelerator and burned on down the road. I pulled into the driveway and I could hear screaming and yelling. It scared the crap out of me. I thought Carl must be in serious trouble and I ran to the barn. There was Carl, with a big stick in his hand. Carl had tied the yet unborn calf's foot and head to a barn pole and he was whipping his cow, trying to make her pull her own calf. The cow had pulled too hard, and the calf was dead from a broken neck and leg. I yelled at Carl and told him he was a dumb SOB for not waiting for me. Carl told me he thought he might as well get something started while he was killing time. And, that was the year of Carl's bad luck."

Dr. Jim and I pulled into Carl's drive. Out Carl came, toting a twelve-pack of beer under one arm. "Let's go, boys," he said. "The sow is in the hog shed."

Dr. Johnson came from a long line of Swedes and he did like his beer. He could handle it, too. Out of a six-pack, he would have five to my one and I would be worse for the wear. Dr. Johnson denied he could ever go five to my one.

Carl got the beer ready while I examined the sow. Johnson joined Carl. The sow was gentle and laid there grunting, as if she knew I was there to help. I put some lube on my hand and gently slipped my fist into her vagina. The diagnosis was easy. The old girl had broken a pelvis and it had failed to properly heal. There was no way she could deliver normally.

"Oh, great, Carl!" I expounded. "This is going to require a caesarean."

"No shit?" asked Carl.

"Let me explain," I said. "It's 2 a.m. Carl, and sows don't have a high survival rate when it comes to caesareans. So, it's either try the operation, or shoot the sow."

"I have faith in you boys!" Carl yelled. "First, let's have a beer."

Considering the evening as a whole, I figured what the hell. A beer couldn't hurt. We restrained the sow and threw down some suds.

Dr. Johnson picked up the knife and went to work. He cut through the skin, the layer of muscle, and the peritoneum to expose the uterus. Jim took another swig. He gently incised the uterus that covered one of the piglets. Dr. Johnson was a good veterinary surgeon but at that moment he was beginning to look more like an artist. He was so smooth! The beer had leveled him out.

Carl had more time to drink, which he did. He also kept a steady stream of advice flowing.

The first piggy was out and alive. One by one, Dr. Johnson would incise the uterus and retrieve a piglet. In the uncoordinated manner of a newborn animal, the little pigs crawled on top of each other. They were looking for a teat from which to drink. I considered the instinct to go for milk a miracle of nature. We put the piglets under a heat lamp where they promptly fell to sleep.

Dr. Johnson sutured the sow. As we cleaned ourselves, Carl handed us the last of the beer and said, "Let's celebrate! I propose a toast to a successful surgery and to a night we can long remember."

We all had one more. The sow and her nine pigs were all doing well and in all of my practice years, I could think of no other occasion when that kind of surgery was as victorious. Carl had set the stage.

When the beer was gone, Jim and I headed for the truck. Carl yelled, "Wait a minute boys. I'll get my wife to cook us some breakfast."

"Oh, no, Carl," I pleaded. "That's not necessary. It's 3:30 in the morning. Let her sleep."

"Hell no, Doc! Come on in," he insisted.

Carl's wife Elaine greeted us like it was Christmas morning. The kitchen was soon filled with the aroma of home raised bacon and farm fresh eggs. We were all feeling good anyway and this sort of topped off the long night. Carl said it was a night to remember.

As I carefully guided the pickup to the end of the drive, I looked up. The snow had stopped and the sky had cleared. The rest of the world was soundly sleeping under a galaxy of stars. Dr. Jim and I both agreed it had been a joyous night.

44

HOW TO BUY
A DEAD HORSE

My attendance was required at every Saturday's sale when I worked as the sale barn veterinarian. I watched all classes of livestock being bought and sold and it gave me a slight advantage. I could spot a bargain.

My wife and I owned one Shetland pony for our three kids, the oldest of which was five. One Shetland didn't go far for our kiddie rides and I had decided we needed another horse. One Saturday, an older gentleman backed up to the unloading dock at the sale barn. He was driving an old Chevy pickup with a homemade stock rack on the back. In the back of the pickup stood a nice looking, year-old Palomino stallion.

There were very few people at the sale that day. It didn't appear I'd be bidding against a mob as I set my sights on owning the horse. The stallion was not broken to ride but he seemed to have a gentle demeanor. Of course, he was still a stallion, but I could take care of that.

Sale time came and the pretty little horse was led into the ring. The stallion didn't pull much interest from the few who had gathered, and the offers started slowly. I was just about to signal a bid when Dean Beemer, the sale barn owner, threw in a price of $75. For diplomacy sake, I kept quiet. "Going … going … gone," cried the auctioneer. The stallion was sold.

I sauntered over to Dean. "How bad do you want that horse?" I asked.

"If you want him, you can have him," Dean answered.

"It's a done deal," I gleefully replied.

Living in a small town has its advantages and disadvantages.

News travels fast, with accuracy lagging far behind. It wasn't long before my wife, Kay, came barreling up to the sale barn. In less than an hour, she had heard I had bought a stud horse. That part was true. From what my wife had pictured, I had purchased a renegade killer stallion.

"What in the world were you thinking?" she accusingly asked.

Finding myself on the defensive I stammered, "but … but!"

"But nothing! You are not bringing that stud horse home. I won't let it near our little kids. That is final!" Kay dictated.

I knew I was fighting a losing battle. "I'll have Beemer take him back," I told Kay.

I went to Dean and explained the situation I was in. No money had exchanged hands and he agreed to keep the horse. Because I had backed out of our bargain I offered Dean a favor. "I'll castrate the horse for free since you agreed to take him back," I told him.

I took out my surgical instruments and gave the horse a shot in a vein for anesthesia. Dean and I quickly tied the horse's legs together and castrated him.

"Let him go," I commanded. The boys untied and dropped the horse's legs. The colt died on the spot, apparently intolerant of the anesthetic. I knew who owned him now.

That horse had changed ownership four times. The original owner sold to Beemer, Beemer sold to me, I sold back to Beemer and when the horse died, I had the privilege of paying for a dead horse. You win some and you lose some.

Word spread like wildfire the local vet had bought a dead horse.

A client of mine chortled, "Look at it this way, Doc, your feed bill won't amount to much."

And from another friend, "Yeah and you won't have to clean up after it. And, he won't buck you off."

An older buyer remarked, "You could sell raffle tickets on that dead horse. Just make sure you give the winner his money back."

Owning a dead horse pleased my wife to no end. She was pretty darn sure the stallion wouldn't hurt anyone.

45

LIGHTNING

"What else could it be, Doc?" asked James. "I couldn't find the cow for about a week and that was about the time the storm went through. And then I found her dead."

James was looking for an answer from me. What he wanted to hear was "lightning."

Farmers carried disaster insurance on their herds. A claim could be made if an animal was lost due to lightning, drowning or accidental shooting. This was how farmers viewed a loss, according to an unwritten rule. If a cow died on a hill, it was from lightning. If it died near a pond, drowning was the sure cause. If it was hunting season, the cow had died from an accidental shooting. The insurance company saw it entirely differently. There could be no "possible lightning" cause of death claims. It was either lightning or it wasn't, conclusive.

James had a decomposed bag of bones left of his cow. From that, I was supposed to determine the cause of death, for insurance purposes. There were a hundred different ways that cow could have died. James would disagree with each one of them, except for lightning. It was impossible for me to say what the cause of death had been as I had no tissue to conduct a post mortem. I would leave this one up to the adjuster.

I didn't like being caught in the middle of the farmer, the insurance company and the insurance agent. An insurance agent wanted a veterinarian to give his client the benefit of the doubt. After all, the insurance agent didn't want to lose his customer, nor did I. Home offices of the insurance company required, in the name of fairness, an accurate opinion from the veterinarian. In order to provide that, an autopsy on a fresh carcass was necessary. Fresh, I hardly ever saw, particularly during hot summer months. Decomposition of a carcass occurred within a few short hours.

If I were in a predicament, I would ask the insurance agent what he wanted me to do. That would take the pressure off of me. In a lightning death, there were a few things I could look for on a carcass without opening it up. There would be no lesions, for example. I also looked for other visible symptoms of disease. Performing a full post mortem on a 2000-pound bull was not an easy task anyway. Without the aid of another person, it was nearly impossible. I often asked insurance adjusters to go along with me to check a carcass. They would ride along, but they would not assist. They were the first, however, to criticize me for not performing a complete autopsy.

An insurance agent accompanied me on a questionable lightning death call. I was to perform a post mortem for the farmer's claim. The cow was big and she had been dead for about 48 hours. I stuck my knife in her paunch and the swollen carcass nearly exploded. Ten turkey vultures hopped around us on the ground, waiting to finish their feast. They had already dined on the cow's eyeballs and teats. Coyotes had eaten away at her vagina area. When the rotten tissue and fluid exited the knife wound I had inflicted, the agent vomited.

"Let's go," he said weakly as he walked back to my truck. "I've seen enough."

The agent was very quiet during the drive back to town. I dropped him off at his car. He got out of my truck, turned and said to me, "Doc, you call 'em as you see 'em." I never had to call him for a consultation again.

There were neighborhood quacks, feed salesmen and alcoholics who could always determine a lightning death, just by looking. "The lightning blew out her top teeth," one told me.

Cows don't have top incisor teeth. "Her lower teeth were loose," was another tale. A cow's lower incisor teeth were always loose.

"There was a big burn mark on her belly," another declared.

Most cows have that mark which is called Stephanofilarisis.

My favorite was, "Her hooves came off." Decomposition caused hooves to rapidly drop and lightning could not blow them off.

I received a cause of death request in the mail from a farmer. A neighbor of the farmer's had told him that if hogs would not eat a carcass, the death had to occur from lightning. The farmer was so confident in the advice he included a stamped return envelope for me to mail back the report. This was the letter.

Jim,

I want to write you about a heifer that could have been struck with lightning.

Les found a young cow that had just had a calf. Both were dead. Les just thought that calving had killed them and drug her to a lot with 140 shoats in it and ripped her open. Five days went by and she was stinking. Just as we were pushing her to a brush pile to burn her, two men came. They said this cow just had to of been struck with lightning for no hog had touched her. The insurance adjuster agreed, but said he would have to have a statement from a veterinarian.

Of course, all you could do would be to write a statement that hogs will not touch an animal struck by lightning. These two men would make a statement to what they saw.

The adjuster at Maryville said he about run Dr. Pierce down inspecting dead animals after this electrical storm.

I can not see where this could get any of us into trouble.

Thanking you until you are better paid,

I am yours truly.

Incidentally, I could not call it a lightning death.

I had a client who worked very hard at creating insurance claims. For lightning, he would literally put burn marks on a carcass or climb a nearby tree, tearing at the limbs to make the tree look like it had been struck. He once had a big calf stuffed down a well. My client wanted me to call death by drowning. Just for fun, I took the insurance agent with me. It was a humorous sight, such a big cow for such a little hole. Both the agent and I would have liked to have been mice and watched that farmer stuff his cow down the well. The agent didn't pay the claim.

Because cows huddled together under trees during storms, it was not impossible for the whole group to get struck by lightning. The biggest struck herd I ever saw numbered eight. The cows were practically on top of each other. They had died instantly. A college classmate of mine had a client who lost 34 cows at once from lightning. In some cases, carrying insurance was very beneficial.

A cantankerous Athelston client of mine counted every penny, then counted them again. He had a habit of purchasing vaccine from the feed store and then hiring me by the hour to do his processing. I often took Donnie along with me to run the chute. When old Vilar, the client, was within earshot, I would say to Donnie, "work slow!" The old guy would cringe and keep poking his cattle as fast as he could.

It was a bright sunny day after an Iowa storm that had come out of nowhere. The storm formed from searing heat and humidity. It brought vivid lightning and gusts of wind that knocked down trees. A tornado may have been a part of that storm as debris and junk had been scattered. Vilar called saying he had a cow killed by lightning. I hoped for an easy time with Vilar on this consult. After all, there had been a violent storm and lightning could have caused the cow's death.

"She's out in the pasture," Vilar hollered as he opened the gate.

Vilar and I drove for miles back through rough pasture filled with tall musk thistle. I drove around terraces and dodged washouts. I wished I had called the insurance agent so it would have been his nice new vehicle taking the thistle beating instead of mine.

"She's across this ditch, about 30 yards," Vilar blurted out. "Never saw anything like it," he continued, "the lightning caused the cow to blow the calf out of her ass and blew the whole calf bed, too."

I gathered my posting tools and Vilar and I went for an early morning walk through the weeds. The storm had left the air cool and fresh. Six turkey vultures lurked around the dead cow. One of the vultures stood rigid, with its enormous wings spread. "Is he protecting his find?" I asked Vilar, not expecting an answer.

"Nah, he's just drying his wings," Vilar said, as if to say a vulture wouldn't waste his energy, the same as Vilar wouldn't waste a dime.

We walked up on the dead cow. Her uterus was prolapsed and her dead calf lay behind that. It was obvious from the position of the carcasses she had trouble calving. She must have strained pushing her dead calf out. Her uterus had popped, and then she probably died. It was not possible to conclude that the animals had suffered a lightning death. I didn't want to argue with Vilar over my decision so I merely told him to contact his insurance agent for direction. I never received a death claim form from Vilar's agent. I knew what the agent had said.

I had my own personal fear of lightning. I was known to play outside during severe storms, working metal chutes around steel fences. I kept one thing in mind all the while. If I saw the flash and heard the boom at the same time, I knew I was too close to lightning.

46
WHITE
FANG

It was an unusual family evening. Kay didn't have a meeting to attend, all the kids were sitting at the table and I hadn't been called away. We had a catch-up session and Kay and I found out who was doing what and where and with whom.

The conversation turned to the movie White Fang, the story line of which revolved around a white wolf that was saved from the wilds by a family who raised him domestically. The wolf eventually left the family's camp only to return later to save their lives somehow. White Fang was rated for the general public and was coming to the local volunteer-run theater in town. Our family enthusiastically and with optimism made a date to attend the movie together.

The night had arrived. Jamie, Shelly and Matt decided they wanted to go with their friends. Kay was busy with volunteer work which left Joe and I. We would catch the early show, we decided. A large crowd was expected at the first showing and no one was disappointed. The movie house volunteers scurried around and found a seat for all as the projectionist began to roll the film onto the screen.

Joe and I were settled in our seats. I wondered what my odds were of getting called out of the show but I'd decided not to worry about it. A third of the way through, the P.A. system squawked, "Dr. Lucas, you are wanted out front."

I swore under my breath and said to Joe, "Well, I'm sorry but we're going to have to leave." Joe told me he was sort of tired anyway.

We walked together to the lobby. The call was from Fred Wall who had a cow calving and needed help. Joe and I headed to his farm, just a short drive from the downtown theater.

Mr. Wall had the cow haltered and tied to a post. The calf was a normal presentation and all I had to do was hook on and pull for the calf to come. Joe and I cleaned up and gathered our tools. On the way to the truck I asked Joe, "Do you want to go home or back to the movie?"

"Let's go back to the show," he answered with sparkle in his eyes.

We waltzed back in to the darkened movie house and I stood at the door for a moment to adjust my eyes. I spotted one open seat in the center of the row toward the back. Joe and I excused ourselves as we squeezed our way past several pairs of legs. I sat down and put Joe on my lap. White Fang was just at a point of excitement and I realized we had not missed that much of the plot. Our attention was immediately refocused.

Behind me I heard a baby cough and whimper, the kind of noise I'd recognized as the beginning of something big. The coughing turned into a gag and the baby began to wail. I sensed the physicality of the baby's mother standing up behind me. All of a sudden, in a projectile manner, the baby vomited right on top of my balding head. From there, the stream ran down my forehead and eyes, around my ears and down my neck. It was enough to make me gag. In disgust, I thought about the fact there was one damn seat left in the whole place and I had to be sitting in it. I grabbed Joe by the hand and told him, "Let's get the hell out of here."

I never knew who the lady with the baby was. The next day at the office, my secretary said, "Oh, Jim, some gal called and said to tell you she was really sorry about what happened at the movie last night."

I never forgot White Fang and wondered what the wolf saved the family from.

47
A DASTARDLY DEED

Veterinarians are not perfect. As in life, mistakes are made. Euthanasia, while being controversial in its implementation, is a service of mercy veterinarians must perform. The methods used for a painless, happy death are fraught with happenstance.

Euthanasia has come a long way with the advent of injectable drugs, making the stout-hearted deed more humane. It wasn't long ago when the only tools available were a gun and an axe.

Animal rights in veterinary science had yet to become nationalized when the theatrical Dr. Roy Shultz demonstrated how he'd euthanasia a pig. Dr. Shultz held the meeting to illustrate methods for the administration of death in order to keep tissue intact to conduct a post mortem exam.

He began. "You may give a shot of succinyl choline which seems to precipitate a quick death." Dr. Shultz then injected his demonstrator pig. The pig died quickly enough. He continued, "or, you can just cut its throat and let it bleed to death. And, of course, a hammer will work, except that's pretty hard on the brain if you need to save the organ." With a second pig, Dr. Shultz demonstrated a hammer death.

"As a last resort," he calmly said as he reached down in his leather grip, "you can always shoot the SOB." Dr. Shultz pulled his 45 revolver from the grip and shot a pig in the head. Kaboom! Everyone was taken by surprise. In the meeting room, the shot sounded like a cannon in a rain barrel. There was never any napping during a Dr. Shultz demonstration.

A common euthanasia vet call occurred with a downed cow, one that was unable to get back on its feet. The cow was usually toothless and somewhere between 15-20 years old. Without teeth, the cow could not chew well, which caused ineffective digestion of feed. If the cow was carrying a calf, the fetus took what little nutrients there were, leaving the cow weakened and diseased. The cow almost never responded to treatment and its health was irreversible. If a fetus was mature enough, I recommended taking the cow's life to spare the calf. I would deliver the calf by caesarean. With my scalpel in hand, I then reached through the caesarean incision up to the cow's aorta. By severing the aorta, the cow instantly bled to death.

Ted Brook called me to attend an old cow of his. I examined the toothless animal and explained the situation to him. Ted accepted the diagnosis but did not want to be a witness. I injected his cow with a local anesthetic along the incision line, and opened the cow's abdomen. The calf fell out. With my helper, Donnie, we picked the calf up, drained the mucous from its respiratory tract and Donnie rubbed it down. I breathed a sigh of relief, having promised Ted a live calf. I then turned to the old cow, wishing I could do more to help her. Knowing help was but a dream, I reached up along her spine and located the aorta. I could feel the pulsation from the huge vessel with each beat of the cow's heart. I reached down to the ground for my scalpel. As I brought the scalpel across her bony spine, its blade broke. The cow would unnecessarily suffer it seemed, if I took the extra time to look for another scalpel. Instead, I reached in my truck for a double bit axe. I had used the axe many a time when I was in such a pinch. I measured for the spot to aim the axe, where I could sink the blade into the cow's brain, causing instant death. I raised the axe and was bringing it down when I heard a blood-curdling scream come from behind. The axe in hand continued on its path and the cow was soon dead. I turned around to see from where the scream had come.

Without my knowledge, Ted's wife had walked down to see what was going on. Tears were running down her face and she was pulling at her hair. I, too, was almost in shock. Her scream had scared the pudding out of me.

"Oh, Mrs. Brook," I said, "I am very sorry you had to see that."

As nice as she could be for the moment, Mrs. Brook answered. "Oh, that's okay I had never seen anything like that before. The sight of the huge incision frightened me. But what a beautiful bull calf you saved for us."

I was relieved Mrs. Brook understood. In the future, I made sure there was never a surprised or unwilling participant if death had to come from my hand.

I hardly ever carried a gun even though a bullet in an animal's brain is about as humane as a death can be. Humane, that is, if you know your anatomy and where to place the bullet. One night around 11:00 p.m., I received a call from the Taylor County Sheriff. He asked me to meet him as quickly as possible at the east edge of town. There had been an accident. A thoroughbred horse belonging to Marion O'Connel had strayed from its pasture and was on the highway. A pickup truck came roaring through and hit the horse. It was an ugly sight. The horse was badly cut and one if its rear legs had been broken around the hock. The leg was just dangling there and the horse was in a great deal of pain.

The sheriff handed me his 45 revolver, as the decision had already been made. Horse's legs do not heal well and putting the animal out of its misery was the only recourse. I was sizing up the horse's head, looking for the right spot to fire the bullet when Mr. O'Connel said, "I'll do it."

I handed him the pistol. After all, it was his horse. Marion raised the gun and pointed it between the animal's eyes.

"Marion," I interrupted, "You need to aim the gun higher than that."

"I've done this before," he said.

He squeezed the trigger and fired. The horse had been standing on three legs when the sheriff's revolver with Marion behind it, blew an inch-sized hole between its eyes. The force of the bullet knocked the horse back about five feet but it never went down.

"Here, Doc," Marion said as he handed me the gun, "You'd better do it."

I drew an imaginary line from the medial canthus of the horse's eye to the opposite ear and then measured the same from the other eye. That crossing point was where the horse's brain would be. I figured it was about four inches above the spot Marion O'Connel had aimed for. I pulled the trigger and the horse died instantly. I handed the gun back to the sheriff with remorse.

As I drove back to town, the pardonable death reminded me of another.

The clinic was boarding a large St. Bernard dog that had bitten a town resident. For two weeks we held him, checking him for rabies. After the quarantine, the dog's owner decided he should be destroyed, rabies or not. The dog appeared to be gentle, but his 150-pound stature was very intimidating and he did have a bite record, after all.

I was going to need help holding the dog if I was to inject him with a lethal drug. I asked for volunteers to enter the dog's pen with me but could not find one. I could have reached him with my five-foot pole syringe but I didn't have it available. Dr. Johnson and I then decided shooting the animal was the safest avenue for us. Dr. Johnson left to get his 22 pistol.

When Johnson returned, the St. Bernard was sitting puppy-style on its butt with its tongue lapping, looking as content as could be. Johnson carefully aimed the pistol and squeezed the trigger. The bullet traveled through the dog's sinus cavity, totally missing its brain. Without changing its posture, the friendly dog just looked up at us. Johnson fired again and that shot did the trick. We were not at all proud of ourselves.

"Don't feel bad, Jim," I said. "One time in the outside dog runs, I was about to give a dog a lethal injection when it tried to bite me. That startled me, I jumped back and lost my grip on the animal. I kept jabbing at the dog until finally I delivered the drug. The dog took off running and ran as fast as he could up Main Street. He died right in the middle of the street. I had to go get the carcass while many onlookers stood by. They knew what had happened." At least the botched attempt at shooting the St. Bernard was just between Dr. Johnson and myself. No one else had to know.

Old Doc Anderson was one of my partners who practiced veterinarian science in the old-fashioned way. He would, at times, invent his own treatment in order to get the job done. There were many stories he had to tell and I doubt euthanasia was in his vocabulary. Those were the days when you just put animals "to sleep."

Two widowed sisters lived together and shared their love with a Cocker Spaniel. The Cocker Spaniel was getting as old as the sisters were and suffered from untreatable cancer. They called Doc Anderson to come put their dog in puppy-dog heaven. Doc Anderson obliged and made a house call. When he arrived, he realized he would have no one to hold the dog down for him. The ladies ushered old Doc into a garage where the recumbent dog lay. Alone, Doc tried to hit the dog's vein with a needle. The dog began howling and barking at Doc. As Doc was a sensitive person, he did not want the ladies to hear the howling dog. He reached for the dog's neck and choked it to unconsciousness. Then, he made the injection. Death was the goal after all, and the choking was part of the humane act and was almost as instantaneous.

In Bedford, Doc Anderson lived across the street from a Mrs. Hook. Mrs. Hook owned a big blue-colored cat named Ol' Blue. Everyone knew Ol' Blue, as the cat more or less owned the whole neighborhood. The older Blue became, the more decrepit he was. Blue suffered from arthritis. Soon, younger, healthier cats began taking over his majestic kingdom. The younger cats fought Ol' Blue and he was left with deep scars and abscesses. Mrs. Hook realized the plight Blue faced, and called Doc Anderson. She made plans with Doc to deliver her cat to the clinic, where Doc would put Blue "to sleep."

Mrs. Hook dropped Blue off one afternoon and left. Doc Anderson took out a syringe filled with sodium pentathol and gave Blue an overdose. When the cat had stopped breathing, Doc put him in a box and set the box outside in a barn stall. One day passed and then another. Doc's wife, Marian, noticed nothing had been done with the cat's remains.

"Now, Don," she blurted, "that thing will stink up the whole town. You get it out of here, right now!"

"I suppose I just as well do it," Doc answered her.

Doc and I took the cat in the box to the fairgrounds. We dug a shallow grave and scantily covered the box with dirt. "There," Doc said, "that will take care of that."

"Yep," I replied. It's a good thing Marian noticed the box still sitting there. It would have been one stinking mess."

The next day, Mrs. Hook phoned Doc Anderson. "I thought I told you to put Ol' Blue to sleep for good!" she emphatically stated.

"I did just that," Doc replied. "We just buried him yesterday."

"Well," came Mrs. Hook's gruff voice, "Blue is sitting right here on my front porch, purring up a storm."

All Doc could say was, "I'll be right there to pick him up. I'll have to try again."

Doc fetched me and said, "I just can't believe this! You have to come with me."

We drove the quarter-mile to the fairgrounds. There we found the box with a hole scratched out of it, just big enough for Blue to have made his getaway. The cat had slept away a two-day barbituate snooze, woke up and went back home.

Mrs. Hook was so impressed with Blue's will to live she let him run another year. When the neighborhood cats had once again beaten Blue down, Doc Anderson's second attempt did not fail.

If I ever thought Doc Anderson didn't have the right tools at his disposal, I was reminded of a story I once heard.

There was a rancher out of the West who had a big spread and farmed it with mules. He loved to trade for mules and had a high turnover rate. Naturally, in his swapping, he would end up with injured or unmanageable mules he would have to get rid of. This rancher had more dynamite than bullets and more explosives than brains. I heard he would tie a quarter of a stick of dynamite to the mule's halter, tie the halter to a post and light the fuse. The explosion would instantaneously kill the forlorn animal.

One day, the rancher lit a stick of dynamite that had been tied to its halter, and the hissing noise spooked the mule. The mule must have been bitten once by a rattlesnake. Anyway, the mule's rope broke and the animal was free to run. Run he did, about 50 yards, right into the rancher's barn. The barn blew up. The rancher was lucky the mule didn't chase him. Either way, the mistake the rancher made was never repeated with another mule.

48

TWEET, TWEET, DANGER

I dreamt I heard voices buzzing around my head. The sounds were sometimes muffled and sometimes loud and I wondered if I was in a padded room. I tried to move around to get away from the din but I couldn't change position. My muscles were as limp as rags.

Had I remembered the kick in the jaw from the 700-pound bull, I would have known I wasn't dreaming. I was lying on the floor of my cattle chute, knocked out cold. Somewhere between consciousness and swoon I distinguished two voices. The first one whispered, "Drag him out so the bull doesn't stomp on him."

A second trumpeted, "Should I call Kay?" Kay, my wife, was a paramedic.

I was down for a ten count but it seemed like an eternity. I could never get used to the experience being cold-cocked and time escaped me. I regained my senses, sat up and saw Donnie holding onto the bull's tail. I had no one to blame for getting kicked, except of course for the bull. And then, I was thankful for the favor he had granted me, imprinting in my mind what a dangerous place it was to stand behind a big bull calf.

I stepped out of the chute and took an invigorating breath. I looked all around until I got my bearings. I was standing at a once stately homestead that had two brick structures at its entrance. Cement posts were in position around the perimeter meaning that Mr. Crum, a banker, had owned the property at one time. His trademark cement posts were all that remained of the structure.

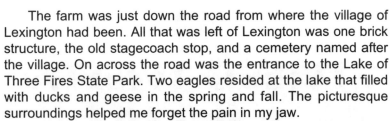

The farm was just down the road from where the village of Lexington had been. All that was left of Lexington was one brick structure, the old stagecoach stop, and a cemetery named after the village. On across the road was the entrance to the Lake of Three Fires State Park. Two eagles resided at the lake that filled with ducks and geese in the spring and fall. The picturesque surroundings helped me forget the pain in my jaw.

As Donnie and I were driving down the long lane heading home, I thought of how perilous my profession really was. Man was the superior species and by nature animals were not the aggressors, unless it was a matter of survival. I took things for granted too many times and as a result, I put myself at risk.

Richard Brand had scheduled me to vaccinate, castrate and dehorn his big calves. I picked up Donnie and Ray and headed for the 102 River Valley. When we drove in, Richard was herding the cows toward the lot. He needed an extra body or two to close some holes so the three of us climbed in to help. Richard should have been taking it easy after his two open-heart surgeries but it was an impossible task to convince him to slow down. After we cornered the calves, they needed to be sorted away from the cows. The sorting was going well when I noticed a big steer wearing a set of the strangest horns I'd ever seen. The horns, instead of being tipped forward, were sticking horizontally straight out of its head.

"What in the world is that thing?" I yelled at Richard.

"He's a wild SOB that has gotten away from us the last two years. Watch him because he is one crazy steer," Richard yelled back.

I realized then I was standing within ten feet of him and I teetered on the fence for protection. The steer paid me no attention and instead focused his eyes on Richard. No one had time to do a thing before the steer charged. The steer rammed Richard in his rib cage and threw him up in the air, the picture of which is forever embedded in my brain. Richard must have flown a good five feet, straight up. When Richard came down, the nasty steer tried to gore him with its horns and stomp him with its feet. I found a club and ran toward the steer as fast as I could. I hit that steer on the ass and yelled and screamed to divert its attention. My charge worked and the steer turned to come at me. I high-tailed it for the fence, out of reach of the steer's horizontal horns.

"Open the gate and let him go," I yelled.

The steer was indeed one demented animal and for the third straight year, he got away.

I spoke to Donnie as we attended Richard, "Of all of us, Richard is the one who needed this the least."

Richard was short of breath and nearly unconscious. He talked very little and his tone was soft. I called for the ambulance. Hospital x-rays showed Richard had several broken ribs but no damage to his heart. After a few painful weeks, he mended.

The steer wasn't as fortunate. Richard's boys immediately called the butcher who shot the steer with a high-powered rifle. The sons hung the steer's head on a fence post in effigy.

While steers were dangerous enough, they didn't compare to the mean and mighty boar. Boars grew long tusks that pointed upward in a curve out of both sides of the mouth. When angered, a boar lowered its head, threw it powerfully back up and the tusks would cut open anything in their path. Its teeth, too, were razor sharp from constantly being ground together.

When I worked as the sale barn vet, it was my job to de-tusk all boars prior to auction. It was a preventative measure, for in the past I had seen cows and horses with legs and bellies torn open from one boar swipe.

One Saturday, Dr. Johnson went to the boar pens for me. Jim was just ready to step over the fence when his toehold slipped and he tumbled into the pen with a 500-pound boar. The boar was alarmed. He lowered and then threw up his head. Jim was gored at a spot just under his kneecap. He screamed in pain. I heard the wail and ran over as fast as I could. The boar was going after Jim a second time.

"The SOB got me!" Jim cried to me. The boar's second thrust missed Jim who had somehow reached the top of the fence, just a few inches out of harm's way.

"I'm getting you to the doctor right now," I told him.

The doctor cleaned Jim's wound and sutured it closed and

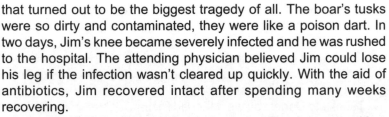

that turned out to be the biggest tragedy of all. The boar's tusks were so dirty and contaminated, they were like a poison dart. In two days, Jim's knee became severely infected and he was rushed to the hospital. The attending physician believed Jim could lose his leg if the infection wasn't cleared up quickly. With the aid of antibiotics, Jim recovered intact after spending many weeks recovering.

As a souvenir, Donnie and I presented Dr. Johnson with a fresh set of tusks handily removed from one sale barn boar.

49

SOME PEOPLE JUST PISS ME OFF

A new bank had opened in our beautiful little town. One of my best friends, Don Vawter, was to be the manager. The bank had an open house to welcome Don and introduce him to the community. A nice lunch was to be served and my wife, Kay, accompanied me. It was an unusual event for us to be able to share the time together. Kay and I had just filled our plates when I saw Robert Galey coming our way.

It doesn't matter where a veterinarian is or what he is doing. A vet can just expect a question or two to arise during his free time. Sure enough, Robert had spotted me and I had nowhere to hide.

"Here it comes," I told myself.

"Hey, Doc, I got a question for you," Robert stated.

"Go ahead," I said reluctantly.

"I have this 70-pound pig and his belly is as big as a 5-gallon bucket," Robert leaned over whispering, "and I think he can't shit." Before I could make a comment, he went on. "My Indian wife, with her 250-pound frame, jumped on the pig's belly and it was like letting the air out of a balloon. The pig went pfft, pfft, thh, thh, and the shit just flew."

A lady standing behind me had overheard Robert and she began choking on her hot dog lunch.

Robert's wife, Edna, blurted in and said, "I do not weigh 250 pounds!"

I ushered Robert outside and said to him, "Your pig has F.O.S. and that stands for Full Of Shit, just like you."

More than likely, the pig had a rectal prolapse. It sounded as if the prolapse had healed on the inside meaning waste could not travel out. I told Robert the pig was likely to die and he just as well butcher it and be done with it.

"Thanks, Doc," Robert said, "sorry to bother you."

I felt sorrier for the lady choking on her hot dog.

Robert was about as F.O.S. as anyone I had ever met. One day as I was driving down our town's brick streets, I heard, "Heyyyy Doctor, pull over a minute. I have something to show you."

I pulled over and got out of my truck so Robert wouldn't get in with me. I leaned up against my truck and said, "Shoot, Robert."

Robert's F.O.S. began this way. "Well, Doc, you know I have a ranch down in Texas with a lot of purebred Brahma cows on it. Them ornery ranch cowhand cusses took this old horny goat, injected him with hormones and turned him in with ten sows. That goat bred them sows over and over until he wore the hair off their sides."

"Yeah?" I said in a disbelieving tone.

"Well, in about three or four months, those sows went to pigging and here is what they bore," Robert said.

Robert reached in his pocket and got out a photograph. I looked at the picture. It showed offspring that had pig bodies and goat heads. The litter had short noses like pigs with wattles on their jaws like goats.

I remembered my genetics classes as I thought to myself, "This isn't supposed to be possible!"

I thanked Robert for the glimpse at a remarkable animal. I never did believe what I saw in the photos, but I wondered about it.

Two years later, a Missourian unloaded a bunch of pigs at the sale barn. Those pigs all had wattles.

"Sir, could you tell me where those pigs came from?" I asked the fellow from Missouri.

"Sure," he answered. "This breed is raised down south. I bought a few sows with wattles and they passed it on to their pigs."

YOU CAN'T TRUST ANYONE

One mystery had been solved just as another surfaced.

It was a nice Saturday. A junk sale was being held across the street from the veterinary clinic. A lot of folks were in attendance and several loads of 'treasures' had been dropped off. I always enjoyed looking over the lots and the people. The crowd represented the many facets of life. There were well-dressed people looking for antiques, farmers looking for bargains and the low-lifers looking for anything that was free. Included in this day's bounty were puppies, Banty roosters, rabbits and geese.

Robert Galey sidled through the crowd and bumped up against me. "Hi, Doc, how ya' doin'?"

"I'm just fine, Robert, how about you?" I asked.

"I'm pissed Doc," Robert blurted.

"What about, Robert?" I inquired.

Robert said, "Did you see those geese over there? Well, I got cheated out of them."

"Oh, how is that?" I asked.

"This woman came up and started talking to me. She started talking about sex and you can guess what happened," Robert explained.

"No, I haven't the foggiest idea what happened," I answered. "What did happen?"

"I got screwed out of my geese."

There was more than one Robert in my world.

On a close, hot day in July the clinic was really slow. I was thinking of taking a little time off to check my farm. I was almost out the door when the phone rang. It was on slow days when the worst calls came.

Julie, the office assistant yelled, "It's Clarence Vincent. He has a cow calving on the north place."

"OK, tell him I'm on the way," I said begrudgingly.

Driving to Vincent's, my mind wandered to what a worthless person he was. I decided I must have been willing to make the call for the benefit of the cow alone.

I pulled into the lot and was surprised to see Clarence had built a corral with a head catch. The head catch was tied to a post with baling wire. I reminded myself to be careful because I was nearly killed in Missouri once with a similar set up.

"The cow's in the big lot," Clarence mumbled. "If you'll park your truck in that hole between the steel bin and fence, I think we can to get her in the corral."

"No!" I exclaimed. "Let's put your truck in that hole. I don't want the cow on the hood of my truck."

"Aw, she wouldn't do that," Clarence assured me.

"I am not putting my truck in that hole," I said matter-of-factly.

Clarence got out his old Datsun pickup and closed the hole with it. The first time around, the cow jumped on the hood and windshield, digging her way off. The second time, she nearly cleared the truck as she jumped at it.

The cow, by then, was wearing down a little and she began looking at the corral as a safe haven.

"Just stand there, Clarence, and let her look," I instructed.

She paused, looked again and quietly walked in. Clarence and I delivered her live calf. Sometimes cows show more consideration than people do.

IT REALLY HAPPENED

I was never very selective when it came to clients. I always felt I needed to serve every one. As a result, I had some customers who had no boundaries when it came to inconsideration. They were rude to me, to my family, my secretary and most people in general. As chance would have it, the worst clients seemed to show up at the clinic on the very same day.

In walked Paul Hamblin. Paul only sought out a vet when he was in desperation, when all that was left to do was administer last rights to a dying animal. If the truth were to be told, his cows usually starved to death. Paul raised worthless hay. He would never attempt to prevent disease with immunizations. He always expected a miracle and medicine to go with it in order to save an animal. I often wondered why he called me. He frequently blamed me for misdiagnosing and would declare, "That's not what's wrong."

Before Paul had finished lecturing me, in walked Greg Johnston. Greg was a windbag and often repeated stories. Greg boasted how he had lost his farm in the 80's, and still raised ten kids. Greg was the only man I'd ever known who had built a barn lot out of bedsprings. No animal could walk through that lot without bouncing back in.

Greg interrupted Paul's lecture with a question directed toward me. "I have a small calf that is bloated. Do you have a shot for him?"

Paul was listening and before I could answer, he blurted out, "You just as well shoot the son-of-a-bitch between the eyes 'cause he is going to die anyway."

All three veterinarians in the clinic were standing there. We made stinging eye contact.

To top it off, in walked Oliver Hooper. Oliver was an Arkansas hillbilly. He farmed with horses and lived alone in a windowless house surrounded by eight-foot weeds. Oliver was a nice guy to visit with but always asked a lot of dumb questions. On this day he had a problem with some of his calves. The calves had rectal prolapse, which is sometimes caused by an infection in the bowels. The infection creates diarrhea and as the bowel becomes more and more irritated, the calf strains, causing the rectum to pop out.

Greg Johnston began striking up a conversation with Oliver. He was inquiring about Oliver's problem with his herd.

"Well," said Oliver, "I have these calves that are so wormy that the worms are pushing the rectum out."

Dr. Young interrupted, "Do we have any more of that bloat vaccine?"

"Nope," I answered, "we'll have to use bullets. I'll get Oliver some calf wormer and you get Mr. Johnston some smooth muscle relaxant for his bloated calf, and I'm getting the hell out of here."

Oliver paid his bill and said, "Thanks, boys."

He left to start his Ford pickup that was parked in the lot. We heard a rrrr-rrrrrrr-rrr-rrrrrrr, pip, pop, chug-chug, rrrrrrrr. The old truck fired and then backfired and belched out a big black cloud of smoke. Away Oliver went, bucking down the street.

Blanketed by the big cloud of smoke, I got the hell out of there.

The office had filled with the truck exhaust and just maybe, I was guessing, the other people that had just pissed me off were smoked out as well.

50
PROFANITY

There was just something about it. Working with large animals brought out the vulgar side of veterinarians and producers alike. In my vet practice, I tried to hold my tongue and not let loose with my learned rhapsody of strung together cuss words. When I was alone with my own herd it was a different story. There I practiced until I was sure I could stand up against the best of the blasphemers, until I could teach the curse course.

Dr. Jim Cummings and his wife Rosalyn had been caught in a veterinary practice that fell on hard times. Vets and farmers mirrored each other in economics. Farmers practiced prudent livestock management during the good years. When the weather had cooperated, crops came in bountiful and the market price held. Coins jingled in their pockets and trickled into the hands of vets. If farmers had a bad year, the vet was about the last person to be called.

It had been the second, third or fourth bad year in a row for Jim. The Cummings family returned to their hometown of Bedford and set up a practice in competition with me. Jim and I always got along and after a period of time, we joined in partnership. Dr. Cummings had an excellent Christian upbringing and probably had never run across the likes of my vocabulary before. It took some time but Cummings eventually picked up on my habit of verbally unloading on animals. The penchant carried over from his work to his home. Jim's daughter, Carla, once told my son Joe that her dad had certainly changed since he joined my practice.

"In what way?" Joe asked innocently.

"Dad cusses now," Carla replied. I was especially proud of my influence when Jeff, Carla's brother added with self satisfaction, "Yeah, and he even lets us cuss too!"

Chris Fletchall owned some pretty ornery cows that pushed me to the limit. The cows were willing to try my chute but if I got too close, they lashed out at me. One of the cows hooked me in the ribs with her horns, hurting me more than a little bit, and my swearing picked up steam. One older gentleman was standing by and watched the whole operation with intensity. As Chris and I finished the herd, I asked him who that elderly gentleman happened to be.

"Oh, he's the minister down at the Christian Church," Chris answered. "Wow, I'll bet I really impressed him," I said with all the guilt I could muster.

Chris assured me not to worry, the minister had heard it all before.

On down the road, I worked some cattle for Don and Cora who were Christian people and lived by the Good Book. I was making conversation when I told them about a new restaurant my wife and I, along with our kids, had tried out the night before.

"Don't they serve alcoholic drinks there?" Cora asked.

"Why, yes they do," I replied.

"WELL! I'd never take my kids in there!" she said haughtily. I dropped the subject right there and then.

Don, Cora and I ate lunch together and then went out to chase their cows into the corral. The cows worked well for a while before they began to get testy. The herd was going everywhere except where we wanted them to go. One ran right by Cora and she yelled, "Why, you son-of-a-bitch."

Another cow headed her way but rather than enter the corral, it jumped over the fence.

"Well, I'll be god-damned," Cora cursed, "What the hell is wrong with these bitches today?"

The cows had gotten the best of the Bible-thumping Cora. At that point, I yelled at everyone to cool down in hopes of settling the cows down as well. Don grabbed for a bucket of corn. With it, he led the hungry cows into the corral. WELL! I was relieved Cora didn't have the chance to offend me any further. She cussed with the best of them but was strict in applying the sacraments toward the consumption of alcohol.

One of my best workers, Ray Mercer, had a little humor in him but he was a man of steel when it came to cussing. He had no regard for who was within earshot when he'd let out a complete sentence stream. The longer he worked for me, the more he thought he was the vet. He knew it all and had an answer for everything and everyone. The kindly Mrs. Mack walked into the vet clinic one morning to ask about treating her dog for fleas.

Before I could answer her, Ray blurted out, "Hell, I just feed my dog a little garlic every day and the fleas are gone."

My secretary, Julie, wasn't paying much attention to Ray. She set some pills on the counter and said gently to Mrs. Mack, "Give one of these per mouth and that should control the flea problem."

Ray butted in again and said, "I'd just use garlic. That gets rid of the little bastards."

Mrs. Mack was by now confused and asked, "Garlic or pills, what am I supposed to use?"

Finally, I couldn't stay out of the conversation any longer and while I froze Ray in place with my stare I said, "I believe you'd better use the pills. They'll rid the dog of the fleas for a longer period of time. Good day."

I was called a lot of names in my lifetime but I preferred nicknames the best. "Doc" was the most natural as it was easy, quick, and sounded personal enough for the folks who weren't really sure of my first name. They would say, "Hi, Doc," and act like we were long lost buddies even if I'd never seen them before in my life. Some people called me "Max," a leftover from the people acquainted with my dad. I was called "Don" when people confused me with my brother or my partner and my macho friends called me "Luke." Then there was "James" and the one I liked best, "Jimmie." When someone called me Jimmie, I knew they had known me forever.

ROWE, ROWE, ROWE YOUR BOAT

Doc Anderson was yelling at me. "Jimmie, come and go with me. We have a couple of horses to castrate for Wilbur and Patty Rowe."

Doc and I jumped into his 1961 Ford car, his version of a vet truck. We drove up the Rowe's long lane and were met by their Rat Terrier guard dog. That dog would fight a bear to protect the Rowe turf and Doc and I sighed in relief when we'd safely passed. Wilbur had his two two-year-old horses tied to a fence. They were good looking animals, nicely filled out and their coats glistened in the sun. Doc and I were laying out the vet equipment when I heard a faint yell coming from the barn. It was Patty.

Patty was a good farm wife who spoke fluently and never lacked for words. "Jimmie!" she yelled in greeting as she walked out of the barn.

Patty, overdue with her pregnancy, had just finished hand-milking the cows and she carried two three-gallon pails of milk with her. She hadn't spilled a drop when she half pointed at Wilbur and said, "Jimmie, I wish you'd castrate that son-of-a-bitch. I'd be glad to pay you extra for that."

We waited for Wilbur to laugh and when he did Doc and I joined in. Patty made her way to the milk separator where she would spend the next half-hour dividing the cream from the milk.

Before the development of a horse anesthesia that could be used in castration, veterinarians used a casting harness. The harness was attached to the stallion and then, by brute force, the horse was literally thrown to the ground, turned and castrated. The new drug made the surgery more humane and less dangerous to the life of the horse. It also worked very fast. Once it was injected, a vet had three to five minutes to finish the operation before the horse would be back on its feet with only a slight awareness of what had happened.

Doc and I had finished up the horses when Wilbur asked, "Can you guys work some cattle tomorrow?"

I told Wilbur I would return by 8:00 a.m. the next morning.

At 7:30 a.m., I picked up my helper, Donnie, and we headed for the Rowe farm. The day had all of the appearances of being a beauty. The roadside ditches were filled with blooming wildflowers.

Donnie opened the gate to the lot so I could drive over to the corral. The corral itself was empty but was surrounded by several of Wilbur's neighbors who would help herd the cows into the pen. Wilbur and his daughter, Donna, worked the cows from atop their horses. Wilbur and Donna had the cows running as fast as the horses and they were all headed toward the lot. Donnie and I knelt down and hid to avoid scaring the animals away. Before Wilbur could get the gate closed, the cows had rounded the lot and half of them had run back to the pasture.

Wilbur began to cuss. "Patty," Wilbur roared, "get your ass over here and when we bring the cows back, open the gate and let them in. Don't let the other cows out either, by God."

The herd had been gathered in a group at the mouth of the corral when Wilbur came galloping up on his horse. The penned up cows stirred and Patty hesitated. Should she open the gate now or not? She made a decision and gallantly flung open the gate. The inside cows ran into the outside cows and the whole herd was loose.

Now Wilbur let Patty have it. "Damn you woman, you let 'em all out. I could kick your ass."

Quick as a fox, Patty yelled back, "You'd shit too," and she climbed into the truck with me. I tried to apologize to her for Wilbur's words and explained to her that he was just too upset to know what he'd said.

"Piss on him," Patty said, "That son-of-a-bitch don't bother me none."

We once again went back out and herded the cows, headed for the corral, and in they went. Patty said to me, "Jimmie, you're so cool." After all, they were Wilbur's cows, I thought to myself.

Patty was the head cook at the Saturday sale barn and Wilbur worked out back sorting cattle and hogs. Both jobs were tough. Wilbur had a restless nature and after the sale he wanted to hurry home to chore.

"Come on, Patty," he'd urge, "let's go."

"I've got to clean up the counter and grill first before I can leave," she civilly answered back.

Wilbur left the kitchen, paced around the arena, and when he soon enough returned, he insisted to Patty that she quit scrubbing to leave with him.

"If you don't hurry up," Wilbur told her, "I'll tell everyone here we had sex before we were married."

"Go ahead," Patty shot back, "but don't tell them you were first 'cause that would be a lie." Wilbur's ears turned crimson red. He walked out, and without saying another word, waited patiently in his pickup for Patty to finish.

51
WHERE IS
BILLY?

Before the mass exodus of the small-acreage farmer, neighbors helped neighbors. Every country mile was dotted with 40 to 50-acre plots and farm families lived on each one. A farmer could spread the word he had hogs or cattle to work and five to ten neighbors would show up to help. After the work was done, refreshments were served. A certain amount of orneriness livened up the work and was made a part of the occasion.

Mason Township, ten miles west of Bedford, was one of the liveliest neighborhoods of that time. The neighborhood was made up of, to name a few, Herman O'Dell, Wilbur Novinger, Merle Travis, Vern Timberlake, Doyle Cooper, Dale Ingram, Dewey Morehouse, Cobron Payne, R.D. Timberlake, Carl Cummings, Leslie Yearous, and Alvin Pershing. Most of these men owned well-bred, big wrangler horses that they used to farm. The horses and the farmers were about the same, in stature and disposition.

One afternoon, the neighbors got together to work cattle at the Dewey Morehouse place. Of the group, Dewey was probably the most timid. He was somewhat tongue-tied and when he spoke he was difficult to understand. Dewey's herd consisted of 50 Shorthorn cows who were wild and nervous and that day, he had them crowded into a small barn. Dr. Anderson, the attending vet, set the chute at a small door on the south side of the barn. My uncle, Herman O'Dell, and Alvin Pershing crawled inside the barn. Their task was to chase the cows in to the chute. The cows were very worked up from the noise and the yelling going on and the pair of men weren't having much luck performing their job. As a matter of fact, they were becoming a little bored with the whole thing. Uncle Herman spotted an old set of bed springs tied in the rafters, right above the cows and he yelled, "Cut down the bed springs!"

"Oh, hell, no!" answered Alvin.

"If you won't, then I will," Herman shot back.

With the help of a reluctant Alvin, the two cut down the springs. When they fell from the rafters, the springs landed on top of the backs of the packed-in cows and bounced up and down. The cows bellowed and bucked in an attempt to get out from under the coiled metal. The whole herd had turned in to a bunch of Tasmanian Devils and when a herd of cows starts to push, it can move a mountain. The cows leaned up against the side of the barn until it collapsed. The cows ran out of there as fast as they could and the neighbor's work was done for the day.

All Dewey could say was "By dawd, da tows dot oht!"

One of the neighbors purchased an old Billy Goat at the sale barn one Saturday. Billy Goats were the stuff legends were made of. They enjoyed urinating on their whiskers and face and most had huge curving horns. Basically, Billy Goats were ugly and stinking beasts. You could tell by the smell if you were within 50 yards of one. Best of all, when you were least expecting it, a Billy would lower its head and butt you in the rear. Early one morning, Wilbur Novinger walked out of his house to a terrible odor. There stood old Billy, tied in his yard.

Novinger was having no part of that goat and when night fell, Billy was passed to a neighbor, who passed him on to another neighbor until Billy had made the rounds. Not one word was ever spoken about the goat or its travels. Eventually, Billy ended up on my Uncle Herman's doorstep and from there he disappeared, never to be smelled again.

A few months later, the O'Dell's invited everyone to a neighborhood get together. There was food and music and the usual good time. For the first time, the subject of Billy came up. Carl Cummings read this poem written by Doris O'Dell.

The Truth Will Out

Listen, ye children, lend me your ears
For this is a story you'll all want to hear,
Concerning a gang of six lads and six gals
That all loved to play good jokes on their pals.

The fun all began one day at a sale—
The livestock they auctioned would make you turn pale
The auctioneer cried till his throat it was sore
To get just four bits—no less and no more.

"She's sold!" he cried gaily, "just tell me who took'er"
"Why" said two young laddies "she goes to Doyle Cooper"
Doyle stoutly protested, "That goat I'll not take,
Let's take 'er over to Bill Timberlake."

But Bill must have heard of that cute little plan
'Cause they changed their ideas and got a new man
A man who had just bought some sheep, as you know
And built them a shed to keep out the snow.

"Now that's just the place," they said, "all is well"
"We'll just take 'er over to Herman O'Dell."
So they threw a big party at Maxine's and Murphy's
While Wilbur delivered the goat in a hurry.

And then came a new little kink in the fun,
For Lester O'Dell started out with his gun
He had seen something huge with the first of his glances
And said to himself, "I am taking no chances."

The next morning came, as sure as you're born,
And with it came Murphy to sell us seed corn
Then Wilbur came down—I don't know what for—
They stayed and they waited and then stayed some more.

But never a word had come from the throat
Of the boy who, supposedly, had a new goat.
"Did your goat come home, Wilbur?" Dad finally said
(And I'm here to tell you two faces turned red!)

The story from there is a matter of history.
The goat's whereabouts has been quite a mystery
I've heard they have searched the whole county o'er
And just about canvassed from door to door.

Perhaps, they all figured, she's hunted new ground
But nowhere, oh nowhere could Billie be found.
They've asked and they've wondered and looked till they're
weary
But always decided they had the wrong theory.

And I think they did, for old Nanny's been thriving
A few miles away where she's found a good living
She must have been put there by ghosties or witches
But tell me dear friends, DO YOU LIKE GOAT SANDWICHES?

Consternation reigned! And even more so when Doyle was awarded the booby prize of goat horns.

Many years had passed by when I drove on the wandering roads where old neighborhoods and neighbors used to be. There were but a few of the old family farms left and even fewer young farmers trying to make a start. Around the turn of the century, Taylor County had a population of 25,000 people. Now as the century is ready to turn again, the population has stalled at 6,700. The small farms were displaced by large landowners and the farm families had to go, never to return.

52
THE D.V.M. OR
M.D.? THE M.D.
OR D.V.M.?

This was one big fiasco for such a small community. But then, statistics showed that it only took six people before a common thread was found.

Dr. Janson was a veterinarian colleague from the small town of Gravity. In Bedford, there was a Dr. Hardin, the M.D., who ran a solo practice. When Doc Hardin was out of the office, he referred his patients to Dr. Jensen, M.D. practicing in the neighboring town of Clarinda.

Dr. Anderson, my DVM. partner, and I were sitting around one day, shooting the bull. Seymour Straight walked into our clinic. Dr. Anderson and I kept talking, right through Seymour's stone silence. Finally Dr. Anderson asked, "Anything we can help you with, Seymour?"

"Well, by dab, there is," he answered.

"What's the problem?" Doc asked.

"Well, by golly, it's my wife, Jenny," he said.

"Oh?" Doc responded with question in his voice.

"Yep, she's constipated alright. And that ain't all. She's got blood in her urine and sometimes some yellow pus. Boy does she squeal when she tries to go to the bathroom," Seymour kept on in vivid description.

Doc Anderson and I were on the edge of our seats wondering

what was coming next. "Why in the devil are you telling us about your wife's problems? We are veterinarians, not doctors," Doc proclaimed.

"Well, by dab," Seymour said slowly, "I went up to Doc Hardin's office. He was gone and had a sign on his door to go see Doc Jensen. I figured it was closer to come down here instead of driving all the way to Gravity. So I just came down here." We explained the mix-up to Seymour and sent him on his way to Clarinda to see Dr. Jensen, M.D.

It was not unusual for Doc Anderson and I to get asked about a human health problem. One lady came in and told us about a sore her husband had. She wanted some sulfa salve to treat him and when I asked her why she didn't see her doctor she told me, "Because, that Doc charges an office call and you don't."

Doc Anderson and I laughed and told her we could not legally dispense sulfa for her husband's sores. In just a little while, she came back into the office and told us she had a horse with a cut and wondered if she could buy some sulfa salve. We sold it to her.

At the clinic, we had a husband and wife for clients whom we nicknamed the Jack Sprat pair. Of the couple, the wife was as obese as the husband was skinny. One day the wife came in to the office and asked, "Do you have something for my husband's jock itch?"

"We don't dispense medicines for humans," I told her, "but I know I can trust you. Try this." A week later, I happened to run into her husband. I couldn't help myself when I asked, "Did that medicine clear up your jock itch?"

"Did my wife tell you that was for me?" he asked with a tilt of his head.

"Why, yes she did," I answered.

"Well damn her, that medicine was for her. It must be potent, 'cause she had a big area to cover, and it cleared up right away," the man blurted out in laughter.

A Clarinda M.D. by the name of Johnson owned a herd of swine he kept just west of town. One farrowing season, one of his sows delivered five ruptured piglets. Instead of calling a vet, Dr. Johnson decided he could do the required surgery himself. He took his tray of sterile instruments, very carefully anesthetized the pigs, did a sterile prep, and surgically repaired the ruptures. All five of the piglets died. He never understood it.

I wasn't sure what had gone wrong either after he had explained his meticulous preparation and surgery. My professional theory was the surgery shock was just too much for the piglets to handle. What I told Dr. Johnson was that the pigs succumbed from the sterile environment. They were just way too clean.

53
SMART
DOGS

Just how smart could dogs be? I tried to figure that out most of my life. Dogs could associate words with action. They must be smarter than human beings. Dogs chased cars, were lazy, and barked all night. They were the dumbest animals on earth. One thing I knew for certain, as companions, dogs had unfailing faith.

I owned a hunting dog, Duchess. She was housebroken and followed the rules when we let her inside. On a hunt, she was as bullheaded as any dog I'd ever seen. She had trouble following my directions. I lost my temper with Duchess on one particular prowl. I gently kicked her, pulled her ears and spanked her hard to get her attention. She hunted pretty well the rest of the day.

When I returned home from work on the very next day, I found a hole in the screen door. I stormed inside in search of the dog, as it was her unmistakable mark left in the screen. Duchess could normally be found in the middle of the living room. I did not find her there. Instead I found what she'd left, a big pile of feces.

Duchess was hiding in her doghouse. She was in it, more than one way. I figured what had happened. She dug her way through the screen door to get into the house. From there, she proceeded to the living room, waited for nature to call, and crapped on the carpet. She exited through the same hole back to the doghouse. In her mind, she was even with me, for the scolding I had given her just the day before.

Our kids had a German Shepherd dog named Princess. I spayed her myself when she was a puppy and mistakenly left behind part of one ovary. Consequently, she came into heat every six months. Every free running male dog in the neighborhood scurried to our house when Princess called. When I had enough, I injected Princess with a drug that kept her neutral. She acted like a big baby from the pain caused by the hypodermic. All I had to do was mention the word "shot" and Princess hunkered down and looked for a place to hide.

Farris and Patsy Gray were good friends and clients. They owned two dogs, a beautiful black and white Border Collie named Sarge and a little mixed Poodle, Muggins. Sarge had few health problems and I only saw him annually, for his booster shots. Muggins, on the other hand, had an ongoing medical problem. Her anal glands plugged. Anal glands were like a human's appendix in that they weren't necessary for life. Once they were plugged, they could become infected. Muggins needed to be expressed two to three times a year. She hated the vet clinic. She hated me.

On a beautiful late spring day, the Grays hosted a fund-raising supper to support the high school's American Foreign Exchange Student program. My wife and I were invited to attend. Fifty guest chairs sat in a big circle. I had been hovering around the refreshment area and was one of the last persons to take my seat. My lap held a filled food plate. Muggins took her place in the middle of the circle and pranced around as if she were the entertainment. Then she saw me. Muggins sat down in front of my feet and barked and barked, and barked some more. She let the entire crowd know her opinion of me. The crowd found the display amusing. If only Muggins had known me on a personal level, I sighed to myself.

After the program, Farris and I chuckled over Muggins antics. He said, "Did you know that old Sarge always chases your truck when you drive by?"

"Yep," I said, "I've seen him. He goes round and round chasing his tail until I get close and then he chases me down the road."

"Well, Doc, you are the only one that Sarge chases. I suppose that means that Muggins and he have discussed you and they stick together with their assessment," Farris concluded.

"It's nice to be so loved," I said.

There was one known fact about canines that didn't apply to

any other animal species. It was instinctive for animals to go to the rescue of their young or the young of their own species. Only dogs would go to the rescue of man.

My Uncle Ralph and Aunt Vadonna lived on a farm where they milked cows and tended a few old sows. Ralph was milking the cows when his 4 year-old son, Richard, decided to go watch. Richard didn't know that an old Hampshire sow had a litter of piglets. He ran right by the sow on the way to the barn. Forever protective, the sow took off after Richard, knocked him over and attacked him. The family dog, a little Rat Terrier named Prince, went to the rescue. The dog grabbed the sow by the hock, growled and barked and distracted her. Richard got up and ran to the safety of the barn. From then on, Prince was a treasured part of the family.

Years ago, my father-in-law, H.K. Russell, had a stray dog come to his house. H.K. tried and tried to find a home for it but had no success. One day H.K. needed to make a road trip to Nebraska and he decided to take the dog along. After he crossed the Missouri River, H.K. opened the trunk and dumped the dog out. H.K. drove away. Five days later, the old hound reappeared on H.K.'s porch. The dog had made a 120-mile trip to return home to a master who was much less loyal than he. I always wondered how he crossed the Missouri river.

Dr. Mark Emmerson, one of the worst professors I ever had, taught obstetrics at the university. He stood for an hour in the front of the classroom and read his entire lecture. One time, he read the same lecture he had read the day before. I slept through it.

Dr. Emmerson got off track only once, I remember. He told us he knew for a fact that a dog could smell at least five miles.

Emmerson owned one male and one female dog. When the female came into heat, he hauled her five miles to his brother's farm to keep the two separated. He and his brother put the female up in the haymow for her own good. Well, the male dog ran that five-mile distance, climbed up into the haymow and bred the female. That was Emmerson's case for a dog's ability to smell for five miles.

I had no trouble remembering Dr. Emmerson's obstetrics final exam. While group studying, I was handed the answers to a final that had been written in 1940. I thought the exam was a good review and I memorized it. I aced the exam. The 1940 test and the one I took were exactly the same.

Some people were as lazy as dogs.

54
SEX
AND ANIMALS

Sex, and its impact on the daily lives of humans, animals and birds, can never be underestimated. Vocabularies, customs and rituals, mannerisms, populations and seasons revolved around breeding.

Farmers had single word descriptions for their animals when they were showing heat or estrus. When a mare was coming into heat, farmers said she was horsing. When a cow came in, she was bulling. A sow ready to mate was boaring while a ewe was ramming. The words couldn't have been more appropriate. The expression fit the pattern of nature perfectly, and suited the brevity farmers were famous for.

Doc Anderson and I about cracked a rib laughing on the day Clarence Sleep came in to talk about his ewes.

Clarence said, "I never seen the likes at what I see'd this morning. I went out to check my "yos" and they were all a bucking." Doc Anderson and I weren't sure if Clarence meant the ewes were literally jumping up and down or if they were coming into heat. Some farmers did not fit the norm and confused one animal's sex act with another.

Jap Lyom was a character in his time. For a living, he bought and traded livestock to small farmers. Jap had a reputation of buying problem animals and then reselling them and the problem to an unsuspecting person. He once sold a bull to an old widow woman. It wasn't long after when his phone rang.

The widow said, "Jap, that bull is sucking the cows."

Jap asked her, "Isn't that what you bought him for?"

"Damn you, I said he is *sucking* the cows," the woman yelled.

I once provided a cow breeding artificial insemination service. Pam Calfee, a local farmer's wife, was instructed by her husband to schedule me for his herd. Pam worked at the bank and she waited for me to show up there to make the appointment. The bank was full of customers and Pam was not sure how to word her husband's request in the middle of a mixed crowd. She winked as she said to me, "We have a cow acting strange."

"Oh, really," I joked with her, "I have a wife like that!"

Everyone in the bank's lobby and I knew what Pam was talking about. That only made matters worse for her. Pam was red in the face and said, "Oh, you know what I mean." I was enjoying the game and answered her, "I'm not sure I do."

"Darn it Doc," Pam impatiently said, " my husband wants you to breed her."

"Oh! Now we are getting somewhere," I said. "You mean he wants her artificially inseminated?"

Pam wished she'd thought of those two little words and saved herself all that embarrassment.

A client of mine, Roger Brummett, had a stallion that was getting old and was crippled in one front and one rear leg. I had three mares to mate so Roger and I reached an agreement. I would bring my mares to his stallion for pasture breeding. The stallion was surely not incapacitated in matters of the heart.

I loaded my mares and pulled up to the pasture gate. From a distance, I saw a feeble looking specimen of a horse plodding up a small hill. The horse could hardly move, suffering as he did from depression and pain. First he hobbled on the back leg and then on the front.

"My Lord," I said to the mares, "that critter is ready for the bone pile." I wondered what I had been thinking as I unloaded my horses. One of them gave a whinny.

The stallion raised his head, took one look at those mares and stood straight up. With a proud arch in his neck and head he turned into a canter. Once again, he was a beautiful show horse without a wish of a limp.

No more beautiful word had ever been spoken than that mare's whinny.

55

BAD-ASS DOC

I was not always a hero nor was I perfect. What I was, I discovered, was a sun person. Lack of sunshine changed my mood in a hurry. When the surliness arrived, I merely had to count the number of days it had been since the clouds got in the way.

I had purchased a set of portable corrals strictly for the benefit of my clients. If my customers needed them, the corrals were there to loan for free. I even bought a new trailer to carry them away on. I wondered, at times, if the corrals and trailer would be returned considering the absence of a deposit or fee. One day, John Garfield asked to borrow the set. I was in an exceptionally bad mood and while I agreed to let him use the corral, I refused to loan him the trailer. Based on nothing but air, I somehow felt he would keep the trailer longer than I wanted.

"Yes," I had said to him when loaning him the corrals, "but I can't let you have the new trailer."

John thought for a minute and asked hesitantly, "Would you let me borrow all ten panels?"

My stubbornness was persistent. "Yes!" I snapped, "but how in the world do you intend to carry them?"

John drove his old automobile around the back and loaded the ten corral panels on top, tying them on with baling wire. If that wasn't a funny looking sight! He fired up the compact car and away he went. John made it to the edge of town before he hit a chuckhole. All ten panels flew off the Datsun's roof. Patiently, he loaded the panels back on top of his car, securely retied them, and away he went for the second time. In a very short while he returned the panels, carefully hauling them back to town within the confines of a stock trailer. John was very nice about the whole affair. So nice, in fact, I felt he was owed an apology.

"Dang, John, I am sorry for the trouble I caused you. If I'd let you take the trailer, you wouldn't have had that much work. I'm really sorry," I said frankly.

"I never much thought about it," John replied in his slow Missouri way. I knew he was sincere.

There were countless things and a variety of places that would set me off. Phil Dwinell was a client of mine who ran a herd of wild Charolais cattle. He called me to check a cow, in his opinion, that was a little off. Phil had a head catch in his barn, but that day the Charolais refused to be driven in. When I arrived, I tried to help but the cow kept running around both of us. After several more fumbled attempts, I was disgusted. It was my immediate notion that Phil had purposely placed me in that time-wasting situation one too many times. Still, we had to keep trying.

Phil positioned himself on one side of the barn and I manned the other. The cow was really getting nervous and she put her head over the top fence board as if she wanted to jump out. I looked over my shoulder to see if Phil was watching. He was looking the other way when I kicked the cow in the butt and made her jump over the fence and run for the pasture.

I met Phil on the other side of the barn and told him innocently, "That rip jumped out!"

"Well," Phil said, "I'll have to get her in the barn myself next time."

"Yep," I replied, "that would be best." My mood had turned me into a liar but I was very pleased I didn't have to pasture chase the cow that day.

Thelbert and Chester Kendrick were brothers. Each one lived separately on the land their heirs had homesteaded. The ancestral soil was the poorest crop production land in the county. Their farms were scarred with humps and hills created and left behind during the coal mining days of the 1940s. The boys were good fellows and never got overly excited about anything. Thelbert had a habit of ending every sentence with a phrase. His 'so it did,' 'so it is,' 'so you did,' or 'so I did' tickled me, so it did. The Kendrick brothers each owned a herd of Hereford cows.

I was called to vaccinate and castrate the Kendrick herd's calves. The calves had been penned in the barn and were ready for the vet. Donnie and I set the cattle chute and it was with apprehension that we began working. The rain that was falling was the product of an isolated thunderstorm, typical for Iowa. The rapidly developed storm carried the risk of lightning, high winds, torrential rain, and tornadoes. I never liked working inside a metal chute when lightning was part of the weather prediction. I hoped Thelbert's two boys could help so we could finish before the storm's fury was unleashed. My hopes were dashed when Thelbert told me his boys were afraid of the cattle.

I was left to plead with Thelbert. "Please hurry," I said to him, "we have to try to beat this storm."

Sensing the storm itself, one of the bellowing calves became unruly and began chasing the frightened boys. My temper was short and it got shorter by the second. I grabbed a two-by-four and went after the calf. The calf turned on me and tried to give me a butt. I stepped back, loaded the two-by-four and popped the calf on the top of its head. I knocked the calf out cold.

"I believe you've killed him, so you did," said Thelbert. The longer the calf lay there, the more I began to think I had bought him. Still a little groggy from the board, the calf finally got back on its feet. I took advantage of its diminished capacity and headed it toward the chute. The calf was powerless to alter his course and went right in.

The storm was coming nearer and nearer when we began working a second calf. Donnie, my helper, held a tail while I castrated. In an instant, a big flash and then a boom came from out of the sky. The second flash seen was Donnie and me crawling into the barn. The barn didn't offer much protection but it was a darn sight better than hanging onto a metal chute and a calf. The wind blew the rain our way, and we were drenched. I was still trembling from the bolt of lightning but I was alive, and so was the calf, so he was.

I dished it at times but I could take it too, except in certain circumstances. I handled face-to-face criticism well but I had an extreme dislike for belittlement that occurred behind my back. My mood was a little on the black side one afternoon after I had just returned to the office from a very tough OB call. Julie, my secretary, was on the listening side of some nasty verbal abuse that was delivered over the phone by Burt Yanda, a client. I knew Burt's bark was worse than his bite but Julie didn't know him like I did. On top of being clouded in black, I was now irritated.

The problem between Burt and I began when he called about a cow calving. I had driven like hell to get there in time and Burt met me at the farm gate.

"Doc, that old cow done went ahead and had her calf so I didn't need ya' furtha but since youins have your catching contraption with you I'd like for you to mouth a cow and tell me how old she is," Burt told me.

I drove down in the hole where Burt's little barn sat. The barn gate was about eight feet wide and I had difficulty backing up the chute against the barn door. It took several attempts to get the chute even close. I got out of the truck and said to Burt, jokingly, "The next time I'm down here I'll bring my chain saw and make that gate wider." He didn't respond.

Burt's old cow chased several hens out of the barn before she climbed in my chute. There were two steps required in mouthing a cow. First I had to count the number of front teeth she had and then 'guesstimate' her age by the amount of wear on the teeth that remained. When a cow's teeth were really short and worn down, accuracy was impossible. This cow of Burt's was anywhere from ten to twenty years old. I explained to Burt why I couldn't be exact. Burt wasn't happy with my explanation and bluntly told me he didn't know any more than he did before I started. I pulled out my chute and handed Burt an invoice for $30 for the call. He thought he had been robbed! The cow had already calved and didn't need any help from me, I couldn't tell him how old she was, and what was the $30 for anyway!

I doubled up on my error and called Burt on the phone. I told him I was unhappy with his attitude and from then on, he could call another vet and I hung up on him. Shortly thereafter I received a letter in the mail from Burt. The letter was a classic and I realized then what a caring individual Burt really was. I had jumped the gun and felt badly enough that I drove to Burt's place to talk it out with him. We had a lively discussion that concluded in the agreement that we both could forgive and forget the incident. We did just that Here is a copy of the letter.

To Jim

I am sorry of what I said. But you have said thing I sure never like enoughter.

I didn't like what you said about bring your chain saw down and sawing my gate down, the gate I made.

And about you coming down on a Saturday and I Pauline was the one you called back and told you not to come on as the reason was they had doun pulleb the calf and seen on reason for you to come on doun. Afther her calf was hear I did say I hate when you came down and look at the cows mouth and he he didn't hear you say what. And he did know any more about the cows mouth when you left as before you came.

P.S. I all righty have a veterinary clinic and I think he propley be a good veterinary.

You have to do what you have to do and I have to do what I have to do.

Theres only one thing for sure. We have to died in our live. I will have to die and you will have to die sometime all do. But God knows on that when he call.

For sure we all have to die sometime in life.

Allso some people say thing and only what they make out of thing is the why it told back and then thing get in a bad as you say bad mouth.

If you think the our way I am quite sure I'll make out just fine. We I way was going to pay you that day but you never mape it on doun hear where c very you where at as the cow done had calf pulleb or you where ni coming any so much for this. Sending you check in this letter.

From: Burt

56

HOW TO
CUT A CAT

I had a client named Steph Parman who was really ornery. One day I met up with her in a crowded grocery store. She yelled, "Hey, Doc, what are you doing?"

"Oh, I'm just picking up a few groceries," I said.

"Well, how's it hanging anyway?" she blurted out.

I felt my face flush and turn twenty shades of crimson. I tried to hide myself in the narrow aisles.

"What's the matter, Doc, can't you get it up anymore?" Steph continued undeterred.

I normally had rapid comebacks in my repertoire but Steph had left me speechless. I was down right afraid to answer her.

Two or three weeks later, Steph brought some pups to the clinic to be castrated and de-tailed. With the surgery finished, I placed the leftover tails and testicles inside of a cardboard box, wrapped the box neatly, and had it hand delivered to the bank where she worked. Inside the package, I placed a note that said, "Shame on you, meany."

I heard through the grapevine the note had left Steph speechless. She did not mention it to me for a very long time.

Steph's husband, Dale, asked me one day, "How much does it cost to castrate a tom cat?"

I told him it depended upon the method that was used.

"What do you mean?" he asked.

I explained, "If I use anesthesia, castration costs $20, if I don't use it, it's only $5."

Dale brought the cat. I held it down, and my partner, Jim Johnson, castrated it in about five seconds.

Case closed for the cat, I thought. He wouldn't be subjected to Steph's embarrassing grocery store question.

57
IT'S BEEN
ONE HECTIC DAY

I had my own definition of a hectic day at the office. It was when the shit hit the fan. I often suspected there was a hectic monster who crouched down, hid and waited patiently at the fan's on/off switch. When I was in a weakened condition, at the point my nervous system had collapsed, the monster tweaked the switch a little to the right. When I was the most vulnerable to surprise, the monster flipped the fan's switch to the highest position. I had developed a tremor in my left hand doctors diagnosed as "essential tremor" or the early stages of Parkinson's Disease. The hectic monster had me at a disadvantage.

I was rousted out at 5 a.m. to help an early calving heifer that was having a very difficult time. I tranquilized the heifer to get the calf and at the end of it all, the heifer threw out her uterus. I was relieved, a few hours later, when I got everything put back together. I drove back to town and stopped at the clinic. Parked outside in the drive were five trucks. Goosebumps shot down my arm as I thought of the pressure of handling all of those customers at the same time.

I puffed out my chest in bravery and walked inside. Julie, the office assistant, was in the back fetching some milk replacer for one of the customers. I glanced at the clientele before I headed toward the ringing phone and what I saw frightened me. I didn't see a friendly face among them. Marvin Sleep blocked my path and yelled, "You're late for work, Doc." I shuddered as I thought about how much I hated the sound of that old broken record statement. I answered the phone.

It was Mrs. Weil, an older lady who thought I was the greatest vet that ever lived. And, her dogs and cats thought so too. Mrs. Weil told me her blood pressure was high, what her doctor had said about it, and what medication she was prescribed. I didn't tell her that my blood pressure was rising by the minute. Mrs. Weil then told me the history of her 17-year-old dog named Queenie, the depth of her grandson's love for the dog and how neither of them could bear the thought of ever losing it.

"It is inevitable the old dog will die," I told her rather unsympathetically, "you had better prepare your grandson for the worst."

Nervous Marvin paced the floor, going from one room to another. He pestered Julie with questions. "I have a sick calf," Marvin told her, "should I give it some liquid sulfur or 'commonbiotics'?"

Julie told him he'd better wait until I got off the phone. I was only half listening to Mrs. Weil by now. Finally I convinced her to bring the dog to the clinic and I hung up.

"How can I help you, Marvin?" I turned and asked.

Marvin spun around on a dime and walked over to look in the cooler. He said, "I gotta sick calf. Should I give him some liquid myacin or some of that dog stuff? Should I give all the calves some coccidiosis medicine in the feed?" The questions kept coming in rapid fire and I nary had time to answer any of them.

The clinic door opened and in walked Mrs. Rauch. By the way, her last name suited her to a T. Accompanying Mrs. Rauch were her five infamous ill-mannered kids with their dog, Laddy.

"God, it stinks in here," Mrs. Rauch said in greeting.

"All vet clinics smell this way," one of the kids said.

"What's this stuff. You sure have a lot of stuff," another piped in.

"You kids shut up!" Mrs. Rauch commanded. "Can I talk to you Doc about our collie dog?"

I knew the dog and it was the best mannered of the whole lot of them. I answered her, "Yes, but I have to take care of this man first. Why don't you take your dog and the kids into the surgery room and I'll be right with you." I answered most of Marvin's questions, gave him what he wanted and sent him on his way.

Now I could plainly hear all the filthy talk coming from the surgery room. The kids were peppering their mom with questions. I walked back with trepidation. "This is free, ain't it?" shouted one of the loudmouthed kids as he helped himself to a pop from the cooler.

"Yes, I guess it is," I said with lips pursed, "Now, what is Laddy's problem?"

"Laddy can't shit," shouted Ramon. Mrs. Rauch ordered Ramon to watch his mouth.

I lifted the dog's tail to take a look and as I did so, my left arm began trembling. The oldest boy yelled, "My god, Mom, look at him shake! I'd hate to have him cuttin' on me."

I could have killed the little bastard of a kid on the spot. "The problem with your dog, Mrs. Rauch, is he is not being groomed. Fecal matter has dried in the long hair around the rectum and it is acting like a cork. The dog can't defecate," I explained knowing I didn't have time to groom the poor animal.

"What's defecate?" yelled a kid.

"In your book, kid, it's shit," I said. "And," I told Mrs. Rauch, "I think it would be a good job for your son there to brush the dog clean."

"OK," Mrs. Rauch said. "How much will that be?"

I told her the fee was $10. To which she replied, "I left my checkbook at home. I'll stop back one of these days." I had no hope of ever seeing the $10. "No wonder vets are so rich," Ramon added as he looked up at me in a disgusting way. I'd have forgiven the $10 fee if it meant I never had to see that group again.

The five bratty kids were barely out the door when Alberta Cornell charged in, carrying a dead hen in her hand. Alberta was one of the hill people who lived close to the Missouri State Line. She was so ugly she could stop a train. Alberta was aware of her bad looks and in an attempt at beautification, wore rouge and big dangly earrings. She must have forgotten to do her hair that day and it stuck out every which way. There was no doubt she had skipped her bath as well. Alberta liked me very much and she constantly flirted. She tried to rub elbows but I was too fast for her. From time to time I would run into her at farm sales where she was forever running up and grabbing my arm. I'd jerk away as fast as I could, hoping all the while no one had witnessed her affection.

"What's the problem today, Alberta?" I asked.

"Oh, our goddamned chickens are dying," she said.

I lifted the dead hen off the table where she had placed it and began to look it over. The hen's feathers were burnt and I asked Alberta why.

She spun around and said, "That goddamned Calvin threw her in the wood-burning cook stove to try to get rid of the carcass. I told Calvin I wanted the hen posted, so he dug her out."

The mental image tickled me so I asked, "Did the burnt feathers smell?"

"Oh, hell yes," Alberta answered, "it stunk up the whole damned house."

Hmm, I thought to myself, that must have been an improvement. "I'll post the hen," I told her. "I'll get some gloves and my posting knife." I looked and looked for the knife but couldn't lay my hands on it.

"I've got a knife out in the car," Alberta offered.

"No, that's OK. I'll find mine," I said as I kept on searching.

"Oh, shit, I'll go get mine," she said and out the door she went.

Julie had been watching and she rolled her eyes at me. Alberta flew back through the door, knife in hand, and said, "Here's mine and be careful, you could cut your f——— throat with this one." She handed me the oldest, most jagged edge butcher knife I'd ever seen and it was as dull as a post.

Julie saved the day and found my knife for me. I proceeded to post the hen and when I opened its craw and stomach all I found was weed seed and straw. "What are you feeding your hens?" I asked Alberta.

"The sons-of-bitches just eat what they can find," she told me.

"Well, that's got to change. This hen has literally starved to death. You'll have to feed your hens grain. I'll send you home with some high nutrition vitamin supplements and you'd better get some grain," I prescribed.

"I been telling that god-damned Calvin we needed to feed them better," Alberta said in her loud voice. "It's his fault."

I discovered another of Alberta's endearing qualities as she was paying the bill. Alberta pulled out her checkbook and had Julie fill in the amount section which, in a small town, was not that uncommon of an event. Alberta then very carefully studied her name on the pre-addressed checks. She copied it in block print as close as she could. Alberta couldn't even sign her own name. She couldn't read or write.

The phone rang again and again that hectic day. Julie handled the calls as I suddenly remembered I had an appointment in the country. I yelled to Julie over my shoulder, "I'm out of here. I'm not sure where to, but, I'm outta here."

Outdoors the birds were singing, my old Ford truck was chugging and the frogs croaked. The gentle breeze whispered a quiet melody. The hectic monster had turned the shit-blowing fan switch to off and returned, for the time being, to his hiding place.

58

HUNGRY

COW

Back in the 1970's, after two back-to-back years of dry weather, Southern Iowa was hit harder from the drought than the rest of the state, or maybe it just seemed that way. We watched the corn and soybean crops wither before our eyes. Green pastures turned brown and quit producing new shoots. Cows had to be kept in those parched pastures. The herd nibbled away at the remains until the grass was grubbed into the ground. The land, the animals and the farmers awaited rejuvenating rainfall.

There were two obvious choices for cattle farmers caught in the middle. They either sold their herds at a reduced price or bought feed for them. Either choice was an economic hardship. While waiting for rain, some indecisive farmers unintentionally starved their herds to death.

A farmer didn't like to hear his cows had starved. He was more likely to believe there was some exotic disease at work. I performed many post mortems during those two years and when I told the farmer the cause of death was starvation, he typically got angry and called another vet. I should have put it to him this way, *the cow died of chronic idiopathic progressive malnutritional hypophagia of environmental origin,* the scientific description of starvation.

I wasn't in a hurry the day I headed back to the clinic after one of those fruitless calls. I looked over the burnt countryside and didn't see a very pretty sight. The pastures were so barren you could have easily sighted a golf ball if it had been driven on any part of the ground. I saw a small group of cows under a tree, gathering what little bit of shade there was. One cow walked out of the pack and stopped to look at a big old withered bull thistle. I said to myself, "Now, she won't eat that bristly old thistle, will she? Naw, she couldn't." That old cow started ripping away at that thistle like it was her last meal. She chewed and chewed until she forced it down her throat. She took another bite, chewed and swallowed until the thistle was gone. Now, that old cow was a hungry one.

Farmers had it just as bad in the years that the weather was too wet. There was ample grass for cows, but the grass was washy and had less food value. In the winter, the abundant baled grasses were low in nutrition. Cows starved to death then, too, if the bales weren't supplemented with purchased feed. It was a slower process than that caused by drought but the result was the same.

Good and bad times were a roll of the dice in farming. There were some years when animals, farmers and vets all got hungry together.

59
1980'S
FARM CRISIS

During the farm crisis in the early 80's, a Des Moines news correspondent wrote, "Southern Iowa farmers can withstand the hard times better than Northern Iowa farmers because Southern Iowa farmers are used to being poor." The statement angered me, until I saw the truth in it.

The farm crisis was not a happy time. It became extremely difficult to find anything to laugh about. Young farmers' dreams of owning a farm, raising the kids on it and becoming solid community members were shattered. I was close to many farmers during the crisis, both personally and professionally. I had people break down and cry on my shoulder. I was their leaning post.

One day I was headed to the local coffee shop for a cup when I met a client in the parking lot. He threw his arms around me and cried like a baby while telling me his woes. I took him back to my office where we talked and he unloaded some weight off his shoulders. After he finished, he sat there in my chair the rest of the afternoon, staring at the walls.

There were divorces, murders, bankruptcies and suicides. The crisis made thieves and cheats out of honest people. One of my clients owed around $700. He told me, "Doc, I am not going to pay you but I have a cow and her calf in my corral. If you want the cow, go get her."

I called my wife and told her to be ready. We were going to steal a cow.

"Say what?" she asked.

"We are going to get a cow that was given to me," I said, even though I was pretty sure the cow was mortgaged at the bank.

Another client sold nine cows at the sale barn in my name to settle his bill. I never asked questions.

Farmers hid money, machinery and personal items. When they had to leave the farm forever, they had the shirt on their back and anything they could hide.

60
GOOD OL'
MOM

For the first years of my veterinary practice, my wife Kay was my secretary. As the years went by and our four kids were born, the pressure of being a mom and secretary was too much. Kay needed relief.

My good mom, Dorothy, consented to become my secretary. She learned the job rapidly and became very proficient. She worked cheap.

When Mom came to work for me, Dad and I were partners in the family farm. Jerry Baker was the man we hired to do the farm work for us. While Mom never told me how to run the veterinary business, she had a lot to say about the farm partnership, especially when it came to Jerry. She wanted to make sure he was kept busy.

On a particularly slow day at the vet clinic, several of my friends and clients saw my truck parked outside. It was as if the café sign was hung. Five or six of them joined me for coffee and a bull session. Jerry happened to stop in as well.

As the conversation continued, Jerry became tired of standing. He slid under the counter and sat on the floor. Mom was working hard that day and ignored most of the comings and goings. She heard the door slam and assumed Jerry had left. She knew he had work to do at the farm.

Somehow the subject of hired hands came to be the topic. That picked up Mother's ears and she said, "I'm glad Jerry left to get back to the farm." I tried to make hand signs to tell Mom that

Jerry was still in the office. She ignored me. She spoke again, "He surely has more to do than loaf around here." And then she concluded with, "The little bastard isn't worth his salt."

"Mom!" I exclaimed and pointed down.

"Oh, he's not here … is he?" she inquired.

I pointed down again. Mom was beside herself. It was her most embarrassing moment. I gave her a hug and told her to forget it.

When she told Dad, he said, "It's just good enough for you!"

We all had a good laugh, including Jerry.

61
SUMMIN'
IT UP!

A good friend of mine, Brook Turner, summed up my veterinarian practice for me by comparing the vet practice with that of a medical doctors.

The M.D. strolls into his $10 million office around 9:30. He asks his secretary what's on for the day. She says that Mrs. Smith is scheduled to have her baby, and she's put her in for 2:00 that afternoon, giving the doctor time to make his 10:00 tennis match, noon lunch and nap and make the 4:00 country club tee time.

The vet walks into his $10 thousand dollar office at 8 a.m. after having already delivered two calves. He asks his secretary what's on for the day. "You have an appointment at the Ford garage to get the window put in your truck at 8:30. At 9:00, you have to declaw a cat and you're out of anesthetic. At 10:00, you need to run a hundred head of cows through and mouth them. I'll pack some day old donuts and Pepsi for lunch. At 1:30 you've got 15 bulls to cut. Old man Johnson called and said he had a cow prolapse. You're scheduled for 3:30. Oh, and your wife called. She has a PTA meeting this evening and sure hopes you can go."

The M.D. finishes his tennis, lunch, and nap. He strolls into the office at three minutes until 2:00. He says to Mrs. Smith, "I know this is your first child and you're a little nervous, but everything's going to be fine. Please step into the other room, put on this robe and the nurses will help you prepare for the wonderful event." Mrs. Smith is 9 months pregnant and weighs all of 120 pounds when soaking wet.

You get through your truck appointment, the cat, the 100 cows, the day old doughnuts, the bulls and the prolapse. You stroll into your office at three minutes until 5:00. The secretary says, "Mr. Smith called. He has a cow calving and she is shut up in the little pasture." You're half-asleep but you drive there anyway. Mr. Smith's little pasture is 80 acres of honey locust and hedge. The cow is 9 months pregnant, weighs 1200-pounds, soaking wet, and the reason she is soaking wet is just from the sight of you. You reassuringly tell the cow, you know this is her first child, that she's a little nervous, but if she would step up and put her head in the chute, everything will be OK.

The M.D. saunters into the delivery room and asks if Mrs. Smith is prepped. He sits down and starts reading a book. He tells the assistants to get Mrs. Smith's feet in the stirrups and to give her a shot of petocin.

You finally get a rope loop around the cow's horns. She puts her feet in the stirrups but unfortunately they're the same ones attached to the genuine hand-stamped leather, silver conch Hereford saddle that you're sitting atop. With a little maneuvering, you get safely to the ground and dolly the cow to a hedge tree and give her a shot of oxytocin.

The M.D. continues reading his book and gives an occasional look to the progress of Mrs. Smith.

You are running back and forth between the pickup and the hedge getting your stuff.

The M.D. can just begin the see the baby's head. He lays his book down, puts his gloves on, grabs, twists, pulls, pushes, and pulls again. He says to his assistant "foreplay", er, I mean forceps. She smiles coyly. He reassures Mrs. Smith and gives another pull. The baby's head is out.

You put on your gloves and grab the OB chain. You pull, twist, push and pull again. Nothing happens. You look at your assistant, D.B., and you make damn sure you say forceps to him. You give another pull and the nose is out.

The M.D. grabs again, twists, pulls, and pushes. One shoulder, then two appear. Pop! The baby is born.

You've gotten down on the ground and braced your feet against the cow's rump. You pull on the OB chain and nothing. You yell to your assistant, get the calf jack. You put the jack on and tell the cow to push. She does and you crank, she pushes, you crank. The head's out. You crank some more, she pushes. The shoulders are out. You crank some more. You crank and crank but the hip locks. You're devastated. The cow is now tired and she quits pushing. You're tired too, having been up since 5:00, and you just realize you've missed the PTA meeting. You talk reassuringly to the cow ... "you canner and cutter and cross S.O.B.!" You push the calf jack to the ground and crank again. Nothing. "You Hereford, hippopotamus, cross-nothing excuse for a cow," you soothe her with. Then it hits you. You remember something that your new, just-out-of-vet school partner told you. If a calf hip locks, twist the handle of the calf jack around side to side and back and forth and the calf will pop right out. So you twist and twist and nothing happens. You've twisted the cow around until you're whispering in her ear. "You piece of black baldy beef jerky," you tell her. She's offended and lunges toward you trying to drive her horn into your side. That causes her to push and whoosh, the baby is born.

The M.D. tells Mrs. Smith, it's a baby boy! He hands the baby to the nurse and she weighs him, 8 lbs., 6 oz. The nurse uses a suction bulb to remove any fluid. The M.D. gives his patient a couple of suppositories and a shot of a drug with a long name. The nurse hands the baby to the new mother. She instantly takes the child to her bosom and the bond begins immediately. The M.D. says he's 'gotta go. Tee time is in 45 minutes. "That'll be $3,000 and please make arrangements for payment before you leave," he tells Mrs. Smith.

You run behind your patient and grab the baby before the cow stomps on it. All you can think about is getting the fluid out. You grab the hind legs and lift until the calf's butt is off the ground. You reach into the very bottom of your heart for more strength. You have to get the baby lifted so it can drain. You get the tail off the ground and about half the rib cage and that's about all the energy you've got left. It's an opportune time to sex the baby. Big boy! The calf weighs 125 lbs. you figure. You tell your assistant, D.B., to get over here. You hand off the baby to him. Donnie lifts the calf off the ground until its front feet aren't even touching earth. Donnie remarks with his usual candor, "What's the matter, Doc, he only weighs 3 lbs."

You give your patient a couple of suppositories and a shot of something with a short, cheap-sounding name. You get the calf standing and it nuzzles up to its mother. She kicks it. You try to reassure the new mother and say, "you no-claim calf kickin' crowbait shell-shocked silage swallowing sailor." You kick her in the side to get her attention. The rope breaks and she takes after you, D.B. and farmer Smith. You're all running around the pasture from tree to tree like your heads are on fire and your ass is about to catch. The cow is closing in. You jump up and grab a honey locust limb not caring that the thorns are poking you and tearing your flesh. You're finally high enough in the tree to escape the cow's horns. You sit there for two hours, pulling thorns while the cow keeps guard below you. Mr. Smith asks, "How much will it be, Doc?"

You say $45.

Mr. Smith says, "Could you add it to my bill? My wife just had our first child today and you know how much those M.D.s charge."